MISSING PIECES

LAURA PEARSON

AGORA BOOKS

ABOUT THE AUTHOR

Laura Pearson has an MA in Creative Writing from the University of Chichester. She lives in Leicestershire with her husband and their two children. *Missing Pieces* is her first novel.

facebook.com/LauraPAuthor

twitter.com/LauraPAuthor

instagram.com/LauraPAuthor

MISSING PIECES

LAURA PEARSON

First published in Great Britain in 2018 by Agora Books

Agora Books is a division of Peters Fraser + Dunlop Ltd

55 New Oxford Street, London WC1A 1BS

This book is for Paul, who never once said,
'Why don't you choose an easier hobby?'
Or, in fact, referred to my writing as a hobby
when it's clearly much more of an obsession.

PART I

5TH AUGUST 1985

21 DAYS AFTER

The coffin was too small. Too small to contain what it did, which was not only Phoebe's body, but a large part of Linda, too.

At the funeral parlour, a man touched Linda's arm and asked, gently, whether she wanted to see Phoebe, and even as she was nodding her head, she knew that it was a mistake.

'Are you sure?' Tom asked.

Linda knew that this was a decision she couldn't unmake. Knew, instinctively, that she was wrong. She would wish, later, that she hadn't seen their daughter like that, because no matter how peaceful she looked, she was still gone. Knew that the memory of her lying there, surrounded by silk and dressed too immaculately, would interfere with the memories she held of Phoebe laughing and running. Alive. And still, she nodded her head and followed the man down the corridor towards a lifetime of regret.

Linda looked back, once, at Tom and Esme. They were standing hand in hand, quite still, dark heads bowed. Esme's fringe needed cutting, and it was covering her eyebrows and, when she looked down at the thick carpet, her eyes too. This is my family, Linda thought. This is what's left of my family. And then she looked down at her swollen belly, touched it as her baby flipped over like a fish, felt nothing.

When they reached the room, the man told her to take as long as she needed. He opened the door for her and then disappeared down the corridor like a ghost. And Linda approached the coffin slowly, looked in at the girl who couldn't possibly be Phoebe. Who was too small, and still, and quiet, to be Phoebe.

And Linda felt like getting inside it, curling up with her daughter and going to sleep.

But the coffin was too small.

13TH AUGUST 1985

29 DAYS AFTER

Linda set her hands on her rounded stomach, interlaced her fingers. Tom was beside her in the sparse, white waiting room, and neither of them reached for a magazine, and neither of them spoke. The receptionist was eating her lunch, and the smell of her egg sandwiches made Linda feel sick. She unlaced her fingers and gripped the sides of her chair, willing the waves of nausea to pass. She'd given birth to both of her daughters in this hospital, had sat in this room waiting for numerous scans, and she'd always found it cold. That day, though, it seemed stuffy. She thought about standing and opening a window. She lifted her thick hair from the back of her neck, rooted in her bag for a band to tie it up.

When her name was called, Linda stood. Tom held out a hand for her to take, but she didn't reach for it, and he let it drop, followed her down the corridor. When they opened the door, the doctor stood and offered them a kind smile.

'I'm Dr Thomas,' he said.

'You were here when Phoebe was born,' Linda said. 'I remember.'

He smiled again, but didn't confirm or deny it. He saw

hundreds of babies being delivered, Linda told herself. He wouldn't remember hers. She sat down on an uncomfortable blue plastic chair and crossed her legs. She couldn't look at Dr Thomas, and she couldn't look at Tom, and so she set her eyes on the abstract painting that hung on the wall to the left of Dr Thomas's head. Every time she blinked, she kept her eyes closed for a fraction too long, trying to ignore the strong smell of ammonia that hung in the air.

'I heard about your daughter. I'm so sorry.'

Linda wanted to ask why he didn't say Phoebe's name.

'Thank you,' Tom said. 'It's been very hard.'

Since Phoebe's death, almost everything anyone said seemed ridiculous to Linda. She wanted to shake Tom, to punish him somehow for reducing their pain like that.

'Of course,' Dr Thomas said. 'That's why we wanted you to come in today and have another scan. The stress of something like this can be very tough on a baby. We just wanted to have a look and check that everything's all right. Try not to worry, though, I'm sure it will be. Now, Linda, would you like to get up on the bed?'

Linda did as she was told. As she pulled her legs up, the paper that was covering the bed tore a little, and it sounded loud in the quietness of the room. Six weeks ago, they'd come here for her twenty-week scan. Esme and Phoebe were being looked after by Maud, their next-door neighbour. Tom had closed his travel bookshop and they'd driven to the hospital, and Linda had felt a clutch of excitement in her throat, like she had on the day they'd run away from their families, when Esme was growing inside her. On the way to the appointment, Tom had turned the radio up loud and they'd sung along, the car windows open and the breeze whipping Linda's dark hair against her face.

It was hard to reconcile that memory with the question that wouldn't go away. The question that had come to Linda, formed and ready to be spoken, a few nights before. That was rising up in her throat, like bile.

'Dr Thomas?'

He turned to her, and she met his eyes for the first time.

'Yes, Linda?'

'Is it too late to have an abortion?'

Linda heard Tom's intake of breath and saw the flash of shock that Dr Thomas tried to hide. She wouldn't back down, or retract the words. How could she? How could she be expected to have this new child, and love it, when her love for Phoebe had brought her to this? When she could barely take care of her remaining daughter, barely look Esme in the eye?

Dr Thomas cleared his throat and the sound brought Linda back into that room, and she glanced at Tom. He was looking at her like he didn't quite recognise her. Squinting slightly, as though trying to work out whether he'd seen her somewhere before.

'It is too late,' Dr Thomas said. 'But if you don't think you can care for this baby, there are options we can discuss.'

'Adoption?' Linda asked.

She considered this, briefly. Going through the labour, feeling the baby emerge from her like a miracle, and then handing it over. Would she hold it first? Would she be told the sex, be given a chance to think about a name? No, she decided. That option wasn't for her. But before she could speak, Tom spoke for both of them.

'No,' he said, his voice soft but firm. 'We're having this baby, and we're keeping it.'

'Let's get this done,' Dr Thomas said. 'And then we can talk some more.'

He smeared the cold jelly on Linda's stomach and she almost laughed at the tickling shock of it. She waited to be told what she knew, that the baby was fine. She was aware that Tom was worried that her grief, her refusal to eat properly, and her inability to sleep, had caused the baby harm. But she could feel it moving, turning and probing. And more than that, this baby was a part of her, and she felt sure that she would know instantly if there were anything wrong. Just as she had known, that night, that something had happened to Phoebe.

And so, when the image appeared on the screen and Dr Thomas said the heartbeat was strong, Linda wasn't surprised. But she saw Tom, saw his hand fly to his mouth in pure relief, saw the love in his eyes that was ready and waiting. It was simpler, somehow, for him.

Despite what Dr Thomas said about it being too late, she knew there were ways to rid yourself of a baby. Ways that women had relied on for centuries. Painful and dangerous ways, but possible. But she wouldn't do it, because of Tom. She closed her eyes briefly, tried to imagine herself as the mother of a newborn again. Tried to imagine them being a family of four again. But it didn't feel right, when Phoebe wasn't one of them.

'Well,' said Dr Thomas, 'everything looks fine here. Come and take a seat at my desk again, when you're ready.'

He wiped the fluid from Linda's belly and she pulled her clothes back into position, pushed herself up and off the bed. Tom waited until she was ready. When she stood, he placed a hand on the small of her back and guided her the few steps back to the waiting chair. Linda anticipated a lecture, a talking to about how she would get through this. How other women had. You don't know, she wanted to scream. She wanted to open the door and let her voice bounce and echo along the empty white corridor. None of you knows.

'I'd like you both to think about having some counselling,' Dr Thomas said.

'It won't change anything,' Linda said.

'Not the situation, no. But I really think it might help you to come to terms with things. To accept what's happened, and start to move on. I'm not asking you to make a decision today. Just think about it.'

Linda took the leaflets he was holding out to her, and stood, ready to leave. When she was at the door, she felt Tom's breath on her neck, and she was sorry, for a moment, that they were leaving together. That they would have to suffer the car journey home, and then the evening, and the days and weeks to come in that too-empty house, with the words she'd spoken hanging there in the air, like a threat.

Tom didn't speak until he was behind the wheel with his seat-belt on. He reversed neatly out of the parking space, and Linda watched him, waiting for the accusations and the blame. He was handsome, this man she'd chosen. His profile was strong. They were both still young, him thirty and her twenty-eight, and yet small flecks of grey were starting to show in Tom's neat, dark hair. Once, he'd mentioned colouring it, and she said that she liked it as it was, and Esme commented that he looked like he'd been caught in a tiny snowstorm, and he left it. Tom must have felt her eyes on him then, and he glanced at her. It was his eyes that she'd noticed first. Green in some lights, grey in others. Kind, open. There was kindness in them still, she saw, even though she expected to be met with disgust.

When Tom did speak, it wasn't what she expected at all.

'I do understand,' he said, his voice calm. 'I lost her too. Just—'

His voice cracked, and Linda watched his face, saw the tears welling.

'—Just try not to shut me out.'

'I'll try,' Linda said, because she wanted to offer him something other than hurt.

THAT NIGHT, after Tom fell asleep, Linda lay awake beside him, listening to the occasional sounds of people and cars on the street outside. Sometimes, even before Phoebe's death, Linda woke up wondering how she'd ended up here, in an unassuming semi on a residential road in Southampton, so far from home. The night before she'd left Bolton with Tom, they had sat in his car with a map of England spread out on their laps. Linda's eyes were drawn to the edges, to the places beside the sea, and she'd pointed at Southampton, smiling. She had known almost nothing about the place. Her grandparents had holidayed there once. It was where the *Titanic* had sailed from. Linda had pictured a crumbling sort of house by the sea. Fish and chips, walking along the beach, her hair salty, being lulled to sleep by lapping waves. And when they had arrived, and it was nothing like she imagined, she hadn't cared much, because it was still a fresh start, a new life. But almost a decade had passed, now, and that freshness had long since faded.

Linda was aware of the sound of her breathing. She watched the clock crawl through half an hour, and when it got to one o'clock, she sat up carefully, trying not to wake Tom. She took her white cotton dressing gown from the hook behind the door and left the room, looking back once to check that he hadn't been disturbed. He was lying on his side, his breathing deep and slow, his mouth open.

She didn't turn the light on in the kitchen. After almost eight years in this house and two babies, she knew her way around in darkness. The kitchen had always been her favourite room. When they had come to look at the house, weary with unsuccessful viewings and the knowledge that they couldn't afford the kind of place she would choose, Linda had gone to the kitchen first. She'd looked around, at the drawings on the fridge that were held in place by colourful magnets, at the old pine table in the corner still messy with breakfast crumbs. The walls were painted a bright yellow and the cabinets were a pale wood, chipped and marked in places. It was the kind of room where a family gathers at the beginning and end of each day. And she'd known, then, that it didn't matter that the bathroom was small and the garden was a bit wild. This was the house where she would have her family.

For a while, Linda stood at the window, watching the stillness of the dark garden. It was mid-August, late summer, and although she was hot with the weight of her pregnancy, she wasn't ready for the season to change. Because when that summer had begun, she'd still had Phoebe. And it still seemed impossible that she was gone for good.

Linda opened the narrow cupboard in the corner of the room, stared at its contents. And then she took out the bottle of vodka and unscrewed the cap. She did it quickly, as though afraid of being caught. The bottle was three-quarters full, and she calculated that it had probably been there since the previous Christmas, when they'd had a party for some friends and neighbours. That night, she'd taken the drinks Tom had handed her, and she remembered feeling light-headed, feeling that the room was spinning slowly, as girls in bright dresses darted in and out of the small groups that had formed. She remembered catching sight of Phoebe, and dropping to her knees, catching her youngest daughter's wrists and kissing her forehead. Phoebe had wriggled from her grip, dashed off after her sister and the other older girls, and Linda had poured herself another drink.

Now, alone in the dark while Esme and Tom slept upstairs, Linda longed for the edges to blur a little, to take a break from the heaviness of her thoughts, and alcohol was the only way she knew. She lifted the bottle to her lips, tipped it, gulped. The baby inside her kicked, a quiet protest. And Linda tipped the bottle again, swallowed, and put it back in the cupboard. She sat down at the kitchen table, waiting for something to change, for some of the darkness to lift.

23RD AUGUST 1985

39 DAYS AFTER

Tom couldn't sleep. There was a kernel of rage deep in his chest and he was terrified of what it might grow to become. He turned in bed, from his back to his side, faced his sleeping wife. There was a tiny part of him that wanted to hold his pillow over her face. The same part that had wanted to hit her when she suggested aborting their child. Wasn't it enough that they'd lost Phoebe? It pained him that, for the next three months, he had no choice but to rely on Linda to keep their baby safe. Linda, whose voice hadn't shaken when she asked about aborting it.

Tom lay still, silently fighting against images of Linda throwing herself down the stairs or stuffing pills into her mouth. Keeping his eyes open was safer. And so it was that, some nights, he lay awake beside her, watching her stomach for movement.

That night, Tom gave up on sleep a little after four o'clock. He padded softly down the stairs, intending to try to lose himself in his book for an hour or two. But as he approached the lounge, he saw through the glass door that Esme was in the room. She was wearing her pyjamas, but she didn't have that sleep-crumpled look he always noticed when he woke her in the morning, and her unruly, dark hair was brushed and pulled into a slightly lopsided plait. He wondered how long she'd been up, sitting quietly in the lounge with the TV turned off and no books or toys to amuse her. As he entered the room, Esme looked up with a slightly fearful expression, as though she'd been caught doing something she shouldn't. And Tom saw, then, what she was holding in her hand, running through her fingers.

Beebee. It was a tatty piece of pink cloth, the size of a hanky. Phoebe had carried it everywhere with her, for as long as he could remember. She'd named it after the way she said her own name, when she was just learning to speak, her eyes full of concentration as she tried to make her slack mouth fit around difficult sounds.

Linda had wanted to put it in the coffin beside Phoebe, and on the morning of the funeral, they had searched for it. The three of them, ransacking the house, upending drawers and moving furniture to look behind. It had felt good, in a way, to be doing something together, to have a common goal. But then, when he couldn't put it off any longer, Tom had insisted that they leave without it. Ventured the opinion that it didn't really matter, not in the way that their late arrival would matter. And Linda had looked at him with pure venom in her eyes – when he closed his eyes, he could still picture that look – and brushed past him out of the door, to the waiting car.

'Hey, Es,' he said. 'Where did you find Beebee?' Tom reached out to take it from her, and she snatched it away, her expression unreadable.

Tom wanted it, then. He remembered how Phoebe had slept with it beside her head on the pillow, how she had sucked at it, twisted it between her chubby fingers. Every few weeks, Linda had stolen it away to wash it, and Tom had tried everything he could think of to distract her from the fact of its absence. He'd staged elaborate plays with her teddy bears, fed her forbidden treats, invented games that involved all of her senses. Still, she'd always noticed, always complained and whined for it. And when it had been returned to her, fresh and clean, she'd always insisted that it was different.

Suddenly, it was clear to Tom that Esme had had it all along. That it was never lost. That she had hidden it, somewhere in that house, to keep something of her sister. He was shocked by her deviousness, softened by her compassion.

'How long have you been awake, Es?'

She shrugged. 'A while.'

'And what have you been doing?'

Tom was careful to keep his tone light. The last thing he wanted was for her to feel like she was in trouble and being interrogated. And yet, he had to ask, because it troubled him to think of her like this, awake and alone in the unforgiving night.

'Just thinking, really.'

'About Phoebe?'

She flinched at the mention of Phoebe's name, and Tom realised that they rarely referred to her, despite the fact that she was at the heart of everything they did or said.

Esme shrugged again.

For a minute or two, they sat together in silence. Facing one another on the shaggy green rug, their legs crossed, his eyes searching out hers, her eyes avoiding his. Tom was astonished by his daughter whenever he took the time to really look at her. She had Linda's wide-set, chocolate-brown eyes, just as Phoebe had, and Linda's slight build, but he could see himself in her facial expressions, in her movements and gestures. And he was constantly amazed that he'd had a hand in creating this sweet and complicated person, that she existed independently from him and Linda, her brain packed with thoughts and opinions that she could choose to share, or hide.

'Where is she, now?'

Esme's voice was soft and Tom had to move his head a little closer to her to hear. He felt his throat swell with tears and he wanted to reach for Esme's small hand, close it up in his and hold it there.

'She's nowhere, Es. She's gone.'

Tom didn't believe in any kind of God, in heaven or hell. And he didn't believe in telling his daughter lies. It was something he'd argued about with Linda. She was a non-believer too, but she questioned whether there was any harm in telling Esme a nice story about Phoebe looking down on them, watching over them. And Tom said that it was important to him that they were honest. But just then, when he saw the lost look in Esme's eyes, he wondered whether it was the right decision.

'And Mum?'

'Mum? Mum's upstairs in bed, Es.'

Esme met his eyes, and there was a weight and solemnness in her gaze that didn't belong there.

'I know, but will she be okay?'

Tom didn't know how to answer that. Some days, he caught a glimpse of the old Linda, in the quick reddening of her cheeks when she was a little too warm or in the way she bent to pull on her shoe. He tried to focus on those moments, to believe that they were a sign of things to come.

'I hope so,' he said.

Esme nodded solemnly, and Tom realised that he needed to give her something more than that.

'You know Beebee?' Tom said, gently taking it from Esme's hand and holding it up in front of them. 'Do you know where it came from?'

Esme shook her head, and Tom saw the beginnings of a smile starting behind her eyes.

'Well, do you remember the Emperor I told you and Phoebe about? The one who paid a lot of money for a new suit, and was too embarrassed to say that he couldn't see it, after it was made?'

'He walked all over the town with no clothes on,' Esme said.

'He did. And when he got home afterwards, his wife told him

he was very silly and gave him some new pyjamas to put on. She'd bought them for him because it was his birthday two weeks later, but she decided to give them to him early because of the mix-up with the new suit. Anyway, those pyjamas were pink with little grey elephants on them. And the Emperor liked them so much that he wore them every night for four years. He used to wash them first thing in the morning and hang them outside to dry so that he was never without them.

'But at the end of the four years, the elephants had almost faded away and the seams were starting to come undone, and the Emperor was very sad. So when it was nearly his birthday again, his wife went to the same shop and they had one pair of the pink elephant pyjamas left, so she bought them for him, and she put the old pyjamas in one of the spare bedrooms and forgot all about them. She was getting a bit old by then, and she'd only gone in the room to water the plants and hadn't meant to leave the pyjamas there at all.

'Anyway, about a year later, you, me, Phoebe, and Mum went to the Emperor's house for a sleepover...'

'We didn't!' Esme squealed.

Tom put a finger to his lips.

'Shhh, Mum's asleep. We did, Es, you must be getting forgetful, like the Emperor's wife. I don't know how you could have forgotten – we had a big tea party and lots of walnut cake. Anyway, Phoebe couldn't get to sleep that night, because it was her first sleepover and she was missing her own bed. Mum and I tried singing songs to her and telling her stories, but nothing worked.'

'What was I doing?' Esme asked.

'You were snoring, like this.' Tom flung himself on to one side and lay with his legs curled and his hands beneath his head, and began to snore loudly.

Esme laughed, then, and it was such a relief to hear that sound, to see her face like that, unburdened and open.

'Anyway, eventually your mum found the old pyjamas on top of a chest of drawers and she gave them to Phoebe to hold, and Phoebe fell asleep that very second and didn't wake up until morning. The next day, we asked the Emperor's wife where she got the pink pyjamas from, so that we could buy some for Phoebe to hold when she couldn't sleep, and she said that they used to belong to the Emperor but they were very old and we could have them.

'And from then on, Phoebe took those pyjamas to bed with her every night, and she never had problems getting to sleep again. But because they were so old, they started falling apart and we had to keep throwing bits of them away, until this was the only piece left.'

Esme held Beebee close to her eyes. 'I can't see any elephants,' she said.

'No, you can't now, I expect. They were almost gone when we first got those pyjamas, and that was a long time ago, now.'

While he'd been talking, Tom noticed Esme's eyes getting heavier and heavier, and when he asked her if she wanted to go back to bed, she nodded. He lifted her, Beebee still clutched in her fingers, and carried her up the stairs. By the time he laid her down and covered her with her duvet, she was asleep.

STANDING ON THE LANDING, Tom considered going back to bed himself, but he knew he wouldn't sleep again that night. Instead, he headed back downstairs, made himself a cup of tea and took it into the lounge, where he pulled a photo album from the bookshelf. Packed tight with memories, the album was heavy. It was the weight, Tom thought then, of his marriage.

Linda had given it to him as a present on his last birthday. The start of May, hot sunshine. Linda sat by his side on an old blanket in the garden as he leafed through the pages, and Esme and Phoebe abandoned their skipping game and crowded in, prodding disbelievingly at pictures of themselves. Linda was pregnant, but they hadn't told the girls yet. Now, just three months later, he was going through it again, alone in the darkness, and the memories seemed to claw at him, taunting.

First, a picture of him and Linda in the early weeks of their relationship, standing in Linda's back garden. Her mother must have taken the picture, Tom thought. But when he tried to picture her behind the camera, he couldn't. It was slightly out of focus, and Linda's waist-length dark hair was blowing in the wind, hiding the left side of her face. Tom's arm was wrapped awkwardly around Linda's waist, and he was looking at her, rather than at the camera, his eyes full of wonder.

Next, Tom standing in front of their house on the day they moved in. He remembered Linda taking this one, remembered her making faces and waving from the pavement, trying to make him smile. He looked stunned, slightly shaken, as if he couldn't believe the house behind him was theirs. Tom lifted the album a little closer to his face, looked intently at the house. An ordinary, red-brick semi, built five years before they bought it in the late-seventies. Tom was twenty-two years old, about to become a father, a new homeowner. And yet the weight of all that responsibility wasn't showing on his face. He looked proud, disbelieving, happy.

His travel bookshop: Read the World. Linda had chosen the name, and she was in the photograph, pointing at the sign with one hand and holding the hand of a chubby, two-year-old Esme with the other. It was a compromise of sorts, the shop. He'd always had itchy feet and longed to see the world, but he had a wife and a family, so he'd settled for renting a dusty unit and filling it with maps and books about the exotic places he'd probably never see.

Tom flicked forward a few pages, searching for his favourite photo of Esme. There she was, lying in his arms, days old. Her eyes wide and her hair thick and so dark it shone. The fingers of her right hand were curled around his thumb, and she was looking up at him, trusting. The backdrop to the photo was the room Tom was sitting in. The same green and white wallpaper, the same battered floral sofa they'd picked up at a house clearance sale and carried home, stopping a couple of times to sit on it, and rest. Tom looked around him. In the years since that picture was taken, little had changed. A couple of new pictures on the walls, a dark stain on the carpet from a spilled glass of cherryade, the addition of the grass-green sofa cushions that Linda made. And yet, the room in the picture looked more like a home, somehow.

A few pages later, and there was Phoebe. In one photo, she was sitting in her highchair in the kitchen, brown mush covering her face and hands. She was crying, her face red, but beaming through the tears. Tom remembered taking that one. Remembered sitting patiently while Linda fed her, waiting for the right moment. Remembered holding up Beebee to encourage that glowing smile.

There were very few photos of the four of them: him or Linda always behind the camera, the pictures showing the other of them flanked by the two girls. But there was one. They were in the garden, and Tom could hear Linda calling across the fence to Maud, asking if she could nip round to take a photo. Phoebe and Esme were wearing matching red dresses, their dark hair pulled into identical pigtails. Tom and Linda were kneeling behind them, Linda's arms circling Tom's waist. Esme was sitting cross-legged and Phoebe had her chubby legs out in front of her. In Esme's hand, a daisy chain. At the moment the image was snapped, she looked at her sister, passed the daisy chain to her. Their eyes met. Tom and Linda were looking at the camera, smiling and relaxed. But Esme and Phoebe were looking at each other. Serious, calm. A girl offering a gift of flowers to her sister. Saying it's yours, because you're mine.

Tom closed the book, carefully slotted it back into place on the bookshelf. He reached for his tea but it had gone cold, and he winced as he swallowed a mouthful. It was light outside, he noticed. At some point while he'd forgotten himself among those memories, the sun had come up. He went through to the kitchen, poured the tea into the sink, and looked out of the window. In the garden, two blackbirds were fighting over a worm, one tugging it from the ground, the other hopping and pecking at it. He'd made it through another night, somehow got to this place, where he was ready to start another day without Phoebe.

On a sudden impulse, Tom took his keys from the basket on the windowsill and left the house. He drove into town, to his shop, and parked in front of it, looked at it for a couple of minutes through the passenger window. It was still early morning and none of the shops on the street were open yet. When he felt ready, Tom left the car and let himself in. He'd missed this place. Just the gentle, musty smell of it was comforting. But it was a mess: teetering piles of unsorted second-hand books strewn here and there, unsightly gaps on the shelves, a fine layer of dust on everything. Tom sat down on his stool behind the counter, opened the till to check that it was empty. It was. But when he walked through to the back room, he found it strewn with order slips and delivery receipts.

Tom's helper, Liam, had been running the place since that night, but it looked like he was struggling. He was just a kid, after all. He'd helped out on Saturdays for a year or more while he was studying, and in the summer, as his graduation was approaching, he'd asked about a full-time job. Tom had struggled with the decision at the time. He wasn't sure whether there was enough work for the two of them. But Liam was keen, and hardworking, so he'd given him a chance. And he was grateful for it now, now that this boy had picked up the pieces as best he could in Tom's time of need.

For the next hour or so, Tom worked. He cleared his mind of what was happening at home and he filed, sorted, and shelved. He swept the floors and got on a chair to dust the lampshades. When he'd finished, the place looked the way it had when he left it.

Crowded but organised. Cluttered but not chaotic. He wrote a quick note for Liam, thanking him for all his hard work, promising to get in touch again soon.

And as he drove the familiar route home, he felt a small swelling of comfort in his chest. Because at last, he'd done something useful and easy. But by the time he pulled on to his driveway, the feeling of rage was back, rising up again in his throat. And he sat for a few minutes after he'd turned the engine off, his eyes tightly closed, not quite ready to go back inside.

3RD SEPTEMBER 1985

50 DAYS AFTER

'Are you sure you're okay with this?' Tom asked.

Linda wondered what he would do if she backtracked and asked him to stay at home. But the truth was, she was desperate for him to go back to work. She felt his eyes on her, wherever she went. And so, though she longed to stay in bed and pull the covers over her head to shut out the world, she had showered and dressed, that morning, to show him she could function. She nodded.

'Go,' she said. 'Liam can't be expected to do it all by himself.'

'I know, but…'

Tom let the unfinished sentence hang there, and Linda silently listed all the ways he could have finished it. …But I don't trust you with Esme. …But I want to make sure you keep the baby safe. … But I know you're not coping.

'Go,' she said, a little more firmly.

Defeated, Tom leaned down to kiss Esme, who was eating toast in silence, kicking her feet against the legs of her chair. When he approached Linda, she thought he might kiss her, and she stood quickly, moved backwards as her chair scraped against the tiled floor. It sounded too loud, too abrasive. Tom shook his head and left the room.

After the front door clicked shut, Esme put her elbows on the table and rested her chin in her palms. She looked at Linda with wide eyes.

'When are you going back to work?' she asked.

Linda drained her strong black coffee. 'I don't know,' she said.

Something in the way that Esme was watching her made Linda want to reach across the table and slap her face. And she was shocked by the intensity of the impulse. She walked over to the kettle, flicked it on. And while she waited for it to boil, she dug her fingernails into the palms of her hands, fighting back tears.

She wanted to have a drink, she realised. It was before nine in the morning, and she felt like she needed to have a drink. To take her mind off it, she resolved to get out of the house.

'Let's go for a walk, Es,' she said, turning around. 'Let's go to the common and feed the ducks.'

'Mum, I'm seven,' Esme said. She rolled her eyes and went back to her toast.

It would be so easy, Linda thought, to crumble. To go back to bed, or to take the vodka from the cupboard and unscrew the top, or to walk down the hallway and out of the house, closing the door behind her, leaving Esme inside. She was on the brink of it, teetering on the edge of being a functioning person.

'Finish your breakfast and put your coat on, Esme,' she said.

And while she waited for Esme to do as she was told, Linda broke up a couple of pieces of bread and sealed them up in a sandwich bag. They would feed the ducks. Such a simple, normal thing. And once they'd done that, she would think of something else to fill the next hour. And slowly, with small steps, she would get through the day.

It was the start of September and the sky was blue and almost cloudless. Summer's last gasp. In a week, Esme would be going back to school. The thought pleased Linda, because there would be no more pretending, no more false cheer. But it scared her, too. With Tom back at work and Esme at school, there would be nothing to make her get out of bed in the mornings, nothing to stop her from sitting quite still, for hours on end, going over and over the events that had led them to this.

When they got to the main road at the end of their street, Linda reached instinctively for Esme's hand, but it felt warm and slightly sticky, and she was glad when Esme shrugged her away. Silently, Linda calculated. Fifteen minutes to get to the common, maybe twenty sitting on a bench while Esme fed the ducks, another fifteen to walk home. Maybe more like thirty if they stopped at the shops to pick up milk and some soup for lunch. She couldn't imagine how the entire day would be filled, how days had been filled before, how she'd ever been rushed and short of time.

They walked in silence, Linda reaching for things to talk about.

'Back to school next week,' she said, feeling like someone who didn't spend much time around children, and didn't know how to talk to them. 'It will be nice, won't it, to see Samantha every day?'

Esme shrugged, and Linda wondered whether something had happened between Esme and her best friend. Usually, they were in and out of each other's houses, trailing their bikes and asking to have sleepovers. Especially in the school holidays. And now, Linda couldn't remember the last time she'd seen Samantha.

'Why don't we call her when we get home? You could go over there this afternoon.'

'She's on holiday,' Esme said. 'In France, until Sunday.'

'Oh.'

Linda realised she'd been hoping that Esme would go out to play for the afternoon, that she would have the house to herself.

When they reached the common, Linda pulled the small parcel of bread from her bag and passed it to Esme. 'Be careful,' she said.

And then she took a seat on the bench and let the sun warm her. Linda watched Esme approach the bank and felt a clutch at her heart. Esme crouched down and pulled a few pieces of bread from the bag. The ducks, swimming calmly in groups of two or three, began to flock towards her as the first pieces hit the water. Linda caught her breath whenever Esme edged a little closer to the water, and a couple of times she stood, ready to dash forward and grab her daughter by the arm, wrench her back to safety. But she resisted, reminding herself that Esme had always been a careful, cautious child, that she was old enough to be given this space. There was a danger, here, she knew, and it was larger than the danger of Esme falling into that shallow water. It was the danger of infecting Esme with more fear than a child so young should have to carry. And so, Linda kept a little distance, and followed Esme's every movement with her eyes.

After a few minutes, the bread was gone, and Esme turned and walked the short distance to the bench where Linda was sitting. In the sunshine, Linda couldn't make out her expression. She was a silhouette with wild, dark hair blowing about her face. As she got closer, Linda saw that she looked bored. She's doing this for me, Linda thought. She's doing something that a younger child would enjoy, for me.

They were turning to leave when a woman appeared in front of the bench, her son silent at her side. Linda recognised her as one of the other school mothers, but she couldn't retrieve her name. Her son was in Esme's class, and they'd crossed paths at the school gates and on sports days. The children didn't acknowledge each other, but the woman smiled brightly at Linda.

'Lovely day,' she said.

Linda tried to force a smile, but her face didn't respond.

'Hi there, Esme,' the woman said, bending a little to look Esme in the eyes.

Linda heard Esme mutter something, and she wished they had left two minutes earlier. They'd come so close to avoiding this encounter.

'Over halfway now, by the looks of things.' The woman nodded towards Linda's bump. 'Where's your little one? Phoebe?'

Linda froze. In the days following Phoebe's death, Tom had phoned a seemingly endless list of people with the news of what had happened. Linda had sat in the kitchen, listening to his side of the conversations, which were almost identical, wondering how he could bring himself to say it, over and over. She'd been amazed at how much there was to do, how many people there were to notify. And still, she realised then, there would always be people who didn't know. Like this woman, who didn't matter and who hadn't loved Phoebe, but who would ask where she was and how she was, and stand there, waiting for an answer.

She wasn't ready. Perhaps, in a few months, it would be easier to say, although she couldn't imagine it. Perhaps, in time, she would have a stock response, one that she could reach for in situations like this. And perhaps she'd be able to dissociate the words from the image of Phoebe in the coffin, and she'd be able to imagine she was talking about someone else's child, or something innocuous like the weather. Perhaps.

'We have to go,' Linda said, putting an arm around Esme and rushing her away.

And all the way home, every step felt like a challenge, and the sun was a little too bright, too warm on the top of Linda's head. She felt the tears running down her face, felt the eyes of strangers resting on her for a moment too long. Esme didn't speak, and Linda was grateful for that, because her head was filled with that woman's voice. She heard her, saying Phoebe's name, over and over, and it was all she could do to keep moving forwards, to keep moving further away from that question. *Where's your little one? Phoebe?*

When she shut the door behind them, Linda felt safer. Inside the house, no one could startle her like that. But there were other demons to contend with. Every square inch of their home held a memory of Phoebe. When Linda sat at the kitchen table, she saw a nine-month-old Phoebe crawling across the floor towards her, a teething ring in her chubby fist. When she lay in bed, she saw a three-year-old Phoebe poking her head round the doorway, asking to come in and cuddle for a while. And sometimes, just about anywhere in the house, Linda saw Phoebe lying still, on her back, the way she had seen her in the coffin.

'Mum?' Esme whispered.

Linda realised how she must look to her daughter. Her face streaked with tears, her eyes frightened, her shoulders hunched.

'Go and play upstairs for a while, Esme,' she said.

As soon as Esme had gone from the room, Linda went to the cupboard and reached for the bottle of vodka. With shaking hands, she poured a large measure and tipped it back, welcomed the warmth of it as it slid down her throat. This time, the baby didn't kick. And Linda wondered, for a second, whether she had harmed it, and she was flooded by a mixture of panic and relief at the thought of that. She poured some more, drank it, desperate to feel her insides soften and turn to liquid. Desperate for her thoughts to stop for a while, or at least slow down.

At the top of the stairs, Linda stood outside Phoebe's room. She could feel her heart knocking in her chest and, just as she reached out to touch the door handle, the baby woke and kicked her. Once, twice, and a third time. She opened the door and slipped inside.

Something of Phoebe's apple-sweet scent seemed to linger, still, in the air. The door had been shut since that day, and Linda felt that, by keeping the room closed off, they'd somehow preserved her. She looked around slowly, taking in the bright colours of Phoebe's belongings, reaching out to touch a favourite book and the teddy bears that still sat at the end of her bed, neatly placed in a row. For a moment, she felt that she would fall, but she gripped the edge of the windowsill and steadied herself. Through the open door, she could hear Esme moving about the room opposite, and she almost went to her.

Part of her wanted to leave the room and go across the hall to her living daughter. She wanted to want that. She wanted things with Esme to be how they had been before, easy and playful and washed with joy.

But instead, she tore a bin-liner from the roll in her hand and started to put Phoebe's things inside. Books, toys, and all those tiny and colourful things that are somehow essential to being a three-year-old girl. She removed the pictures from the walls, carefully picking off the Blu-Tack and rolling it into a smooth ball in her palm. She folded clothes, working fast to distract herself from the tears that had started falling. She wasn't sure when she became aware that Esme was watching, but she realised at some point that she could feel eyes on her. Esme's room was opposite Phoebe's, and both doors were open.

Linda turned and her eyes locked with Esme's, and she saw that her daughter was crying. Esme stood and walked towards her, stopped in the doorway to Phoebe's room, as though she couldn't quite bring herself to step inside.

'What are you doing?' she asked.

Linda didn't know what to say, and so she turned away and carried on with what she was doing.

'Mum, what are you doing? That's Phoebe's stuff!'

Linda turned and slapped Esme's cheek, hard. She stepped back, her hand stinging, and she felt like she was watching the scene from afar, watching Esme's hand fly to her face, her eyes fill with tears. Esme turned and crossed the short distance to her bedroom, pushed the door closed quietly. But Linda had seen the look in her eyes. The look of incredulity, and horror, and hatred. She sank to the floor where she stood, wrapped her arms around her knees, and closed her eyes.

BY THE TIME she heard the key in the lock, Linda was in bed. She'd left Phoebe's room bare and still, with a neat row of black bags against one wall, and she'd opened a window to let in the last of the summer air. To let out the last of Phoebe. And then she curled up in bed, listening to the sounds of Esme moving around downstairs, making herself something to eat for lunch and watching television. She couldn't bring herself to go down there, to find out whether Esme would speak to her, whether her hand had left a mark on Esme's pale cheek. But now, Tom was home. Linda drew her knees up to her chest, and waited.

'There you are,' Tom said.

She opened her eyes and saw him moving towards the bed.

'Esme said you've been in bed all afternoon.'

There was an accusation in his voice, but she could tell that he didn't know about the slap. She imagined Esme, keeping quiet about it, protecting her. She wondered why.

'I was tired,' Linda said.

Tom sat down and sighed heavily. 'Maybe it's too soon. I won't go in tomorrow. We can't leave her on her own like that.'

'She wasn't on her own,' Linda said. 'I was here.'

Tom looked at her, and she could see irritation behind the compassion in his eyes.

'You know what I mean,' he said.

'I cleared out Phoebe's room,' Linda said.

She wanted to provoke him, to see how far she could push him.

'What? Why?'

'Because I couldn't go in there, I couldn't face it. Now it's just a room.'

Tom stood up and she listened as he made his way along the landing. She could picture him, standing in the doorway, surveying the changes.

'I'm going down to Esme,' he called back to her, his voice cold, steely. 'We'll make some dinner.'

9TH SEPTEMBER 1985

56 DAYS AFTER

E sme didn't speak until Tom pulled up outside the school gates, but he could tell by the way she was fidgeting and gazing out of the window that there was something on her mind. She was an easy child, that way. Her feelings showed up clearly on her face, and it was simply a matter of waiting for her to work up the courage to voice them.

'I don't want to go in,' she said, her words hurried and tumbling, tripping over one another.

Tom had expected something like this, and yet he hadn't decided how to handle it. He'd felt sure that he would know what to do, when the time came. And now the time was upon him and he was lost. He wanted to consult Linda, but the old Linda, not the one he'd left at home, sitting with her hands in her lap and her watery eyes fixed on the wall. He considered starting the car again without a word, driving Esme to his shop, where he knew she was happiest.

'Why not?' he asked, instead.

He knew why not, of course. If he were her, he wouldn't want to go in either. Children could be bloodthirsty and hurtfully frank, and it was a dangerous combination. Tom reached across the space that separated him and his daughter, brushed a few stray hairs from her face. He fought the urge, again, to start the car and keep her with him for the day, keep her safe, not just from physical danger but from careless words, too.

'Will everyone know?' she asked. And then she added, unnecessarily, 'About Phoebe?'

Tom had spoken to Esme's teacher, Mrs Lewis, the previous day. The teachers went back a day early to get things ready, and he made a last-minute appointment to see her, to explain. When he told her, her hand flew to her mouth.

'Oh, I'm so very sorry,' she said.

Tom had learned that people didn't know what to say or what to do with their hands when they heard the news. He considered Mrs Lewis's reaction to be frank and open, felt comforted that this woman would be the one to take care of Esme during school hours. He believed, naïvely, that Mrs Lewis would make sure she came to no harm.

But now, sitting beside Esme in the car, he realised he'd been foolish. He snuck glances at Esme, at her composed but apprehensive expression. Mrs Lewis couldn't be there all the time. She was in charge of almost thirty children, and there were break times and lunchtimes and notes secretly passed around the class behind her back. He remembered, just about, how it could be.

Tom turned to Esme, looked her in the eyes. 'Mrs Lewis knows, and some of the other children probably do, I guess. Do you want them to know?'

'I don't know.'

Tom looked through the windscreen, hoping to see Esme's friend, Samantha. He wished for a friendly face, a hand to pass Esme's hand into. She didn't talk, often, about other friends, and Tom always assumed that she didn't need anyone else. He remembered from his own schooldays that girls' friendships could be intense and exclusive, impenetrable, almost like a love affair. He'd never worried about it before that day.

'Do you want me to walk you in?' he asked.

Esme paused for a moment, and then shook her head. 'That's worse,' she said.

Her solemnity made Tom's heart ache, and he sat there, unmoving, for several minutes after Esme left the car and turned at the gates to give him a small wave. He blew her a kiss, and waited until she was inside before he started the car. As he pulled out onto the road, he hoped, fervently, that her day would be smooth. That the other children would be kind.

He was still thinking about Esme when he arrived at the shop. She was carrying too much weight for a seven-year-old, and it pained him that he couldn't lift it. She'd never come out and said that she felt guilty for Phoebe's death, but Tom could see it in her movements and her stillness. When they lost Phoebe, they'd lost a part of Esme too, and he wasn't sure whether they'd ever get it back. He wondered, sometimes, whether Linda had noticed it, or whether her grief had blinded her.

Tom flicked the kettle on, checked the till while he waited for it to boil. When Liam arrived, the two men exchanged nods and greetings and then leaned back against the counter, drinking their first coffee of the day. It was almost time to open up when Tom went into the back room and opened the top drawer in his old chest, looking for an invoice. His eyes fell on the slip of paper at once, and he picked it up, lifted it closer to his face, although he knew exactly what it said. *Marianne 0703 218862.* He looked at her name, the way she'd written it in a hurry so that the letters ran over one another. It was reminiscent of the way she spoke, the words overlapping and fast, unable to quite keep up with the speed of her thoughts. And her accent, almost hidden now, after all these years, but still discernible if you knew to listen for it.

He remembered the way she'd looked as she wrote it, her brow furrowed as though she had to concentrate to remember her own name and number. And how, halfway through writing, she had paused and used her right hand to tuck a lock of hair behind her ear, and the pen grazed a thin black line across her cheek. And he, he had licked his finger and lifted it to wipe away the ink. It had felt strangely erotic, as though they'd crossed a boundary and there was no going back. He remembered that she had rested on the top of the chest while she wrote it. Now he ran his fingers along the smooth wood, hurriedly, feeling for an imprint, but there was nothing there. For a second, he looked at the phone on the wall, almost daring himself to pick it up, but then he slid the paper into his pocket and went back out to the front, to open up.

TOM MADE it through the morning, but when Liam popped out to pick up some lunch, he didn't take his sandwiches from the fridge. He picked up the phone instead, and called Marianne. Because for years, there had been Linda. But before Linda, there was Marianne. A French girl in the middle of Bolton, as unexpected as snow in July. He'd fallen for the way her tongue worked its way around the unfamiliar English words and the way the light seemed to fall on her slightly differently to how it fell on the other girls. Her movements were a series of perfectly lit photographs.

And without warning, eight weeks earlier, she'd resurfaced. Strolled into his shop as though she'd never left him with his heart broken and his life in shreds.

Knowing that he shouldn't call her wasn't enough to stop him from doing it. He knew the number by heart, just from looking at the slip of paper all morning, between serving customers. Without quite believing that he was going to do it, Tom dialled – his heart quickening as he tried to work out what he would do if she answered. What he would do if she didn't. Four shrill rings, and then her voice, and he was seventeen again in an instant.

'Hello?'

'Marianne, it's Tom.'

'Tom?'

She sounded surprised and he thought it might be the first

time that he'd caught her off-guard. This woman, who was so sure and steady, even all those years ago when she was barely more than a child. He wondered what she was doing, whether he'd caught her in the middle of dressing or washing up or reading. He wondered whether her cropped blonde hair was wet and dripping onto her shoulders, whether the light in the room she was in was bright or dim.

'I want to see you,' he said.

His voice cracked a little, and he tried to cover it by clearing his throat. But he could picture her on the other end of the line, knowing how nervous he was, revelling in it.

'Are you at work?' she asked. 'I need to be in town for six o'clock. I could come in earlier. We could have a coffee.'

'Yes,' Tom said. He let her speak, writing down the name of the café she mentioned, the time. And after he hung up, he couldn't remember saying goodbye. He sat down on the stool behind the counter, his lunch forgotten. The weight of what he'd done – what he might do – sitting heavily in his gut, like a meal that was too rich and too plentiful.

ALL AFTERNOON, it rained heavily, and customers were few and far between. Tom retreated to the back room, leaving Liam to read at the counter and take care of customers. He started to price up a pile of second-hand phrasebooks, but he couldn't concentrate, and he soon abandoned them. His mind spun, resting first on Linda, at home alone. Had she stayed in bed today? She was still sleeping when he left with Esme, and he didn't see any reason to wake her. She needed the rest, he reasoned, for the baby. And yet he knew that it wasn't normal, to lie there the way she did, with no colour in her face and no interest in anything. Next, he pictured Esme in the playground at lunchtime, off in a corner with Samantha. He imagined the other children gathering around them, asking Esme questions about Phoebe that she couldn't answer, and he closed his eyes for a moment, desperate to push the image away.

And then, he thought of Marianne. He didn't know the first thing about her life, now. When she'd left him, they were twenty-two. It seemed impossible that he could ever have been so young. But he knew it was true. After five years of being inseparable, of saving money to travel around Europe and of talking about the wedding and the children they would have, one day, she brought his world crashing down. No explanation. No apology. And then she disappeared, as quickly as she'd come. Until now.

At quarter to five, Tom went back out to the front of the shop. Liam had just finished serving someone and Tom waited, leaning against the doorframe, until the bell jangled and the customer had gone.

'Early close,' he said. 'You get off home.'

Liam looked up at him. 'Are you sure?'

Tom nodded. 'It's only a few minutes. And you've done plenty of extra work these past few weeks. I appreciate it.'

Liam was uncomfortable with praise, but he'd stopped deflecting it. Tom cashed up as Liam grabbed his coat and left the shop with a quick parting wave. The café was at the other end of the high street, no more than a five-minute walk. And Tom remembered that Marianne was always late, just as he was always early. He knew why she did it, now. She wanted the person she was meeting to wait for her, to wonder whether she was going to come, and then to watch her arrive. It was a game she played, but he didn't care. He felt as though he couldn't stand in that shop for another minute, wondering what would happen when he saw her.

Tom fixed his eyes on her as she sauntered through the door, shaking a large black umbrella. She looked around and caught his eye, and then she made her way across the room to him, taking in the gingham tablecloths and the greying walls as though she'd never seen this place, despite the fact that she'd suggested it.

'You came,' she said, leaning down to kiss his cheek. 'I'm glad.'

A heavy woman with a notepad approached the table, and while Marianne ordered a coffee, Tom looked at her out of the corner of his eye. There were a few lines around her eyes and the hair he'd once gathered in his fingers had been cut to the length of a couple of inches. And her voice was different, too, that exotic accent he'd fallen for all but lost. But the light still followed her, arranged itself around her, highlighting her cheekbones and her narrow lips. She was still that girl. His girl.

'What are you doing here?' he asked, when the woman had shuffled away. 'In Southampton, I mean.'

'I came to find you. I was living in London, and it was time for a change, and then I ran into someone from school who was in touch with your brother. She said you'd come here, years ago. She told me about the bookshop. That was a surprise, I must say. I thought you'd be living on a beach somewhere in Asia.'

Tom was astonished. For a moment, he couldn't speak. And then the woman returned with Marianne's coffee, and they were silent as she stirred sugar into it, poured in milk.

'You didn't move here, because of me?'

Tom wasn't sure what he wanted her answer to be. He wasn't sure of anything.

'Well, I needed a change of scenery anyway. I've moved around quite a bit. I'm restless. It comes of leaving your home country, I think. But yes, I came here because of you.' She fixed her eyes on him, made sure she had his full attention before she spoke again. 'I came here because I want you back.'

Tom was angry, exhilarated, more excited than he remembered being in a long time.

'I have a wife,' he said. 'I have a daughter.'

Marianne paused, her coffee cup in mid-air. 'Oh,' she said.

'Marianne, it's been eight years. Did you really think I'd just wait around for you to come back?'

He realised, then, that she did. She was used to getting what she wanted. He remembered that about her. She was a little spoiled, a little selfish, and she placed herself at the centre of everything. But this, this was incredible. He kept his eyes on her, waiting for her to say that she was joking, that it was all a coincidence and that she was married, too. But she said nothing like that. She just sipped at her coffee, watching him watching her.

'I didn't know,' she said, at last. 'I came here to tell you that I made a mistake, back then. I didn't know what we had. I miss you, and I want you back. That's all. It's up to you.'

She stood, took some coins from her purse and left them on the table, and before Tom could stop her, she was back outside in the rain. He watched her walk down the street, not bothering to open her umbrella, her hair darkening and moulding itself to her skull. And he wanted to follow her, grab hold of her and kiss her in the street, in the rain. He could see it happening, like a scene from a black-and-white film. But his feet stayed rooted to the floor, and he didn't realise that he was biting the inside of his cheek until he could taste the blood.

The first time she heard Phoebe, Linda was sitting on the sofa, an unread book open on her lap. Esme was upstairs in her room and Tom was making lunch in the kitchen. It was quiet in the lounge, and then it wasn't, because Linda heard Phoebe's laugh, clear and rich. And a moment later, it was quiet again. Linda turned her head from side to side, trying to make sense of it. Then, she kept very still for a few minutes, straining to hear it again.

'It's ready,' Tom called.

Linda stood and walked through to the kitchen.

'I just heard Phoebe,' she said.

Tom was standing with his back to her, wiping the counter with a dishcloth. The sandwiches he'd made were on the table. He'd filled a bowl with crisps and placed the fruit bowl in the centre of the table. He turned, opened the fridge and took out the orange juice.

'What do you mean?' He didn't look at Linda when he said it.

She wondered whether he knew what it had cost her, how hard it had been, to say her name aloud.

'I heard her, Tom. I was in the lounge, trying to read a book. I heard her laugh.'

Tom stopped what he was doing then, and walked towards her. He placed his hands on her elbows and rubbed them up and down. It was something he'd always done, when he knew she wouldn't like what he was about to say. Linda flinched, took a step backwards so they were no longer touching.

'Linda, you know that's not possible. You must have imagined it. Now, let's have lunch and we'll talk about this afterwards.' He opened the kitchen door and called Esme again.

'I'm not a child,' Linda said.

Tom looked at her calmly, but there was a warning in his eyes. 'I know that.'

'You speak to me the way you speak to Esme, sometimes.'

As Linda said her daughter's name, Esme appeared in the room.

'What about me?' she asked.

Linda said nothing. She walked past Esme, out of the kitchen and down the hallway, only stopping to pick up her jacket and keys. And then she walked out of the house without looking back.

Without thinking where she was going, Linda found herself walking the familiar path to the university, where she worked. Treading that path to work every morning seemed like a different life, though she'd been doing it up until just a few months ago. Through the maze of residential streets, on to the wide open space of the common. She found that she could breathe more easily there, and she stopped looking around to see whether Tom was following her. Autumn was in the air; the breeze had a chilling edge to it and the branches of the trees were swaying, their red and golden leaves beginning to fall. Linda concentrated on putting one foot in front of the other, and although she didn't want to, she played memories through in her mind. Memories of walking this route with Phoebe, their hands clasped tight. Once, the previous winter, she and Esme had pulled Phoebe along this path in a sledge that sliced through the newly fallen snow. She remembered the ache in her back, the unbridled joy in Phoebe's voice as she encouraged them to pull her faster and faster. She remembered Esme collapsing on the ground in a fit of giggles, her bobble hat falling off and her hair tumbling down around her shoulders. Why hadn't she clung to days like those? Why hadn't she known?

Linda had never believed in a God or a heaven or an afterlife. And yet now, she imagined Phoebe – or some form of her – wandering the house, watching over them. It was clichéd, disdainful. She didn't care. Despite Tom and Esme and her unborn child, she felt that it was all she had. And still, Tom wouldn't let her have it. Couldn't cross that barrier of sense and reason to believe in the possibility of her hearing their lost child. It was selfish, she thought. Closed-minded. And she was filled with a fury that she didn't know what to do with.

When she reached the edge of the common, Linda crossed the road and carried on until she arrived at the cluster of university buildings. It was a little over two months since she'd been here, and as she passed the familiar library and the union, she realised that she missed it. She missed coming here, each morning, and filing, calculating average marks, talking to the students about their delayed essays and their changed addresses. People depended on her here, and she didn't let them down.

It was Sunday, and the campus was deserted. Linda wandered through the gardens, pulling her jacket tighter around her body as she began to feel cold. She pretended that she was someone else, her younger self, a student. She pretended that she was about to go home to her tiny flat in halls after a long day of lectures and seminars. She'd been that girl, once. At another university in another English town. And then she'd gone home for the summer and met Tom, and a couple of weeks before she was due to go back for her final year, she'd discovered she was pregnant.

Linda heard someone calling her name and looked up, and it

took her a moment to remember where and who she was. Maud Wilson, her neighbour, was approaching across the grass. Linda wiped at her face with her hands, as though she'd been crying. She felt sure that there would be some visible trace, there, of the thoughts that were crowding in. What if she hadn't had Esme? If she hadn't left university? If she hadn't married Tom?

'Hello,' Maud said. 'What are you doing here?' She was a little out of breath and her white hair was lifting slightly in the wind.

'Just out for a walk,' Linda said. 'I had to get out of the house.'

Maud linked her arm through Linda's and Linda flinched slightly at her touch. Was this how it was, between her and Maud? She couldn't quite remember. She didn't say anything, and the two of them walked slowly along the path, back towards the library.

'Arthur used to be a gardener here,' Maud said.

Linda turned to look at her. She hadn't known this.

'I come here, sometimes, to remember.'

It was easy to forget that Maud had recently lost her husband. He'd died in his armchair the same day that they lost Phoebe. Like dominos, one loss had led to the other.

'Do you blame me, for what happened that day?' Maud asked.

'What?' Linda was genuinely shocked.

'If I hadn't called you, it would have been different.'

It was true, of course. If Linda hadn't gone next door, hadn't spent that time waiting with Maud for the ambulance and trying to console her, her own life would be intact. But she didn't blame Maud. She blamed herself, and she blamed Tom. And although she was disgusted with herself over it, she blamed Esme.

'No,' Linda said. 'You couldn't have known.'

'You see that row of trees?' Maud asked, pointing to a neat, straight line of sycamores. 'Arthur planted those. When Karen was young, I used to come here with her, sometimes. We'd bring him sandwiches for his lunch. And if the weather was fine, I'd pack a blanket and we'd have a little picnic on the grass. It was always buzzing with young people. I think that's one of the things he liked about working here. You too, I expect.'

'Yes,' Linda said.

She didn't say that she had once been a student of languages, dreamed of living in Paris or Barcelona. She didn't say that her administrative job in the modern languages department was as close as she could get, now, to the things she'd once wanted.

'I'm going to head back,' Maud said. 'It's getting chilly. What about you?'

'I think I'll stay for a while.'

Maud paused and looked at Linda for a moment.

'Come and talk to me, if you need to,' she said. 'Any time.'

When Maud was out of sight, Linda sat down heavily on a bench. The baby was moving, kicking, and she felt tired. She thought about Maud, who'd brought freshly baked scones over on the day she and Tom moved into their house, and been a good friend to them ever since. Maud and Arthur's daughter, Karen, had gone to university in Scotland, met a man there, and stayed. And so, with Maud missing her daughter, and Linda without a mother, they'd become close, wordlessly plugging the gaps they saw in one another's lives.

Linda wanted her mother, then. She set off for home, and when she saw a phone box, she stepped inside, ignoring the faint smell of urine and the graffiti on the walls. She fed some coins into the slot and dialled the number that was still familiar to her, despite the infrequency with which she used it.

Her mother, Christine, answered after four rings. 'Hello?'

Linda opened her mouth to say it was her, but found that she couldn't. She stood there, listening to her mother's breaths, trying to force herself to speak. Christine said hello again, and then once more, and then she hung up. And Linda stood in the phone box for a long time, the phone still in her hand, the flat dial tone eventually replaced by a shrill beeping.

When Linda was young, people always expected there to be a

special closeness between her and her mother. She was an only child, and she'd never met her father, who left shortly after discovering that Christine was pregnant. But that closeness just wasn't there. The two of them had lived together in an odd sort of near silence, like strangers who happened to share a home. Linda remembered realising, at the age of twelve or thirteen, that her mother blamed her for her father leaving. That she was a cruel, daily reminder of him. And now, years after leaving home, Linda found that she needed a mother more than ever before, and it was too late.

When she let herself back in to the house, Tom and Esme were in the lounge, playing a game of cards. Esme looked up, her cards fanned out in her hand, when Linda appeared in the doorway.

'Dad ate your sandwiches,' she said. 'Where did you go?'

'I went for a walk. I had a headache, but it's gone now.'

Tom looked at her, and there was a sadness in his eyes.

'You can play if you like,' Esme said. 'But I'm winning.'

'I think I'll go upstairs and have a bath,' Linda said. 'I'm feeling a bit cold.'

She ran the bath and slipped down into the water. There was a time when she'd have taken a book in with her, but she was well practised, by then, at sitting or lying with nothing to distract her. Linda sank back into the steaming water, closed her eyes and heard Phoebe's laugh again.

Phoebe was an attention-hungry child, always competing with Esme, always falling short. Esme was faster, taller, stronger. She knew more, understood more. There were three years between them and yet Phoebe was constantly striving to find that one thing that she could win.

You've won, Linda had always wanted to say to her. You've won at this. I love you more. It was true. Esme was her first baby, but Phoebe was her favourite. Linda had wanted to tell her to slow down, calm down, catch her breath, stop competing. She'd wanted to tell her that she was perfect exactly as she was. And she'd held back, for fear of hurting Esme by showing her preference, and she knew that that was the right thing, what a mother should do. But now she'd never get to say it, and Phoebe would never know.

Linda looked down at the mound of her belly that rose above the bubbles, and cautiously, she let herself wonder about this child. She let herself start to hope for a boy, because she didn't want to make any comparisons between this child and its sisters.

Tom was sitting on the bed when she emerged, wrapped in a towel.

'I'm sorry,' he said.

'Where's Esme?'

'She's watching a video. Did you hear me?'

'Yes.'

Cautiously, Linda reached out a hand and touched the top of his head, ran her fingers slowly through his hair. And that was all it took. For the first time in months, they were kissing and he was whispering her name through her hair and tugging at the small towel that covered her.

And it felt right to Linda, at first, it really did. She felt a rush of desire and she didn't want it to stop. She wanted to close her eyes and be ruled by her hands and her mouth. She let Tom pull the towel off her, felt, when he kissed her, that his desire was a match for her own and that there was nothing to do but let it take over. As long as they didn't stop, and she didn't open her eyes, and she didn't think, it would be okay. She felt sure that Tom would know that, would understand.

But he didn't, and when he paused to look at her, she opened her eyes to see why he'd stopped, and that was it. Linda pushed him lightly away from her and sat up. And still, he didn't realise. He embraced her from behind, and she felt his erection hot against her naked back. She removed his hands, stood.

'Sorry,' she said, and she went back to the bathroom and stood under the shower for twenty minutes. She didn't wash her body or her hair, she just stood there, the water as hot as she could bear it, running in small rivers over her skin.

It was late that night, at two or three in the morning, when Linda woke from a rare deep sleep, her heart knocking fast. She looked around her, blinking as her eyes adjusted to the darkness. Almost under her breath, she whispered Phoebe's name. And she knew, as clearly as she knew her own name, that Phoebe was there. That she was watching.

Almost a month had passed since those strange moments Tom had spent with Marianne in the café. He'd thought about her almost constantly, had closed his eyes at night and imagined forbidden encounters. When he thought about what she'd said, about coming to Southampton to find him, he couldn't quite make himself believe in it. He knew that he would see her again. It was only a matter of time.

And then, one Friday, while Liam was in the back room making coffee, he found himself reaching for the phone. She answered after the first ring and he was taken aback. He cleared his throat before speaking, and when he did speak, his voice was unrecognisable to him.

'It's Tom. I want to see you.'

'Now?' she asked.

She didn't sound surprised, and Tom was a little irritated by that. Despite what he'd told her, about his family, she had remained sure that he would get in touch. Sure about his weakness.

When Liam came through with a steaming mug of coffee in each hand, Tom was sure that his betrayal would show in his face.

'I've got a meeting in an hour, with a supplier,' he said.

'Oh? I didn't see it in the diary.'

'No,' Tom said. 'My fault. I forgot. Will you be okay here?'

'Of course.'

Liam tilted his head to one side and kept his gaze on Tom for a few moments, and Tom wondered whether he knew. No, he reasoned, Liam didn't know. He was too young, too honest. Since Phoebe's death, Liam had been a little awkward around him. It was possible that he thought today was one of the harder days, and that Tom just couldn't see it through to the end. His guilt ran a little deeper, as he considered this.

'It might take the rest of the day,' Tom said.

'No problem. I can lock up if you don't make it back.'

'Thanks, Liam.'

Tom drove the four miles to the address she had given him. Four miles. It wasn't far enough to afford him the time to consider what he was doing, what he was about to do. It wasn't far enough for him to count up all the reasons why he shouldn't. It was only far enough for him to play and replay the memory of Linda pulling away from his touch a couple of weeks before, leaving him aching with a want that was fast becoming a need.

Marianne opened the door wearing a short, silk dress, her legs and feet bare. She led him down her flat's narrow hallway, and Tom looked down to find that his hands were shaking. When she reached the kitchen, Marianne turned.

'Tea?' she asked.

They were almost touching. Tom took one step closer and reached out to touch her cheek, and the trembling stopped. When she kissed him, she tasted of strawberries and toothpaste. They stumbled back along the corridor, kissing like teenagers, the way they'd kissed all those years ago, when they had nowhere private to be and more lust than they knew what to do with.

Marianne opened the door to her bedroom and pulled him inside, gently. She stood at the end of the bed, kept her eyes on him as she unzipped her dress and let it fall to the ground. And then she reached behind her to unfasten her bra, stepped out of her knickers. Tom was amazed by the ease with which she carried herself. She'd never been shy, but when he'd known her before she'd had that slight awkwardness that all teenagers carry. Now, she'd grown into her body and learned the power it afforded her.

Tom was frozen, unable to move or speak. Marianne came to him, unbuttoned his shirt, slowly. Pushed him backwards on to the bed and straddled him. The window was open, and Tom could feel the autumn air on his chest as she kissed him again. It was like something from a dream. His first love, resurfacing like this, still wanting him. Tom closed his eyes and gave in to it, trying to push away the doubt that lay on his heart like lead.

'WHAT TIME DO you have to leave?' Marianne asked, afterwards.

Tom traced the bumps of her spine lightly with his fingertips.

'Soon.'

Tom realised that although she knew about Linda and Esme, she didn't know that Linda was heavily pregnant and she didn't know that his world had caved in on the day she walked out of the past and into his shop and stood on tiptoes to kiss him on both cheeks. Tom felt sick, and sorry, and yet satisfied. Throughout his life, he'd known men who did this, who cheated and betrayed, who lied and hid things from the women they claimed to love. And never once had he thought that he would be one of them.

Tom stood and began to pull on his clothes. Marianne's bedroom was in shadow, lit only by two tall candles on the dresser that reminded him of his childhood, of Sunday mornings in church. There was a chair, covered with clothes, and a window that looked out on a small park. And behind him, that enormous oak bed where he had carelessly risked his marriage.

He wanted to ask how she'd known to arrive in his life now, when Linda was retreating from his love for the first time. But it didn't matter, not really. She was here, and he had gone to her, and now he had to go home with the image of her resting behind his eyelids. Waiting to taunt him, whenever he closed his eyes.

He felt her arms snaking around his waist, turned to face her.

'Stay a little longer,' she said.

He wondered, then, whether she was lonely. For the first time, he questioned why she was alone in the world. Why other men, like him, hadn't been captivated by the tricks she performed with even the greyest of English light. Perhaps they had. Perhaps there had been a parade of them, strolling through her life. Perhaps there was one even now, working in an office nearby, unaware that she had undressed for Tom in the middle of a Friday afternoon. That she had shivered slightly when he entered her and kissed his eyelids when he came.

And the release of that, the sweet release of holding her hips and emptying himself into her.

She was asking him to stay, and he wasn't ready to face his family so soon after his betrayal, and so he did. They drank coffee in her kitchen and laughed about the clumsiness of their teenage romance, their badly timed and unsatisfying attempts at sex. The people they'd known and what they knew of the way their lives had turned out.

'What do you do?' Tom asked, realising with a start that he didn't know.

Marianne leaned across the kitchen table and poured herself another cup of coffee. She added milk and stirred, and Tom watched her, wondering what her answer would be. When they'd been at school, she had struggled a bit. She was quick and bright, but she was lazy too, and the language was an obstacle for her. Many an afternoon, they'd skipped their lessons, spent long hours kissing: in the park, when it was sunny, at the back of the cinema or in bus shelters when it rained.

'I'm a waitress,' she said, 'at a French restaurant in town. I bring a touch of authenticity. The chef's from Croydon.'

Tom laughed, imagining her stacking plates neatly, reciting specials, emphasising her accent. But it saddened him slightly to think of her at work – the long hours, late nights, rude customers. He pictured her coming home to her empty flat in the darkest part of the night, her feet sore and no one to rub them. No one to talk to about her day's frustrations and high points, her loftier dreams. Or perhaps he was being dramatic, and she was happy with her life the way it was – a low-stress job, a nice home and no one to answer to.

It was easy, he thought, being with her. Easier than it had been back then. And easier than it was to be with Linda now, when everything he said or did was somehow wrong. But when he looked at his watch and saw that it was approaching six o'clock, he said again that he was leaving and she didn't try to stop him. At the door, she kissed his lips and he pulled away, knowing that he was in danger of going back inside and pretending his life was not what it was.

'Thank you,' he said.

And she frowned, and held up her hands as if to say that she didn't know what he meant, but he was walking away by then and he didn't go back. On the drive home, he told himself over and over that it was a one-off and it was wrong and he would make sure it didn't happen again. Knowing, even as he did so, that he wasn't that strong.

When he arrived home, Linda was sitting at the kitchen table with her head in her hands.

'What is it?' he asked, going to her. 'Is it the baby?'

If something had happened to the baby while he was with Marianne, he would never forgive himself.

Linda looked up at him, her eyes a little watery, a little glazed.

'Nothing,' she said. 'I've got a headache, that's all.'

Tom frowned at the sound of her voice. Slurred, slow.

'Have you been drinking?' he asked.

Linda's head snapped up and she locked her eyes on his, held them steady.

'No.'

'Sorry, I don't know what made me ask that. Where's Esme?'

'She's in her room. I think something happened at school. She's been up there since I brought her home, but she won't talk to me about it. She said she doesn't want anything to eat. She just wants you.'

Tom nodded, ignoring the resentment in Linda's voice, and walked up the stairs. He knocked on Esme's bedroom door and then opened it slowly before stepping inside. Esme was sitting on the blue rug beside her bed, her legs crossed, doing a jigsaw puzzle. One of her plaits had unravelled and the other one was still in place, and it made him smile. He kneeled down opposite her.

'Can I help?'

'I want to do it by myself,' Esme said, her voice quiet.

'That's very admirable. Can I watch?'

Esme shrugged her small shoulders.

'Thank you,' he said. 'And perhaps, while I'm watching, I could tell you about the international jigsaw championships I once attended, as a judge.'

Esme didn't look up, but she gave a small nod. He watched her as she separated out the pieces of blue sky from the pieces of green grass.

'The finalists were William Wasserschlanger from Germany and Mrs Wilson from next door, and the competition was held in your school hall. They had half an hour to try to complete puzzles with five thousand pieces. William Wasserschlanger's puzzle was a picture of a world map and Mrs Wilson's puzzle was a group photo of a one-hundred piece orchestra. I started the timer and they got to work, and after a couple of minutes I noticed that they were both looking confused and not getting very far.'

Tom saw that Esme had stopped working on her own puzzle and was looking directly at him, her eyes wide.

'It was Mrs Wilson who realised. Somehow, the puzzles had got mixed up, so Mrs Wilson had lots of bits of Africa and William Wasserschlanger had half a tuba and some pieces of cello. William Wasserschlanger was all for calling the whole thing off, but Mrs Wilson wouldn't hear of it. She insisted that they work together, and that's just what they did. And between them, they finished both of those puzzles with one minute and three seconds to spare. And we named them joint international jigsaw puzzle champions and all came back here to celebrate with cups of tea and a pineapple upside-down cake your mum had made.'

'That didn't happen,' Esme said, smiling.

'Esme, I can assure you that it did. Your problem is, you don't believe in things that happened before you were born, or things that you didn't see yourself. Next time you see Mrs Wilson, you ask her to show you her trophy.'

'Okay.'

'Good, I'm glad that's settled. Now, how was school today? You didn't find any stray bits of Sweden from William Wasserschlanger's puzzle in the hall, did you?'

'No.'

Esme paused and looked back down at her puzzle pieces. She picked up a piece of sky with the edge of a cloud on it and twirled it between her fingers.

'There's a boy at school who's mean to me, sometimes.'

Her voice was quiet, steely. Tom took the puzzle piece from her hand, placed it on the floor and held her hand between his.

'What does he do?'

'He just says things, about Phoebe.'

Tom felt an anger beginning to boil inside him. He closed his eyes for a moment, willed himself to stay calm.

'What kind of things?'

'He said that everyone knew it was my fault, that she died.'

Tom was still holding Esme's hand, but her head was bent low and her hair was hanging over her face. He heard the shake in her voice, and he saw a tear drop from the end of her nose and land on the rug. He stood and pulled her to her feet, held her close to his body, and he stroked her hair rhythmically as she sobbed into his chest.

'You know that's not true, Es. I don't know why he would say that, and I'm going to talk to the teachers and make sure it doesn't happen again, but the most important thing is that you remember it's not true. It was an accident, what happened, and it could have happened when I was here, or your mum. It was nobody's fault. You know that, don't you?'

Tom put his hands on Esme's shoulders and held her at arm's length so he could look at her eyes. They were watery, puffy, heartbreakingly sad.

'Yes,' she said.

And Tom didn't believe her, and he thought that she probably knew he didn't believe her, but he didn't know what else to say, to make things better.

21ST OCTOBER 1985

98 DAYS AFTER

Linda went into Esme's room each morning to find her lying on her back, eyes wide. And the first words out of her mouth were always the same. I don't want to go.

Tom had been down to the school, more than once, to try to get to the bottom of it. But Esme's teacher, Mrs Lewis, said she wasn't aware of any name-calling or teasing, or of anything that would explain Esme's reluctance to attend. Her work had slipped a little, Mrs Lewis said, but that was to be expected after such a difficult time.

Linda wished she could be there, with Esme, to catch the things her teacher was missing. Unseen, like a shadow. She wished she could follow her daughter like a shadow and find out what was happening to make her uneasy and steal her sleep. Sometimes, she told herself that there might really be nothing, that the time Esme had cried and confessed to Tom that someone was picking on her might have been an isolated incident. That the difference in Esme might stem from losing her sister, from her family being violently altered, from her mother's silent blame.

Linda knew, in her rational mind, that Esme wasn't to blame for Phoebe's death. That it was her fault, if it was anyone's, for leaving the two girls alone together when they were too young for that responsibility. Or Tom's, for coming home late, for not being there at the time she'd come to expect him. But Esme was the one who had been there, who'd let it happen, and Linda couldn't quite forgive her for that, no matter how much she wanted to. She tried to keep that ugly blame hidden deep inside herself, never voiced it, and yet she feared that it was clear to read on her face when she looked at her daughter. That it was harming her.

One morning in late October, Linda found the morning battle particularly hard. By the time Tom left the house with Esme in tow, she felt exhausted, ready to crawl back into bed. She went into the kitchen, poured the remains of a bottle of vodka into a glass and drained it, her hands shaking slightly. And then she wrapped it up in old newspaper and hid it at the bottom of the outside bin. She told herself that that was it, that it was over. That it wasn't working.

But an hour later, she walked to the off-licence and bought another bottle, an identical one. And she wasn't sure whether she was replacing it in case Tom noticed its absence, or because she needed it. She stood there, in the kitchen, her coat still on, and she looked at the bottle for several long minutes before unscrewing the top and taking two long slugs. And then she hated herself, because she knew. It wasn't over. It was only just beginning.

Linda gave in to the urge to go back to bed. She stripped off her clothes and lay beneath the covers in her underwear, closed her eyes. And that was when she heard it. Just when she'd stopped expecting to.

'Look at me, Mum.'

Phoebe. The soft lilt of her voice, the pride. Linda opened her eyes and looked around the room, willing her daughter to show herself. Silently begging to see her, one last time. To see her smiling and moving and alive. If she could see her that way, Linda thought, it would take away the pain of seeing her in the coffin. It would erase that image that she lived with, that haunted her. She wondered, briefly, whether she could have fallen asleep. Whether it could have been a fragment of a dream. The room was empty, of course. And so Linda closed her eyes again, and reached out for the comfort of sleep.

A little later, Linda awoke, feeling suffocated. The words were still there, on her lips. *Look at me, Mum.* She dressed hastily and moved through the rooms of the house, opening windows. It was a cool day, and as she began to feel a breeze against her skin, she calmed a little. But it wasn't enough. She needed to be outside, to feel the air all around her. She opened the back door and stepped into the garden, feeling goosebumps rise on her bare arms.

'Linda?'

She looked up and saw Maud standing on the other side of the fence that separated their two gardens. Linda forced a smile.

'What are you doing out here in the cold? Do you want to come over for a cup of tea? I've been gardening, but I was just about to put the kettle on.'

'No.'

'You look tired, dear. Is the baby keeping you up?'

Linda looked down at her stomach. Her bump was mostly hidden beneath an oversized jumper. Sometimes, she almost forgot about it, was oblivious, for small snatches of time, of the countdown that was ticking away in the background of her life.

'I'm fine,' Linda said.

She was being rude, she knew. But she couldn't remember how to act, what to say. She lowered herself on to the garden bench, took a few deep breaths.

'You know,' Maud said, leaning her elbows on the fence, 'I had this dream last night and, in it, the whole thing was an elaborate scheme of some kind. Arthur and Phoebe were alive. They'd been together somewhere, and they came back, laughing and joking about how they'd tricked us. And we were so angry, you and I, about what they'd put us through, that when they tried to come to us, we turned away.'

Linda said nothing. She knew that the story wasn't quite finished. There was a lump, growing, at the back of her throat. She bit her lip, desperate to keep the tears inside.

'I wouldn't do that, if they came back. If we could have them back, even if it was just for a day, an hour even. I wouldn't care what had happened. I'd welcome them and I'd hold them tightly. I'd tell Arthur all the things I never said.'

'It's impossible,' Linda said. And then she stood up and went inside without saying goodbye.

The phone was ringing. More than anything, Linda wanted to ignore it. But she thought it would be Tom, and he had a habit of trying again and again until she picked up.

'Hello?'

'Mrs Sadler? It's Miss Bartholomew, Esme's headteacher.'

Linda's breath caught in her throat and she thought about how it was possible for lightning to strike twice. She couldn't speak, couldn't order her thoughts, could only imagine another coffin that was too small, another daughter lost.

'Don't worry, Mrs Sadler. Esme's fine.'

Linda heard the words but still didn't quite believe them. She remained half trapped in a waking nightmare, still convinced that Esme had been taken from her because she hadn't been the mother she should have been. She stood, and then felt her legs start to buckle beneath her, and she gripped the doorframe for support.

'Mrs Sadler, are you there?'

'Yes,' Linda said. 'Yes, I'm here.'

'We'd like you to come in and collect Esme, if you can. She's a bit upset. She got into an argument with another child in the playground, and, well, she bit him. We haven't managed to get the full story out of her, but she's quite worked up.'

Linda said that she was on her way, hung up the phone. And then she called Tom and asked him to meet her at the school.

She'd been waiting for something like this, hadn't she? Waiting for the fragile silence to break. As she drove, she tried to imagine what this faceless boy could have said or done to drive her placid daughter to violence. And without knowing who he was, or how it had unfolded, Linda hated him.

Tom was in the car park when she arrived, leaning against his car. He reached out to take her in his arms, and for the first time in a long time, she let him hold her. There was a comfort in standing there like that, their unborn baby between them. It felt like they were a family, or like they were ready to become one. Linda could feel Tom's heartbeat pulsing in his neck, and she kissed him there, lightly, and then took his hand to lead him inside.

They found Esme sitting on a chair outside Miss Bartholomew's office, her legs swinging, not quite reaching the floor. Linda was struck by how young she looked, how vulnerable. But it was Tom who dropped to his knees and took her hands in his, asked her what had happened. Linda wished it had been her, wished that Esme still thought of her that way, as the fixer of bad situations. Esme was silent, and Linda was reminded of herself at seven years old – closed-off, alone. She wanted to tell her daughter that they loved her, that it didn't matter what she'd done, but the words wouldn't come.

Miss Bartholomew opened the door and ushered them into her office, leaving Esme outside. The room was chilly and sparsely furnished, but her smile was kind.

'I'm sorry to have to call you in like this. We just didn't think we could send her back to her lessons. She seems to have calmed down a bit, now, but she was really quite worked up.'

'How did it happen?' Linda asked. 'Did anyone see?'

Mrs Bartholomew bowed her head, and Linda took that as an admission of guilt. This was her school, after all, and it shouldn't have been possible for a playground rift to escalate to this without someone seeing, and stepping in.

'Mrs Jackson, one of the dinner ladies, stopped it. But she didn't see how it started. And the children aren't saying anything.'

'Who was the boy?' Tom asked. 'Is he okay?'

'Simon Treadwell. He's fine. He can be a bit of a trouble-maker, actually. He's high-spirited, excitable. I imagine he must have said something to provoke her, although I can't be sure.'

The name was familiar to Linda, and almost at once she realised that he was the boy they'd seen with his mother that day in the park. His mother was the woman who had asked after Phoebe. She ran through the cruel things he might have said, wondering what could have led Esme to this. She'd always been so gentle with Phoebe. Linda knew, in her gut, that he must have said something about Phoebe. That it was Esme's fault? Maybe that something awful was going to happen to the new baby?

'We'll take her home, try to find out a bit more about what happened,' Tom said. 'We'll let you know.'

'I'm sure you understand,' Miss Bartholomew said, 'that we have to treat any kind of violence with the utmost seriousness. Ordinarily, in this kind of situation, we'd suspend the child.'

'Suspend her?' Linda asked, pushing back her chair and standing up. 'She's seven years old!'

'Mrs Sadler, please. We can't be seen to be giving the message that this kind of behaviour is acceptable. However, I've spoken to Esme's teacher, Mrs Lewis. She told me about your loss. She also said that this is completely out of character for Esme, and that Esme has reported some teasing recently. And since we don't know exactly what happened to provoke it, I'm prepared to overlook it this once.'

Silently, internally, Linda swung between anger and relief. She wanted to pick up on Miss Bartholomew's admission that they didn't know the exact circumstances, confront her about the fact that this had happened when no one was watching. But she clung on to the woman's final words. Esme would not be suspended. It would be foolish to make things worse.

'Thank you,' Tom said. 'We'll make sure she understands.'

'Good,' Miss Bartholomew said, 'because if anything like this happens again...'

'It won't,' Tom said, his voice calm but firm.

Miss Bartholomew nodded, and then she saw them to the door. Esme was still sitting outside, rocking gently forwards and backwards. When they told her it was time to go home, she dropped to her feet and followed them.

Because they'd come separately, they had to drive home in two cars. Esme went with Tom, and Linda wondered what they would talk about on the short journey home, whether Esme would confide in her father once she was out of earshot. Or whether the car would be thick with silence, the way that echoing corridor had been.

A thought struck Linda as she pulled on to the driveway. I don't know how much more I can take. It came to her, fully formed, as if from nowhere, and it frightened her to think that it had been lingering in her mind for an unknowable length of time. It made her wonder what else was hidden there.

When she entered the house, she heard Tom's voice.

'It's important that you understand,' he was saying. 'It's never all right to hurt someone else. Never. If anyone says anything mean, you must tell a teacher, or me and Mum. Then we'll make sure it gets sorted out.'

'You can't,' Esme said.

Linda walked into the lounge. Esme was curled up in a ball on the sofa, her head hidden. Tom was sitting beside her with his arms folded. Linda approached and reached out a hand to stroke Esme's tangled hair.

'We can't what?' she asked.

'You can't sort it out. He's too clever. He'd never say anything to me when there was a teacher nearby.'

'What does he say?' Linda asked, crouching so that she was level with Esme.

Esme shrugged. 'That I'm ugly, that I'm stupid. That I killed Phoebe.'

Tom stood, then. 'He actually said that? He said you killed her?'

Esme looked up and nodded. Her eyes were red, tired. Linda thought of all those mornings she'd found Esme awake, wondered exactly how much sleep she'd missed.

'We'll sort it out, Es,' Tom said.

He sounded confident, sure. Linda hoped it was a promise he'd be able to keep.

30TH OCTOBER 1985

107 DAYS AFTER

'Do you think Esme's any happier, about school?' Tom asked. He was tidying up. He'd noticed things slipping, getting worse and worse, and he didn't want to leave it for Linda. She was big by then, bigger than he remembered her being with Esme or Phoebe, even though she had a few weeks to go. Her ankles were swollen and her arms and legs looked heavy to lift.

'The same, I'd say.'

Tom felt Linda's eyes on him as he picked things up around her. She was sitting on the sofa, her feet up, a mug of tea going cold on the table in front of her.

'I know you want me to apologise, but I won't,' she said.

Tom stopped what he was doing, hugged a couple of magazines and one of Esme's teddy bears to his chest, and turned to face her.

'Apologise for what?'

'For the state of this place. I'm not blind to it. I'm just so tired.'

Tom lifted Linda's feet and sat down heavily on the sofa.

'I know. That's why I'm doing it.'

He wondered why she was trying to start an argument, out of nowhere. It was something she did, every now and then, and there was always something lurking behind it. The first time she'd done it, years and years before, they'd come out of the cinema and she said she hated the film and seemed to blame him for that. Later that night, when Tom was exhausted from trying to work out what was happening to them, she'd revealed that she was pregnant. He knew the signs.

'What's wrong?' he asked.

It was the kind of question that was hard to ask, after a tragedy, when everything was wrong and there were no words to explain it. But he asked it anyway. He wondered, fleetingly, whether his marriage was over. But he didn't believe that it was, not really.

'What do you mean?' Linda asked.

'You seem upset.'

'I'm always upset.' She snatched her feet away from him, curled them beneath her.

'I mean more than usual. Can we talk about it? Have you thought any more about having counselling?'

'Why? Because you think I'm going mad?'

Tom didn't know what to say to that, so he said nothing for a minute or two.

'Where did that come from?'

'I know that's what you think. Ever since I first heard Phoebe.'

Tom took a deep breath. He hadn't brought it up again, because he didn't know how, and he hoped it would just go away, be forgotten.

'Do you really think you heard her?'

'I know I did. And I heard her again, the other day. I know you can't believe me. But she hasn't gone, Tom. Not entirely. There's something of her left here, whatever you think.'

'I know you want to hold on to her. I understand that. I want her to be here just as much as you do.'

He watched as Linda stood and began to pace up and down.

'That's not it. I can feel her. I just wish, for once, you'd stop being so rational and listen to what I'm saying.'

'Okay, I'm sorry. Just, try not to get worked up. It's not good for the baby.'

Linda placed her hands on her bump. It was an unmistakeably protective gesture, and Tom was glad of that. Since that day in the doctor's office, she'd hardly spoken about the baby. They hadn't talked about names, or made plans. He hadn't dared to ask about the practicalities, about whether he should bring the cot down from the loft, whether he should put it in Phoebe's room. Linda had stripped that room of any reminders of Phoebe, but it felt, to Tom, more like an exorcism than preparation.

'I don't know whether I can do this,' Linda said.

Her words sounded loud in the silence that had grown in the room. But her voice was matter-of-fact, too. Calm. Practised.

'What? The baby?'

'All of it. Being Esme's mother. Being the baby's mother. Being your wife.'

Tom fought an urge to get up and leave the room. He'd always been like that, since childhood. He'd always wanted to hide from the hardest things, to pretend they weren't happening.

'Can't we just see?' he asked, his voice choked. 'You might feel differently once the baby's here. And I'll do everything I can.'

When an image of Marianne flashed before him, Tom felt sick. He could hardly believe what he'd done, what he was doing. It wasn't like him. But loneliness was a powerful thing. And he'd learned that feeling lonely when you're surrounded by your family – the family you love and always wanted – was worse than feeling lonely when you were alone. Loneliness was at its worst when you could see everything you'd ever loved slowly disappearing before your eyes.

'I won't leave,' Tom said.

And Linda looked at him, looked in his eyes with a compassion that had been missing from them for weeks. Months. A compassion that could have been mistaken for love, but wasn't. Not quite. Not even nearly.

'I know,' she said. 'But sometimes I wish you would.'

Tom felt the anger start to bubble in him the minute the words were out in the room. He wondered whether she regretted them. He wanted to hit her. And for the first time in his life, he really thought he might do it, so he turned and walked out of the house, got into his car and drove away. He drove in the direction of Marianne's flat without making a conscious decision to do so. And when he was about a mile away, he pulled over, and at the side of a busy road, he balled his hands into fists and punched the steering wheel over and over, until his hands were sore and bleeding.

'What happened?' Marianne asked, her voice shrill with alarm.

Tom reached out and held her awkwardly, keeping his hands away from her body.

'I'm sorry,' he said. 'I needed to see you.'

Marianne ushered him inside, and when the door was closed, she faced him in the darkened hallway, holding him at arm's length.

'You can always come here,' she said. 'Remember that.'

He'd fallen into a habit of driving over here once or twice a week, after he closed the shop. The journey was familiar, now, and the heaviness of guilt and shame was lifting, a little, with every visit. Every time he walked into his house, more than an hour later than usual, Tom silently hoped that Linda would call him on it. But she barely seemed to notice.

Tom's visits to Marianne were always the same, more or less. First, they went to bed. And after, they talked, drank coffee, laughed. He knew that it was about sex, but he also knew that wasn't the whole of it. He needed somewhere to laugh, and be relaxed and peaceful. He wished that Linda had somewhere like it. Things might be different, if she did.

'Let me sort out your hands,' Marianne said.

They walked into the small bathroom, and she turned on the sink's cold tap, held his hands beneath it. While he stood there, watching the blood swirl around the plughole, Marianne crouched down beside the bath, opened the doors to a small cabinet, and began to search for the things she needed.

She was calm, cleaning the wounds carefully as he sat on the edge of the bath, wrapping both his hands in neat bandages.

'Are you going to tell me what happened?' she asked, once she'd finished.

'It's stupid, I was just lashing out.'

'Why were you so angry?'

Tom thought about that. Was it because he thought it might be over, with Linda? Would that really be such a bad thing, given the state of their relationship? Yes. Because not living with Esme and the new baby would kill him. And that was another good reason to walk away from Marianne. He looked at her, her face hopeful. She wasn't judging him. She was just waiting for him to tell her what had happened.

'Linda and I argued. I had to get away. It's nothing, really.'

Tom knew that he'd betrayed Linda in the worst possible way, but he refused to go into any detail about their battles and problems. He looked down at the floor, Marianne's gaze too intense, too caring.

'I should go,' he said. 'I shouldn't have come. But thank you.'

He held his hands up a little to show he was talking about the care she'd shown him.

At the door, Marianne looked at him sadly.

'I wish it didn't have to be a moral struggle for you to come here,' she said.

'Marianne, I'm married. I told you that.'

'I know. I just wish I'd known what I had, all those years ago. I wish I'd kept hold of you.'

She kissed his lips and slipped back inside, and Tom walked to his car, thinking about what she'd said. If he and Marianne had stayed together, there would have been no Linda, no Esme, no Phoebe. They might have children of their own, by now. They might have married. It might have been wonderful, and yet he didn't like to imagine a world into which his little girls had never been born. When he pulled into his driveway, Tom tore the bandages from his hands and stuffed them into his pockets. The bleeding seemed to have stopped. He took a deep breath, and went inside.

He found Linda at the kitchen table. She was clutching her stomach and her face was set in a grimace. Tom felt his heart lurch, felt that it would leap out of his throat if anything happened to this baby.

'What is it?' he asked, moving quickly to her side and kneeling before her.

'It's the baby,' she said. 'It's coming.'

Tom wanted to ask whether her waters had broken, how long she'd been having contractions. He wanted to ask her whether she was sure, to say that it was too early, by several weeks. He wanted to say he was sorry, for not being there when she needed him. Again. But he said none of those things. He kissed Linda's forehead and he told her to wait where she was while he went next door to ask Maud to look after Esme.

He went to the lounge, switched off the television and took Esme by the hand.

'I have to take Mum to the hospital,' he said. 'The baby's coming.'

Esme looked bewildered, and Tom wondered what his own expression looked like, whether she was simply mirroring what she saw.

'I thought the baby was coming next month,' she said.

'Me too, but it looks like it's in a hurry. Don't worry, though, everything will be fine. I'm going to take you next door, to Mrs Wilson's. Is that okay?'

Esme nodded, but she didn't smile. Tom wanted to hold her, to make up a story for her, to do anything he could to reassure her, but there wasn't time. He would make up for it, he promised himself, later.

Standing on the doorstep with Esme's hand in his, Tom listened out for the familiar shuffle of Maud's slippered feet in the hallway. And when he heard it, he let out a great sigh of relief, and Esme looked up at him, and he felt close to tears. Five minutes later, he was back in the house, hurriedly packing a bag, scolding himself for not doing it sooner. When he opened the bottom drawer in the chest in their bedroom, Tom was faced with a sea of white. Tiny vests, socks, hats, all bought or borrowed in the early days of Linda's pregnancy, when there was only hope in their hearts.

In the car, Linda said nothing, but he could tell from her breathing each time a contraction swept over her. They were about six minutes apart. They still had time. And yet, he put his foot down and cursed every traffic light and roundabout they came to. Swore loudly every time he was forced to slow down.

Finally, he pulled into a parking space and turned off the engine. He was about to open the door, to dash inside and find a wheelchair, when Linda placed her hand on his, stilling him.

'I'm scared,' she said.

Tom felt how close he was to crumbling. He was standing on the edge of a cliff, a sheer and rocky drop in front of him, and his stomach was churning. One wrong move and it would all be over. And he wasn't even in control of his own destiny. He was a puppet, and the strings were held by someone else, someone who didn't know or care how much his family meant to him.

'Me too,' he said.

He wondered whether she was talking about the fact that the baby was coming early, or just about the fact that the baby was coming at all.

'I'll do my best,' Linda said. 'I just don't know how good that will be.'

Tom looked at her, at her eyes, which used to dance and sparkle. They were flat and lifeless, and he couldn't see their future in them.

'I'm here,' he said. 'Just tell me what I can do.'

And then he pulled her hand to his mouth, and kissed it.

'Let's go in,' she said, her voice all steel and determination.

31ST OCTOBER 1985

108 DAYS AFTER

With Esme, there was the cruel shock of it, the intensity of pain, like nothing she'd ever known. Linda had sworn and twisted her body, desperate to rid herself of it. She remembered Tom, biting his nails, trying to take her hand, looking helpless.

With Phoebe, she'd been more prepared, known what to expect, and it had been different again. She'd slithered out, fast and easy, and then lain still without crying for seven long minutes. Long enough to make everyone fear that there was something wrong.

This time, this third time, Linda wasn't sure she had the energy left inside her. The contractions had come on so quickly and she was fully dilated, but it seemed that no amount of pushing would entice the baby to finish its journey down the birth canal. The room was full of medical professionals, all with their rigid opinions. Too many, Linda thought, for a normal birth. She questioned what they knew, what they were keeping from her. She wondered about her drinking, about the damage it might have caused. And she longed for a drink, right then, to give that stark white room an edge of fuzziness. To soften things a little.

She felt a new contraction sweeping over her, coming up from her feet, and she pulled her hand from Tom's, clenched her fists and gritted her teeth, letting it come. When it was over, a smile crossed Tom's face. 'Are we still settled on Oliver, for a boy?' he asked. Linda nodded. 'And if it's a girl,' he said. 'What do you think about Beatrice?'

'Beatrice,' Linda said, unsure.

'Bea?'

'Yes,' Linda said. 'Bea.'

When they told her she was losing blood, Linda only nodded. She felt weak, and wondered whether it was psychological, a result of what she'd just heard. For a second, she wondered whether this was how it would end for her, flat on her back on this hard bed. She pictured Tom, struggling with Esme and the new baby in her absence. He would cope, she realised. He was strong, and he would love them in a way that she couldn't. Perhaps, if it was to be, she thought, then it was for the best.

They acted fast, telling her that they were going to use forceps and then, if the baby still wouldn't come, they'd take her into theatre for an emergency caesarean. They asked for her consent, and she nodded. Hoping, secretly, that she might just ebb away. That the baby would survive. She wasn't sure how Tom would get over it if both of them were lost.

Linda felt the cold metal against her skin, felt her flesh tear, but she felt numb, too. She fixed her eyes on Tom, tried to communicate the fact that she wasn't scared, that she was ready for it all to be over, that she was sorry. And then she heard a cry and the baby was out, and she was still breathing, still living. And they were saying that the baby was a girl, that she was healthy.

And then, and then. Linda was elsewhere, submerged in water, barely breathing. If she concentrated hard, she could hear what was going on around her, but she was removed, somehow absent. And beside her, not visible but very definitely there, was Phoebe. Linda felt a hot rush of happiness, and it was so unfamiliar a feeling that it took her a few moments to recognise it. She tried to whisper her daughter's name but there was no sound. It didn't matter, because all she cared about was that Phoebe was there with her, as real as she'd been when she was alive.

Around her, there was a rush of activity. Linda heard the word coma, heard a low, animal sound that must have come from Tom. There were more doctors and nurses in the room, and they were rushing around, checking things and trying everything they could to bring her back.

Linda firmly believed that coming back up to the surface was within her control. She had her reasons for waiting. It was hard, hearing the panic in the doctors' voices and feeling Tom's hand so cold and imagining him feeling lost and helpless. Knowing that she could come back to him, if she tried. But she was the closest she'd been to Phoebe in a long time, and she wasn't prepared to lose her grip on that. And besides, she had to know that the baby was safe. They'd said that she was healthy, but she'd arrived so early and Linda knew how quickly things could change. She had to know that her baby would live, before she made her choice. In the meantime, she tried to send Tom a signal through her limp hand. She willed him to understand.

She thought of Esme. A memory came to her, from a few days earlier, when she'd found her daughter doing a handstand against her wardrobe door. They were running late for school and Esme's cereal was getting soggy in the kitchen, so she'd gone upstairs to look for her, calling her name. And when she opened Esme's bedroom door, there she was, upside down with her grey school skirt hanging to her neck. Her face red, her plaits skimming the floor.

'Esme,' she'd said. 'I don't have time for this. Come downstairs and eat your breakfast.'

And Esme had righted herself, silently, and obeyed.

There was something in that quiet obedience that pained Linda. She could almost feel the weight that Esme was carrying.

Linda knew that Esme should be the trigger, should be enough to make her snap out of this. But she wasn't.

She let herself slip a little deeper into unconsciousness. It was like sinking into a warm bath. Comforting. The temptation to keep going, to go under, was strong. But she didn't give in to it.

Before she'd lost consciousness, she'd caught a glimpse of her new daughter, of Bea, but she hadn't held her or looked into her eyes. She'd looked just like Esme had, Linda thought, small and peaceful. A shock of dark hair and a serious expression. It was like having Esme all over again.

Linda waited for the doctor to notice the change in her. The slip. She didn't have to wait long. Within minutes, the tension in the air around her bed had raised and she could feel the breath of one of the doctors on her neck. She heard Tom whisper her name and then his hand was gone from hers and she wondered whether he'd been ushered out of the room, or whether he was watching from the sidelines.

It was intoxicating, the power. It was the most control she'd had for a long time. She considered slipping again, but she stopped herself, unsure exactly where the point of no return was located.

Linda forced herself to think about what Tom would tell Esme, if she died, if the baby died. It would be too much for Esme to understand. To be told that there was a baby, a new sister, and then to have that sister taken away, and her mother taken too. It would be something she'd never get over. But would it be worse than the alternative? Would it be worse than her spending every day of her childhood with a mother who couldn't quite look her in the eye?

Linda was so young when Esme was born, and everything was a struggle and there was fear, every day, that she was doing it all wrong. But gradually, her confidence had grown and she'd settled into the knowledge that she was a good mother. Good enough, anyway. With Tom beside her, she'd learned and guessed and muddled through. Every day, there were decisions to make. And she believed that, for the most part, she'd made the right ones.

But just then, she was the furthest she'd ever been from her family. And the decision to return to them – a decision she wouldn't have thought twice about a year before – remained unmade. And Bea was out there, somewhere in the hospital, hours old and never once touched by her mother. And never once held, or fed, or kissed by her mother.

Linda noticed that Tom was speaking. Muttering, really.

'Please. Don't leave us. I need you. Esme needs you.'

Linda wondered whether that was true. It was the sort of thing people said, in these situations. But Esme had always loved her father more, and she hadn't been much of a mother to her lately. How much of a difference would her absence actually make to Esme's small world?

There was a lengthy pause, and Linda wondered whether Tom was crying.

'You know,' Tom said then, 'I think I fell in love with you the first day we met. I think I knew, even then, that we'd live our lives together. And I know how hard it's been and I wish I could go back and change things, because I feel like I've let you down. If I could change things, I would. But not very much. Because even though it feels wrong to say it, I think we've been lucky in a lot of ways. Having each other, having Esme. Having Phoebe, for the time we did. And now Bea.'

He'd spoken quietly and Linda had to concentrate hard to catch every word. She thought about the things that people say when they don't think anyone can hear them. She thought about what she'd say to him, if their places were reversed. Would she ask for his forgiveness, or give him hers? Or tell him about the dreams she had sometimes, in which she had a different husband, a different life? And no children.

A doctor came into the room to speak to Tom. 'I just saw your daughter,' he said. 'She's doing well. She's in an incubator on the special care unit, because she's so small. She'll be in there for a few weeks, while she continues to put on weight and gather strength. You won't be able to take her home for quite a while, but things are looking very promising.'

'Thank you,' Tom said, his voice pure relief.

And without quite knowing that she was going to do it, Linda opened her eyes. She saw Tom, saw the tears in his eyes, saw the doctor, turning to leave the room.

'I want to see my daughter,' she said.

They wouldn't let her get out of bed until much later. There were checks to be done, and she had to tell them, over and over, that she felt fine. And eventually, a wheelchair was brought in and Tom wheeled her carefully along the corridor to the unit where Bea lay. It took less than a minute to get there, and yet Linda felt that entire lifetimes were passing as they made the trip. It was agonising to be so close to Bea, and yet not quite there.

And when she was finally beside the incubator, her eyes level with her daughter's, she expected a sense of calm to engulf her. She expected that everything would feel right, suddenly, and that there would be a break from the pain. But as Bea opened her eyes and Linda caught them with her own, she realised with a searing jolt that there was still a hollowness inside her. That even Bea, with her perfect face and her tiny, kicking legs, couldn't fill it.

1ST NOVEMBER 1985

109 DAYS AFTER

Tom woke at seven after four hours of sleep. His eyes drooped but there was a nervous energy in him and he knew he wouldn't find sleep again. Lying there, on Linda's side of the bed, he replayed the events of the previous day. The midwife washing Bea, wrapping her up tight in a blanket. The jealousy he felt towards this stranger who was the first to touch her. He remembered that he could almost feel the weight of her in his arms, the warmth. And he pushed aside the fear that she was too small, that she'd been born too soon. She moved through the room towards him, the midwife carrying her invisible. And he felt his life dividing into two clear parts – before and after he held her. But she was carried swiftly out of the room to the special care unit, and he was left, open-mouthed. Arms empty. And then there was Linda's sudden slip into unconsciousness. And that knowledge that his heart would stop, if hers did.

Tom shuddered at the memory, and then he got out of bed, walked down the landing to Esme's room. He stood beside her bed, reached for the duvet and covered her foot, which was sticking out.

Esme opened her left eye slowly, as if the light hurt her.

'Hey you,' Tom said.

'Hey you.'

'It's time to get ready for school.'

'Where's Mum?'

She reached out her hands and Tom took them, pulled her to a sitting position. He sat down beside her.

'She's in the hospital with your new sister. She needs to stay there for a few days and get lots of rest.'

'Can't she rest at home?'

Tom shook his head. 'In a while, she can. But for now, she's very, very tired and she needs to rest all the time. I'll tell you what. You go to school, and then when I pick you up, I'll take you to the hospital to see them. And then tomorrow, Mum might be able to come home.'

'Bea too?'

Tom paused, faltered. 'We have to wait a bit longer for Bea. She should have stayed inside your mum for a bit longer, so she's quite small and she needs to spend some time in a special glass box until she's grown a bit.'

Esme giggled. 'That's silly,' she said.

Tom reached out his hand and touched Esme's cheek, and then he stood up and started to leave the room. At the door, he turned back.

'If you're downstairs in your uniform in ten minutes, I'll make you a boiled egg and soldiers.'

'Deal,' Esme said, already rushing past him on her way to the bathroom.

Downstairs, he called Liam.

'Hello?'

Tom could tell by the grogginess in Liam's voice that he'd woken him. For a second, he wished he could swap places with this boy. Twenty-one, with no ties and no real responsibilities. He could go anywhere, do anything. He could visit the places that were detailed in the books they sold, rather than just reading about them, as Tom did.

He explained the situation and Liam agreed to look after the shop, told Tom to take as long as he needed. Before he hung up, Liam congratulated him on Bea's birth, and Tom had to bite back tears.

After dropping Esme off at the school gate, Tom drove straight to the hospital. He went to Bea first, feeling that he couldn't wait another moment to see her again. When he'd left the hospital the night before, he had a clear image of her in his mind, but already, the mental picture he held was a little blurry, and he wasn't sure whether he was confusing it with an image of Esme or Phoebe as a newborn.

Bea's incubator was in the corner by the window. She was lying on her back with her arms resting, palms up, beside her head. Her eyes shut tight. Her fingers were curled and quivering slightly, as though she was in the middle of a dream. Tom longed to hold her. He thought of the broken sleep and the difficult times ahead, once she was home, and he couldn't wait for them to begin. And because it was the closest he could get to her, he kissed his fingers and pressed them against the glass.

Linda was awake, her eyes wide and watery. They'd moved her from a private room on to a ward, and Tom walked through bubbles of low chatter on his way to her. When he reached her, he pulled the curtain around her bed for a little privacy, and took a seat.

'How are you feeling?' he asked.

'Tired. Ready to go home.'

'Have you seen Bea today? I just came from there. She's fast asleep.'

'No,' Linda said, and there was an edge to her voice that frightened Tom a little.

'Well, I'm sure you can see her later. Or I could get hold of a wheelchair and take you now...'

Linda shook her head slightly and he stopped talking. The fizz of excitement that he'd felt since waking that morning disappeared, and all of a sudden his limbs felt a little too heavy, and his eyes ached.

'I just dropped Esme off at school,' he said. He had to keep talking, to keep things normal. 'She sends her love. I said I'd bring her after school. She's so excited about Bea. She's even drawn her a picture.'

The picture was of the four of them – him, tall and smiling, Linda, her long hair reaching her waist, the way it had when he first met her, and for the first few years of Esme's life. Esme, standing between them with her hands in theirs. And Bea, a white bundle in Linda's arms. When she showed it to him, he pictured her drawing it, not quite knowing whether to include Phoebe. He wasn't sure whether he was imagining the fact that, in the picture, Esme stood a little closer to him than to Linda, and there was a space where Phoebe should have been.

There was a scraping sound as the curtains were pulled open, and Tom turned to see the doctor who had taken care of Linda the day before.

'Good morning,' he said.

'Morning,' the doctor said. He turned to Linda. 'How are you feeling today? Any pain? Any dizziness?'

'No,' Linda said. 'Just tired.'

'That's good.' He consulted the chart on the end of her bed, and then he replaced it, folded his arms. 'As long as that doesn't change, I think we only need to keep you here for one more night.'

'I definitely can't go home today?' Linda asked.

The doctor frowned. 'No, I'm afraid not. Your body's been through a lot. You need to get plenty of rest.'

'But I can't sleep here!'

Tom tried not to pay any attention to the other patients and visitors who were turning to look their way. He tried to ignore the hysteria in Linda's voice. He reached for her hand, but she snatched it away before he could touch her. He couldn't help noticing the doctor looking away, pretending not to notice.

'I know it's hard, being away from home, away from your family. But this really is the best place for you for the time being. One more day, Linda. I'll come back to check on you this afternoon.'

When he'd gone, Tom stood to close the curtain again, but Linda stopped him.

'Leave it,' she said. 'I feel too enclosed with that thing pulled across. I feel like I can't breathe.'

'No problem,' Tom said. He lowered his voice, unwilling to have this conversation overheard by this roomful of strangers. 'Listen, it'll be time to come home soon, and then we can start getting things ready for Bea. If you feel up to it, that is. You can lie in bed and direct proceedings from there. Esme will help me.'

'I don't want to talk about that,' Linda said, her voice calm, firm.

'Why not?'

Tom couldn't stop himself from asking, even though he didn't want to know the answer.

Linda lay on her back, and there were tears streaming down her cheeks. Tom wanted to take her hand, or wipe at the tears with his fingers, but he stayed where he was, his hands clasped together.

'I don't love her,' Linda said, her voice barely audible. 'I thought I would love her, but I don't.'

She turned so that she was facing away from him, facing the wall. And Tom looked at her back for a while, the way it moved slightly as she cried, and he thought it was like looking at a stranger.

Once he was sure that Linda was asleep, her breathing deep and even, he made his way down the corridor, looking for a pay phone. He looked around him as he dialled, and then questioned himself about what he was looking for. Someone he knew? Linda?

'Hello?'

'Marianne, it's Tom.'

'Where are you?'

Her voice was rich and full, and it calmed him as he'd hoped it would.

'I can't come over,' Tom said, ignoring her question. 'I just needed to hear your voice.'

'I see,' Marianne said. 'Do you mean you can't come over today, or you can't come over again, at all?'

'Today.'

She didn't speak then, but when Tom closed his eyes, he could picture her smiling. He wanted to tell her what he'd been through. That he had a new daughter, that he'd thought he might lose Linda. The things that Linda had said, the way they made him feel. Sick, and sorry. But she wasn't the right person. Why was it, that she was the only one he wanted to talk to, when there was so much he had to keep hidden from her? Tom thought of Linda, then, exhausted and weak from delivering his baby. He felt a cold trickle of shame running through his veins, mixed in with his blood.

'Do you know when?' Marianne asked. 'I miss you.'

'Soon,' he said. 'I'll call you. Listen, I have to go. But thanks for picking up. I really needed to talk to you. Just for a minute.'

'Goodbye, Tom.'

He stood in the corridor long after he hung up the phone, unsure of what he was doing, or where he should go. Linda had made it clear that she didn't want him there, and Bea needed to rest. Needing air, he found the nearest exit and took a walk around the hospital grounds in the fine autumn rain.

LATER THAT DAY, Tom took Esme to the hospital. He wasn't sure how Linda would react to seeing her, but he'd promised, and he wasn't prepared to go back on that. In the car, Esme was full of questions. She seemed nervous, talking fast and constantly moving her legs around in the space in front of her seat. Tom wanted to tell her that it would be okay, that what happened with Phoebe wouldn't happen again. Instead, he made up a story on the spot, never quite sure what the next sentence would be until it was out there in the space between them.

'You know where the hospital is?' he began.

'Yes.'

'Well, years and years and years ago, there was no hospital, and there was a fairground on that piece of land. It was owned by a very rich man called Hugo Handsandfeet, and he built it for the children of Southampton. All the rides were free and you could eat as much candyfloss as you liked. Then one day, the council decided that they needed to build a hospital so they offered Hugo Handsandfeet a big pile of money to buy the land he owned. But of course he didn't need the money, and he wanted the children to have the fairground, so he said no.

'But then, when he was one hundred and thirty-three years old, he got very poorly and he died because there was no hospital to go to. Just before he died, he phoned the council and agreed that they could have the land to build their hospital. The next day, the diggers arrived to flatten the fairground, but the man from the council couldn't bear to see all of Hugo Handsandfeet's rides being destroyed, so here's what they did. They dug a big hole in the ground and they lowered the fairground into it, and then they built the hospital on top.

'Now, sometimes, late at night, after all the visitors have gone home, you can see the ghost of Hugo Handsandfeet skipping along the hospital corridors. He gathers up all the children and he takes them in his secret lift, all the way down under the ground, and he lets them run around his fairground until morning. So when we see Bea, she might be sleepy from being up all night on the dodgems and the merry-go-round.'

'Bea can't go on the rides,' Esme said. 'She's too little. She can't walk yet.'

'She can in the middle of the night, when she's with Hugo Handsandfeet. It's magic, you see. So if she's asleep when we get there, you'll know why.'

Tom stole a glance at Esme, caught her smiling.

Once they were inside and had reached the special care unit, the nurses made a big fuss of Esme.

'The big sister,' they said. 'We've been waiting to meet you.'

Esme acted shy, hid for a moment behind him, but Tom could tell that she was pleased by the attention.

'How's your wife?' one of the nurses asked him.

'She's okay,' Tom said, resenting the lie as soon as he'd said it. 'Still resting.'

The nurse nodded, reached out for Esme's hand, and when Esme didn't take it, she shrugged and walked over to where Bea lay in her cot. Tom and Esme followed. When Tom peered in at his sleeping daughter, he thought she looked a little different. A little bigger, perhaps, a little more beautiful, and he felt a strange pride in showing her off to Esme. He heard Esme's sharp intake of breath, heard her let it out, slowly.

'She's tiny,' Esme whispered.

Tom reached into the incubator, lifted her out. She was so light, so warm, wrapped up in blankets with only her head uncovered. He held her in the crook of his arm and turned so that her face was close to Esme's.

'Can I touch her?'

'Yes. Just be gentle.'

Esme reached out a hand and stroked her sister's cheek with one finger. Bea's eyelids flickered but she didn't wake. Tom wanted her to wake up, wanted Esme to see her eyes, how similar they were to Linda's.

When she was ready, Bea woke up, stretched out her limbs and stared at Tom, and then at Esme. A nurse brought a bottle and when Tom held it to her mouth, she drank hungrily, even though she hadn't cried or even whimpered for it. Not for the first time, Tom reflected on the fact that she needed her mother. That they needed to bond straight away, before it was too late. Before Bea got used to her mother's absence.

He longed to take her home, to grab Esme's hand, get Linda and dash out of the hospital, drive home with Bea cradled on his lap and Linda in the seat beside him. He wanted to say, look at her. Look at what we made. I know what we've lost, and it's killing me too, but look at what we have. You're missing it.

Esme seemed enchanted, and Tom remembered that this was how she'd been with Phoebe – in awe, almost disbelieving.

'Do you want to hold her?' he asked.

Esme shook her head fast, her hair following her movements with a moment's delay.

Tom looked at her, held her gaze. 'Are you sure?'

'Yes. She's too small. I don't want to drop her.'

Tom was saddened, but he didn't want to push Esme into anything she wasn't ready for. He was happy that she'd come, that he had someone to share Bea with, at last. The sisterly love would follow. He was confident of that.

20TH NOVEMBER 1985

128 DAYS AFTER

Those weeks, when Bea was in the hospital, fighting to get stronger so that she could come home, Linda pretended she'd never had her. She ignored the sagging skin of her stomach, the ache of her weeping breasts, and she lay in bed, thinking of nothing but Phoebe. Some days, Phoebe was with her – she could hear her, or feel her. She said nothing to Tom. She was drinking more, sleeping less. Things were spiralling.

Every day, Tom came home from the hospital with his eyes glittering, full of stories she didn't want to hear. He sat on the edge of the bed and told Linda that Bea was getting bigger, getting stronger, and all Linda felt was a heavy stone of dread in the pit of her stomach. Because she knew that once Bea came home, this period of intense grief would be over. There wouldn't be time for it. She'd be feeding, changing, winding, and she'd no longer be able to pretend that she wasn't this woman, this mother.

Linda looked at Tom, at his bright eyes and relieved smile, and she wondered again how he'd done it. How he'd simply transferred his love from one daughter to another. She didn't envy him, though. She wanted to wallow like this. Phoebe deserved it.

'The nurses on the unit always ask about you,' Tom said.

'And what do you say?'

Tom leaned closer to her, lifted her limp hand and held it between his.

'That you're resting at home. That you're getting things ready for her arrival.'

Linda pulled her hand away, turned on to her side so that he couldn't see the hatred that she felt sure was oozing from her eyes.

'I'm tired,' she said, every time. 'I need to go to sleep.'

And then she woke up one wet November morning, and it was Phoebe's fourth birthday. Tom didn't mention it, and Linda wondered whether or not he'd remembered. As he went downstairs to make breakfast for Esme, Linda turned on her side, too empty to cry. She imagined Phoebe as the older sister she should have been. It should have been her turn, now, to be the faster, taller, stronger one. To win and to show and to teach. Linda was sure that it would have changed her, that she would have blossomed.

When Esme came in to say goodbye, Linda closed her eyes and pretended that she was asleep. She could sense Esme standing beside the bed, hear her breathing. And it should have been easy to open her eyes and tell her daughter that she loved her, that she hoped her day would be a good one. After a minute or so, Esme retreated, and when she was sure that Esme had left the room, Linda pulled her knees in to her chest and lay, quite still, listening out for the sound of the front door closing.

It was her cue to go downstairs and take the vodka from the cupboard. And she took it. She poured herself a full glass, her hands visibly shaking, and she tipped it back, welcoming the burning sensation in her throat. And then, the minute she'd finished, she threw the glass against the wall and watched it shatter, watched the remaining drops of clear liquid drip from the edge of the counter.

By the time Tom got back, the glass was swept up and Linda was dressed.

'You're up,' he said.

Linda heard the happy surprise in his voice and turned.

'Yes.'

'Are you coming with me? To the hospital?'

Linda turned back to the sink. She couldn't look at him while she nodded. She couldn't bear to see that look on his face, the one that would give away his belief that it was over, that the worst of it had passed, that they were moving forward. Still, she heard his sigh, the relief in it. She didn't need to look at him to know that he believed something had changed. The thought of leaving the house troubled her, but she was trying not to think too far ahead. She was hoping that if she just did one small thing at a time, that series of tiny steps would lead her to where she needed to be. To the hospital. To her daughter.

Because despite the pain of it all, despite still wishing that the pregnancy and the birth had never happened, Linda missed Bea. She'd taken a mental picture of her before she left the hospital. Bea, her tiny limbs flung wide and her skin so pink. She carried it with her, through all the days that had passed since then, through all the painful memories of Phoebe. And she still hoped that this could be a new beginning, the start of something that would be different from what they'd had, but still something. Something real.

The nurses greeted Linda like a relative they'd lost and then found again, years later. None of their faces were familiar to Linda. It frightened her a little, to know that she'd left this host of strangers in charge of her new baby. One of them, a short and stocky woman with tight blonde curls and ruddy cheeks, took Linda to one side while Tom gave Bea a bottle.

'I lost a child,' she said. 'Eleven years ago. Alexander. He was just a baby. He died in his sleep. No one really knows why.'

Linda froze when the woman paused, sure that she should say

something, but completely at a loss as to what it should be. She pictured this woman, spending her life caring for other people's babies, her heart shattered.

'People say it gets easier, with time. I don't believe that. Not when it's a child. But you do learn to live with it. To live despite it. One day, something makes you laugh when you thought nothing ever would. That was a turning point for me.'

Linda was overwhelmed by the kindness of this stranger. She wanted to say thank you, but she didn't trust her voice to hold, so she tried to convey it with her eyes. And the nurse took her hand and squeezed it gently, and then led her back to the place where Bea lay.

Linda hardly recognised her daughter, and the shock of that jolted her. Nearly three weeks had passed since the birth, and Bea's fine dark hair was getting thicker, her skin was fairer, her legs and arms were more substantial. She was fragile, still, but no longer dangerously so. Linda reached into the incubator and lifted Bea out, held her against her chest. Bea squirmed a little and began to cry, and Linda rocked gently on the spot until she was quiet. She was light, and her head fitted perfectly into the crook of Linda's neck. Linda felt Bea's heartbeat beside her own. They were not quite in sync, not quite as one. But almost.

After a few minutes, Linda broke the spell by laying Bea back down. She changed her nappy, finished feeding her the bottle of milk that Tom had put to one side. These simple things, these tasks that she'd performed countless times before, didn't seem quite natural, somehow. Perhaps it was because she was in an unfamiliar location or because Bea was smaller and more delicate than Esme or Phoebe had ever been. Linda tried to believe that it was something like that. That it was nothing to worry about, nothing to fear. She remembered telling Tom that she didn't love Bea, and she felt ashamed.

When it was time to leave, Linda was both relieved and saddened that they weren't taking Bea with them. She thought of

Tom, leaving Bea here every day, putting up with the wrench it took, saying nothing. Her arms ached from the minutes she'd spent holding Bea. She hadn't had a cushion to support her and the angle had been awkward and she hadn't felt that she could ask Tom to take the baby from her. So they ached, and it felt a little like emptiness.

'Do you want me to drop you at home before I collect Esme?' Tom asked, as they neared the school.

'No, there's no point going back on ourselves. We'll both pick her up.'

They were a little early, parking the car ten minutes before the school day was due to finish. Tom turned off the engine and they sat in the car, waiting.

'So how was it?' Tom asked. 'Seeing her again?'

He wasn't looking at her. He was looking straight ahead, as if he was still driving and needed to concentrate on the road.

'It was hard,' Linda said. She imagined his face falling, his disappointment pouring out. 'And wonderful,' she added.

It was the truth. Bea was a magical baby. Unplanned, ill-advised. When they'd found out that she was coming, Linda and Tom talked about how they didn't have enough money, or enough time, or enough room for a third child. Linda wondered secretly whether they had enough love. And then Bea survived the impact of Phoebe's death on her mother's body, battled for her life after being born too soon. She was remarkable. Stronger than she was fragile. And if it had been another time, and another place, and another life, Linda was sure that she would have loved her the way she should have.

When the car's dashboard clock showed half past three, Linda and Tom opened their car doors simultaneously. They crossed the car park and walked along the pavement to the school gates in silence. Tom tried to take Linda's hand, but she shrugged him off, burying her hands deep in the pockets of her coat. It was a cold afternoon. Winter was coming. Things were dying, shutting down.

A minute or so later, the children poured out like water from a tap, and Linda picked Esme's dark head out of the crowd. She was walking slowly, her head low, and a small group of boys were following her. She recognised Simon Treadwell, a tall boy with spiky blonde hair and freckles. He was obviously the ringleader. Linda couldn't make out the words but she felt sure that he was jeering, teasing, and she thought she saw Esme flinch every time he spoke.

The anger she felt was primal. It swelled up in her, threatening to burst. Linda strode away from Tom, marched through the gates and approached her daughter. Children scattered, but Esme and her tormenters didn't notice Linda's approach. When she got close enough, Linda swooped down and gathered Esme up in her arms, covering her daughter's ears with her hands, desperate to stop her from being subjected to this.

The ringleader boy stopped, looked up at Linda. He sneered. Linda wanted to slap him, to push him to the ground. She lurched forward but then she felt Esme being lifted from her and her arms being pinned to her sides. Tom.

'You leave my daughter alone, do you hear me?'

Simon nodded, not quite meeting her eyes.

'You're a bully. You should be ashamed of yourself.'

'Come on,' said Tom, pulling at her arm. 'That's enough.'

And it would have ended there, if Simon's mother hadn't bustled through the crowd. She was a large woman, red-faced and wearing too much makeup. Linda thought of their encounter in the park, all those weeks ago. Linda felt sick at the thought of Esme having to face her bully that day, and her not knowing.

'Don't you dare go near my Simon. Hasn't your daughter done enough?'

'Do you know what?' Linda said, turning, her face dangerously close to Mrs Treadwell's. 'I know that my daughter bit your son, and I'm glad she did. It's obvious that he's a nasty little shit. And I can see where he gets it from.'

Linda looked around her. The other mothers were staring, many of them holding their children close to them, as if they were afraid of them getting caught up in the fray. Tom was standing off to one side with his arm around Esme, who was crying silently.

'How dare you?' Mrs Treadwell hissed. 'You're not fit to be a mother.'

Linda couldn't respond to that, didn't dare to. She turned and walked away, towards Tom and Esme. And when she reached them, she took a deep breath before she spoke, hoping that her voice would sound calm, controlled.

'Let's go home,' she said.

T om slipped out of the house just after lunch, telling Linda he was going to check on things at the shop. He drove to Marianne's place, with no idea whether or not she'd be there. He was spending most of his time at the hospital with Bea – couldn't miss one day, because he didn't want his little girl to go a full day without seeing someone who loved her.

He hadn't anticipated missing Marianne, but he did. He missed the ease of being with her, the simplicity, the relief of that crushing weight being temporarily lifted. When he knocked on her door, he didn't really expect her to open it, but he wished hard that she would. And then she did, and she looked taken aback to see him, but not unhappy.

'This is a surprise,' she said.

Tom didn't answer. He stepped inside, taking her small step back as an invitation, and he closed the door behind him and wrapped his arms around her, tight. He held her the way he wanted someone to hold him. When he kissed her, it was fierce and hungry, and she gave a small gasp at the shock of it, but then she kissed him back, just as hard, without asking him why. She let him push his

96

cold hands under her clothes and steer her to the bedroom. It was inexplicable, Tom thought, that she was home in the middle of the day, just when he needed her the most. It was inexplicable that she would let him in, let him touch her – that she wanted him at all.

They lay in her bed, Tom's feet pushing against the footboard, the unfamiliarity of it all giving him a rush.

'Why aren't you at work?' he asked.

'Day off,' she said, lightly. 'Why aren't you?'

And he wasn't sure why that prompted it, but suddenly something in Tom cracked, and he found that he was crying. He was overcome, without warning, with great wracking sobs. He was embarrassed, a little flustered. This woman is not my wife, he thought. This is not my place.

Marianne stayed very still beside him. She didn't reach out a hand or say a word. She just let him cry, and when it had passed, she asked him a question, her voice level.

'Will you tell me?'

'Phoebe,' he said. 'We lost Phoebe.'

And because she didn't know anything about it, it was a bit like going back to the start, for Tom, telling her. It was a bit like returning to the centre of his grief.

Marianne sat still, her arms wrapped around her knees and the duvet loosely covering her, while he told her the story of that dreadful night – the same day that she had walked into his shop and he was home late, and when he got there, his life had been torn to shreds. He told her about the pregnancy, about Bea, about the long hours he'd been spending beside her at the hospital while Linda lay in bed, refusing to move.

'You shouldn't be here,' she said, when he was finished.

'Where should I be?'

It was a genuine question, although it sounded flippant. He'd tried doing what he should do, dividing his time between the hospital and home. It didn't make the pain any less. Being with

Marianne, forgetting, for just a few moments, was the only thing that had come close to making the pain any less.

She didn't answer. She lay back, pulled the covers up to her chest, and stared at the ceiling. And they were quiet for a while, and Tom wasn't sure there were any words to break the silence.

'I lost a child,' she said, at last. 'It's not the same. I never had him.'

'When?' he asked, and he looked at her, but her eyes remained fixed on the ceiling. He wondered how much pain there was in them.

'Last year. I was living in London. I was in love, engaged, and then – suddenly – pregnant. I wasn't sure whether it was the right time, but I believed it was the right person, so I got ready to be a mother. We cleared the spare room of all our junk, bought a cot and a pushchair. I read some books. I was scared. I wasn't sure that I was cut out for it. And then, a few weeks before I was due, I started to bleed. And I sat on the bathroom floor, knowing that I was losing him, not quite able to get up or call for help. Sometimes, when I'm alone, I wonder whether it would have made a difference. By the time I got to the hospital, he was gone.'

Marianne paused, glanced across at Tom, and he nodded, encouraging her to go on.

'I had to be induced, had to give birth to him, knowing that there would be nothing beyond the pain but more pain. My fiancé, Robert, was brilliant. He held my hand and brushed away my tears and told me that he loved me. But even then, I knew that it was over. After he was born, the nurses left him with us for a while. He was fully developed, small but perfect, and all those doubts I'd had seemed ridiculous. It would have been easy, I realised then, to love him and to be his mother. It would have been impossible not to.'

She shifted on the bed, turned her body so that she was facing Tom.

'A week later, I packed my things and moved out, moved here.

Robert didn't understand, or said he didn't. He thought we could try again, after some time had passed. He didn't see it as an ending. But I knew that that day would cast a long shadow over us, that I'd never love him in the same way.

'We named him, our son. We named him Isaac. When I'm at my most lonely, I talk to him. I imagine the things I would have taught him, the things we might have done together. He had my eyes and Robert's mouth. It was like a miracle.'

She stopped talking, and Tom wasn't sure whether she'd reached the end or whether she'd just stopped being able to say the words. He lay back and their faces were inches apart, and he looked at the ceiling, and he reached out slowly and took her hand in his.

They fell asleep like that. Tom thought, afterwards, that it must have been the relief of it. To have all that pain laid bare, to no longer be carrying it in silence. Afterwards, when he was driving home, he thought about what Marianne had said. He heard it all again, inside his head. And he concentrated on the part about her knowing that her relationship was over, that it couldn't survive something like that. He wondered whether Linda felt that way. And he wondered, too, whether it would help if he and Linda could do what he'd done with Marianne that afternoon – lay out their individual stories, get to the heart of their sadnesses. Perhaps it didn't work, he thought, if the pain was shared.

Linda was in bed, her eyes empty, glazed. He went to her, lay down beside her on top of the covers. And he tried to find the words to tell her that he'd been shopping, the previous week, and chosen some books for Phoebe's birthday. He wanted to tell her that he'd wrapped them, and written out a card, and then put it all in a bag and hidden it at the bottom of the wardrobe. Because he had no idea what else to do with it. He wanted her to know that he hadn't forgotten.

Before Tom could find the courage to speak, the phone rang, and he got up and went downstairs to answer it.

'Hello?'

'Mr Sadler?'

Tom recognised the voice of one of the nurses at the hospital, and found that he was bracing himself for more bad news.

'We just wanted to let you know that Bea's ready to go home. One of the doctors checked her over this morning, and he's happy with her weight and her progress.'

'Oh,' Tom said, his voice strangled.

He covered his mouth with one hand and sank to the floor in the hallway.

'Mr Sadler, are you there?'

'I'm here. I'm just…so pleased. I'll be there as soon as I can.'

Tom replaced the receiver, but he couldn't bring himself to move for a minute or two. He sat there, stunned, imagining Bea in this house, where she belonged. He would collect Esme from school in an hour, and her baby sister would be in the car. A surprise. A miracle. He rose and took the stairs two at a time.

'Guess who's coming home?' he asked Linda, peering around the bedroom door.

'Today?' Linda asked, her eyes full of panic.

'Yes. Don't worry. I'll sort everything. I'm going to collect her now, and I'll pick up Esme on the way back. Do you want to come?'

Linda said nothing at first, and he knew they were both remembering her last visit to the school gates.

'I think I'll stay here.'

Tom was disappointed, but he tried not to show it. As he turned to leave the room, Linda spoke again.

'It's cold out,' she said. 'Make sure you wrap her up well.'

TOM PICKED up a big box of chocolates in the hospital's gift shop, and when he got to the unit, the nurses thanked him and said he shouldn't have. And he was embarrassed because it wasn't enough, and he knew that anything he gave them wouldn't be enough, to thank them for taking care of his precious daughter. For almost a full month, these men and women had fed and changed and comforted her, and now it was his turn. He reached for her, lifted her into the car seat and covered her with a blanket. Walking out of the hospital, Tom felt like he was in a dream. He'd imagined this moment, but he'd thought that Linda would be by his side, and perhaps Esme too. It was a time for family, for celebration. He thought of Linda, wondered whether she was still lying there, silent and still, or whether the news of Bea coming home had roused her. Just then, Bea shifted in her sleep and he paused on his way to the car, looked at her face. Her head was covered with a tiny white hat, and the rest of her body was hidden beneath the blanket, so that only her face was visible. And for the first time, Tom saw a resemblance to Phoebe in her eyes.

Later, at home, Tom made a salad and Esme sat in the kitchen with him, gazing into the Moses basket where Bea slept.

'What's Mum doing?' she asked.

'She's resting.'

'She's always resting.'

'Well, she's been very tired.' Tom tried to keep the irritation out of his voice. 'Es,' he said, keen to change the subject, 'how are things at school now?'

Out of the corner of his eye, he saw her freeze. He saw her small body tense up, and wondered whether it was fear she felt, or shame, or simply sadness.

'The same,' she said.

Tom sliced tomatoes into quarters, slid them off the chopping board and into the salad bowl. 'Has anybody said anything, about when Mum came with me to pick you up, and got into an argument?'

Esme looked down at her shoes. Tom noticed that her socks were looking a little more grey than white, and her shoes needed a polish. Every couple of weeks, he collected all the black leather shoes, took them into the garage, and cleaned them until they shone. He couldn't remember the last time he'd done it. He would do it after dinner.

Eventually, Esme spoke. 'It's Bea's first day at home,' she said. 'Can we talk about this another day?'

'Yes,' Tom said. 'Of course we can. Whatever you want. Now, this is ready. Do you want to go upstairs and see if Mum feels like coming down for something to eat?'

That night, Bea slept badly, and Tom paced up and down the bedroom with her, muttering stories under his breath. He knew that Linda was awake, but she didn't say anything. With Esme and Phoebe, she was always the one to soothe and calm them in the night. Tom remembered being amazed by her endless patience, her capacity for love. A little before dawn, when Tom had just managed to rock Bea to sleep, he took her over to the bed, intending to pass her to Linda. His body was heavy with tiredness as he crouched down beside Linda, holding Bea out for her to take. Linda's eyes were open, and she lifted them to meet his, then looked down at Bea's sleeping face for a long minute.

'Take her away,' she said. 'Please.'

And that's when Tom knew that his heart was breaking, that it was shredded and torn. That it was beyond repair.

2ND DECEMBER 1985

140 DAYS AFTER

M onday morning, and Tom woke Linda with a gentle shake to the shoulder.

'I'm leaving in a few minutes,' he said. 'I'm going to drop Esme at school and then I'm going to the shop.'

'To check on things?' Linda asked. She was groggy, and a headache was forming behind her eyebrows.

'To work,' Tom said. 'It's almost Christmas. It'll be getting busy. I can't leave Liam on his own any longer.'

Linda sat up in bed and watched Tom retreat from the room. She considered the day that stretched ahead, with only her to care for Bea. And she sank back on to the pillows for a moment, hot with fear. She hadn't breastfed, because Bea had stayed at the hospital for so long. Would that have made the difference? She'd fed Esme and Phoebe, and she still remembered the way her heart had lifted, a little, each time they latched on and began to feed.

Downstairs, Tom and Esme were having breakfast, Bea asleep in her Moses basket on the floor between them. Linda watched them from the doorway.

'She might be,' Esme said, taking a spoonful of cereal. 'How would we know, while she's so tiny?'

'Well, what would her superpower be?' Tom asked. He was eating toast spread thickly with marmalade, drinking black coffee. If he was scared about leaving Bea alone with her, he wasn't showing it.

'That's just it, it could be anything! She's so little that we don't know yet.'

'Okay, but what do you think it might be?'

Esme tilted her head to one side, gazed at Bea.

'I think she might be able to make herself invisible. Or see what other people are thinking. Yes, that. She knows what we're all thinking.'

Linda shuddered at the thought. She entered the room, made herself a strong coffee.

'Dad,' Esme said, suddenly serious. 'I've got a letter in my bag that you have to sign. It's to say I can go on the trip next week, to the wildlife park.'

'Okay,' Tom said. 'Go and get it for me. And brush your teeth.'

Esme darted from the room without looking at Linda.

'She used to come to me with things like that,' Linda said.

Tom looked up at her, rose from his chair. 'I know,' he said.

And then he picked up Bea, who had opened her eyes and was cooing softly. He held her up to his face and kissed her.

'I love you, Bea,' he said. 'Be good for Mummy.'

Esme had returned, and she stood beside her father, her expression tight and considered.

'I could stay at home, to help,' she said.

Linda and Tom shook their heads in unison, and Linda was pleased by this small act of solidarity. But she also wondered how it had come to this. Her seven-year-old daughter, picking up on her reluctance to be left alone with her new baby. Too young to feel the weight of that kind of responsibility.

When Tom and Esme left, the house was suddenly too quiet. Bea had drifted back off to sleep. If she didn't look at that Moses basket, Linda thought, she could pretend that she was alone. But being alone held fears of its own.

Linda moved restlessly from room to room, feeling out of place, adrift. The temptation to crawl back into bed was strong. She could change back into her nightgown, slip between the sheets, maybe even snatch a few minutes of sleep before Bea needed her.

Even as she stood in the bedroom doorway, considering it, Bea woke and let out a strangled cry. Linda glanced at her bedside clock. It wasn't time for a feed yet. But she could be wet, or just seeking comfort. Wearily, Linda went down the stairs and into the lounge, stood over the Moses basket, looking down. Bea's face was beetroot-red, scrunched up. She wailed. Linda picked her up and rocked her in her arms, and Bea snuffled into her shoulder, and calmed.

As Linda walked up and down the length of the room, willing the movement to send Bea back off to sleep, she was surprised to feel like a mother to her, for the first time. To feel a surge of protectiveness, of love. It was small, but it was there. And with that came the comforting possibility of everything being all right. Not perfect. Not easy, by any means. But bearable.

Tom phoned at eleven. And although Linda knew that he was checking up on her, she was pleased to hear his voice.

'Is everything okay?' he asked.

'Yes. She's sleeping.'

'The phone didn't wake her?'

'No, I just fed her. She's fast off.'

There was a pause, and Linda wanted to fill the silence, but she wasn't sure which words would fit. She half-remembered him calling in the early days of Esme, and Phoebe. How they had chatted away, her bursting with anecdotes about what the day had brought. But there was nothing. She'd fed and changed Bea, she'd soothed her. She hadn't had a drink, though she wanted to more than anything. She'd even felt that rush of love. None of these were things she could share, or hold up as achievements.

'How are things there?' she asked.

'Busy. In fact, there are a couple of people waiting now. I should go.'

'Okay.'

'Just call me if you need to, won't you? I don't have to do a full day, if...'

His voice trailed off, the words he hadn't said heavy on the line between them. If you can't cope. Linda wasn't angry. How could she be? She'd given him more than enough cause for concern.

'You'd better go,' she said.

'Yes.'

When she heard that click, followed by the dull purr of the dialling tone, she felt a loneliness threaten to swarm her. To ward it off, she walked over to Bea and stroked her cheek. She was warm, peaceful. At Linda's touch, she twitched her nose and shifted her position slightly, and then settled back to sleep.

Later, Linda wasn't sure when it had begun to unravel. It was as if she'd moved through the rest of the day in a daze, and then woken up, surprised to find the lounge littered with nappies and Bea screaming, her sleepsuit stained with bitter-smelling milky sick. Surprised to find the vodka bottle on the kitchen worktop, the cap unscrewed and a quarter of its contents gone. Surprised by her own reflection, her hair tangled and wild, her cheeks flushed, her eyes glassy.

It was time to collect Esme from school, so she hurriedly gathered up the nappies and empty bottles, replaced the cap on the vodka and pushed the bottle to the very back of the cupboard. Getting Bea into her coat was a struggle. Every time Linda got one arm in place, Bea would curl up and refuse to cooperate. Every time the second arm slotted into place, the first would slip out. Linda checked her watch. If she left right now, she would make it on time.

'Please, Bea,' she said, trying to keep the frustration from her voice.

Bea looked up at her from her position on the carpet, eyes wide.

Three minutes later, the coat was on and buttoned. Linda reached for Bea's hat and slipped it on, and she was just about to lift her into the pushchair when Bea's face reddened and she let out a cry. After three babies, Linda knew that face. She didn't have to wait for the smell to reach her, but when it did, she felt tears start to prickle behind her eyes.

Linda calculated, fast. Five minutes to undress, change, and redress Bea, fifteen minutes to walk to the school. An image came to her, of Esme standing at the school gates, forlorn, her teacher holding her hand. Or worse, Esme being cornered by that Simon boy, being pushed and teased. She would have to drive. Her mind flitted and landed briefly on the vodka, like a fly buzzing around a dinner plate, preparing to settle. She swatted it away.

When Linda arrived at the school gate, she was breathless and flushed. The children were just starting to file out, and she felt an overwhelming sense of relief that Esme hadn't had to wait for her. Still, she imagined she could feel the judgement of the other mothers, felt they knew, instinctively, that she wasn't coping. A couple of women smiled, and Linda smiled back. This was how it was with women, she knew. Everything hidden below the surface. All the pain, all the dissatisfaction.

Esme came out clutching her friend Samantha's hand. Linda looked around for Jane, Samantha's mother, and saw her waiting near the back of the crowd. They'd never become friends, Linda and Jane, despite their daughters' closeness. When the friendship started, in their first weeks at school, Linda assumed that things would keep changing, week by week, so she didn't really make the effort with Jane, who was quiet and a little hard to engage in conversation. She hadn't known that, three years later, the girls would still be clinging to one another like this. And now, it seemed too late, somehow, for the women to strike up a friend-ship of their own.

Esme approached without dropping Samantha's hand.

'Can Samantha come for tea?' she asked.

Linda was irritated. Time and again, she'd asked Esme to give her advance notice if she wanted to bring a friend home. Told Esme not to ask in front of the friend, in case she had to say no. And yet, it was months since Esme had asked to have a friend over at all. And surely it was an indication that she didn't think things were too bad, at home, if she was willing to show that world to Samantha.

'Hi Samantha,' Linda said. 'It's okay with me if it's okay with your mum. Let's go and ask her.'

They shuffled through the small crowd, Linda steering Bea's pushchair. An awkward quartet. When they reached Jane, she stuck her hand out for Samantha and pulled her away from Esme, a little too hard.

'Hi,' Linda said. 'Is it okay for Samantha to come to us for her tea?'

'I don't think so,' Jane said, the words coming out fast and clear. 'Not tonight.'

The girls began to whine, and Jane cut them off with one sharp word.

'Enough!'

Then she turned to Linda.

'Could I have a word?' She raised her eyebrows, indicating that she meant she wanted to talk away from the children.

'Sure. Girls, just wait here for us a minute.'

Linda followed Jane and then stopped, put the brake on the pushchair. She glanced back over at Esme and Samantha, saw their heads bent together, saw them giggle. She wondered what Jane was about to say. This had happened once before, when Jane wanted to let Linda know that she had told Samantha the truth about Santa Claus. She'd asked her not to tell Esme, but couldn't be sure she'd keep her promise. 'You know how girls are, with secrets,' Jane said, then.

Now, Jane's expression was hard to read. There was sympathy there, but judgement too. For one awful moment, Linda was sure that it was about Phoebe. Her death had never been mentioned between them. She wasn't sure she could face it. Her legs shook, and her eyes felt watery.

'Have you been drinking?' Jane asked.

Linda's cheeks burned. It was so unexpected, so direct. No preamble, no niceties.

'I'm sorry to come out with it like that. I wasn't sure how to put it.'

'No,' Linda said, willing her voice and her body to cooperate with the lie.

Jane raised her eyebrows, doubting.

'I haven't!' Linda snapped.

Stalemate.

'Well,' Jane said. 'I'm not so sure. I've thought it a couple of times. And I'm not judging you, whatever you think. What happened to Phoebe was just…awful. I can't even imagine. I just think that maybe you could do with getting some help. And until I'm sure that you're all right, I can't let Samantha come to your house.'

Jane dropped her eyes to the keys in Linda's hand. 'And I certainly can't let her go in your car.'

Linda stood there for a moment, too shocked to react.

'You think you're better than me,' she said, eventually.

'That's not true.'

Linda was aware of other women looking their way, and she didn't care. She wondered, briefly, whether Simon Treadwell's mother was in the crowd. Probably.

'It is true. You've always thought it, and this is just an excuse. Well, you can take your judgements and fuck off.'

And then she turned and walked away, flipping up the

pushchair's brake and grabbing for Esme's hand as she came level with the two girls. She pushed and pulled her two daughters to the car park and she didn't look back.

That evening, after the girls were asleep, Linda dared herself to talk to Tom about what had happened. This was her chance, to tell him that she couldn't do it. That her grief wasn't lessening or becoming any more bearable, as everyone promised it would. That she couldn't forgive Esme for her part in Phoebe's death. That she couldn't forgive Bea for not being the daughter she wanted. That she was drinking heavily. That people were starting to notice, starting to talk.

'What are you thinking about?' Tom asked, walking through to the lounge with two glasses of red wine in his hands.

Linda wanted to tell him. She did. She imagined the relief of having no secrets, of having shared them all. But the words wouldn't come. And part of her was angry with him, too. Why don't you know? She wanted to scream it. Why can't you see?

'Nothing,' she said, taking the glass that he was holding out to her.

'How was today?' he asked.

'Exhausting.'

Tom paused, and she knew that he was waiting for her to say something else. To say that she'd enjoyed it, despite finding it hard.

'What about tomorrow?' he asked, eventually.

'Tomorrow,' she said. 'Go, I'll be fine.'

Tom's relief was visible on his face, almost tangible in the air. Linda felt that she might be able to touch it, if she tried. She knew that it was a financial thing. If money was no object, she was sure that he'd stay at home with her and Bea indefinitely.

'How were things at the shop?' she asked.

'Pretty busy. Liam's been coping, but he looked relieved to see me.'

And with that said, there seemed to be nothing more to

discuss. Linda thought back to their early years, when they'd talked long into the night, sometimes going right through until morning. She had no idea what they'd said, why it had all seemed so urgent and crucial, why it had mattered so much more than sleep. And how they had gone from that to this, with so little warning.

On Christmas morning, Tom was in the kitchen with a mug of coffee before six. When Esme bounded down the stairs half an hour later, her expression pure anticipation, he was relieved. Finally, the typical reaction he'd been waiting to see in her for months. For once, no visible trace of trauma or grief in her eyes.

'Happy Christmas,' she called, flinging herself on to his lap.

'Happy Christmas, Es.'

Tom put his arms around her, breathed in her just-woken scent. Her hair was tangled and untidy, her pyjamas twisted around her legs.

'Has Santa been?'

Tom thought Esme probably knew the truth about Santa. And with Phoebe gone and Bea too young to understand, Tom wondered who she was pretending for. Was it for him?

'Do you know? I think he has. I'll tell you what. Have a piece of toast, I'll go and wake Mum, and then we'll meet in the lounge for presents.'

Tom took the stairs two at a time. He found Linda curled in a ball, her knees tucked under her chin, her hair covering the side of her face. She looked like a girl, Tom thought. She looked the way she used to look, before all this. He lifted her hair and whispered her name, smiled at her as her eyes opened.

'Happy Christmas,' he said, softly. 'Esme's up and we're about to open presents. Shall I get your dressing gown?'

'Leave me for a while,' Linda said.

Tom couldn't believe he hadn't braced himself for this. Every day, it seemed, he believed that things would be better. Every day, a new blow.

'Linda, it's Christmas and she's excited. I don't think we should make her wait any longer.'

'She doesn't have to wait. You'll be there. And I'll be down in a while. I just need a bit more sleep. I was up with Bea in the night.'

Tom stopped himself from saying that he was up with Bea in the night too. He went downstairs, pasted a smile on his face.

'Mum's coming down soon,' he said. 'Want to start without her?'

Esme looked troubled for a moment, and Tom wondered how much she understood. Every Christmas of her life, Esme had opened her presents with both her parents there, watching. She dropped the burned crust of her toast on the plate and shrugged her shoulders. And by the time they were in the lounge, and Tom was pulling presents from under the tree, he knew that the magic of that morning had gone, for both of them. And he was angry with himself, for believing that it could be a normal Christmas. That, for once, it could be a normal day.

When Esme had finished opening her presents, she sat there, with the discarded wrapping paper all around her, stacking her new books and toys into neat piles. Linda still hadn't appeared, and Tom could feel his anger rising. He'd brought Bea downstairs when she woke, fed her. Now, she was lying in her chair, mesmerised by the bright colours in the room.

Tom slipped out of the room, went back upstairs. This time, Linda was in the bath, her hair wet and her expression blank.

'What are you doing?' Tom asked, not bothering to keep the anger out of his voice.

'What do you mean?' Linda looked and sounded startled, as though she'd forgotten she wasn't alone in the house.

'Linda, it's Christmas Day. If there's one day that you should be with your family, it's today.'

Linda glared at him for a long minute, and then she stood and wrapped her body in one towel and her hair in another.

'Do you think I don't know? I can't face it, Tom. I don't understand how you can.'

'Why? Because of Phoebe?'

It was hard, of course. The first Christmas without her. But it was their first Christmas with Bea too, and Tom was furious with Linda for missing it. He watched her as she rubbed herself dry, pulled on a pair of jeans and a sweatshirt. They had a tradition at Christmas. All morning, they wore their pyjamas. Ate breakfast and opened presents and played games with the girls. And then, an hour before the dinner was ready, Tom prepared the vegetables and Linda took the girls upstairs and they bathed and dressed. Linda brushed Esme and Phoebe's hair until it shone, zipped them into the special dresses she'd bought. She powdered her face, applied lipstick and eyeshadow. She stepped into the blue silk dress that Tom had bought for her, years before. When they were ready, they came downstairs. And every year, Tom gasped at the sight of them. He ran upstairs, with only a few minutes to go before everything was ready, washed and changed into his smartest trousers and shirt, knotted his favourite tie, the same blue as Linda's dress.

Tom couldn't remember how it had started, the family tradition of dressing up for Christmas dinner. But it saddened him to see Linda pulling on her clothes without a thought, silently telling him that that custom, like so much else, was over now.

'I've started the dinner,' Tom said, hoping that would jolt something, and remind her. 'The turkey's in the oven.'

'Good,' Linda said.

Tom was just about to leave the room when she spoke again, more quietly.

'Do you miss her at all?'

He spun around. 'That's cruel. Of course I miss her. Just because I'm handling it differently to you, that doesn't mean I loved her less.'

'You just...' Linda said, gulping back tears. 'You just don't show it. It's like we never had her. And I can't bear it.'

A chill ran through Tom's body, then, and it felt like hatred.

'We have two daughters downstairs,' Tom said. 'And they deserve better than this.'

And then he left the room, no longer sure whether he wanted her to follow him.

Tom shut himself away in the kitchen for a while. The Christmas dinner had always been down to him, but it was different now, with no sounds of laughter coming from the lounge. A couple of times, he heard Bea cry and went to the lounge door to see whether she needed him. Both times, Linda reached to pick her up and rocked her back to sleep. It should have been encouraging, but Tom was uneasy. There was nothing behind Linda's eyes when she held their daughter.

When Esme appeared at his side, Tom ruffled her hair.

'Dad,' she said, her voice a little shaky.

'Yes?'

Tom turned the carrots down, gave the gravy a stir. And then he turned and leaned against the kitchen counter, giving Esme his full attention.

'We're not dressing up today, are we?'

'I don't think so. Do you want to?'

Esme shrugged. 'I don't have a new Christmas dress. Mum forgot, I think... Dad, she's not saying anything.'

'What do you mean?'

'She's in the lounge with me, and she's watching Bea, but she hasn't said anything. At all.'

Tom took hold of both of her hands. He wondered whether this was something she'd remember, when she was an adult. Whether all this would damage her, somehow. Have an impact on her sense of family, and love.

'Mum's not very well,' he said, taking a deep breath. 'She's still very, very sad, about Phoebe. And Christmas is a very special day, and she wishes Phoebe was here with us, so she's finding it harder than ever.'

'I wish Phoebe was here, too,' Esme said.

Tom felt tears well in his eyes. He bit his lip, willed himself to stay in control.

'I know, baby. We all do.'

'I made her something, at school,' Esme said.

She left the room, and Tom heard her feet on the stairs. Up, then down. When she returned, she pressed some papers into his hand, and Tom dragged his eyes away from his daughter to look at it. It was a collection of drawings. Phoebe with Tom and Linda. Phoebe with Esme. Tom recognised that these two were copied from photos. It was the third drawing that made him catch his breath. Phoebe, holding Bea. Their dark hair and their eyes the same.

'These are beautiful,' he said.

'I know she can't have them,' Esme said. 'I understand that. But it seemed strange to not have a present for her, for Christmas. I picked one of my toys for her birthday present. But it's just in my toybox, still, like it always was. I don't know what to do with the things I want to give to her.'

Tom watched as a tear spilled from Esme's left eye and ran down her face, dripped off her chin. He felt his own tears coming. There was no stopping them now.

'I don't know, either,' he said.

Esme looked surprised, at that. And he saw it from her

perspective. She still thought he knew the answer to everything. Just then, the oven timer sounded.

'Is it time for dinner?' Esme asked. 'Shall I tell Mum?'

'Yes please,' Tom said, wiping at his eyes. 'And Es?'

She turned, her eyes dry now, but still weighed down with sadness.

'I'll find somewhere safe for these.' He held up the drawings. 'I think Phoebe would have liked them very much.'

Tom found the rest of the day a strain. There was too much silence – over dinner, when they went for a walk to look at the neighbours' Christmas lights, while they played the board game he'd bought for Esme. Christmas had long been one of his favourite days, but when he saw Esme's eyes drooping, he felt a huge sense of relief. He told her a story, like always, but she was asleep before he'd finished it. And he sat, for a while, in the armchair under the window that he'd sat in to tell her stories over the years, thinking about how there wouldn't be many nights like this to come. It wouldn't be long before she was too old for a bedtime story, Tom knew, but neither of them were ready to let go of the ritual. But they would. He could sense that day coming. And he feared it.

Downstairs, Linda was on the sofa, drinking a glass of red wine. Tom had noticed that there were three empty bottles in the kitchen, and yet he was sure that he'd only had a few glasses.

'Are you drunk?' he asked.

Linda met his eyes and didn't flinch. 'So what if I am?'

Tom didn't know what to say to that. He sat down on the other end of the sofa, buried his head in his hands. He was tired, he realised. He'd been tired for weeks.

'I know there's someone else,' Linda said.

Tom froze, and then he lifted his head and sought out her eyes.

'It's okay,' she said. 'I mean, it's not okay, but it's not as bad as I thought it would be.'

Tom wondered how she knew. There had been a few phone

calls, but never from home. Marianne had written him some notes, but they were locked in the drawer of his chest at work, and he knew Linda would never look there. Had he told her, somehow, with his actions, his demeanour? He was sorry. Sorry that he'd betrayed her, and sorry that she'd found out. It was obvious all along, of course, that this might happen, and yet he hadn't dwelled on it. In his mind, his time with Marianne bore no relation to his marriage. It was something entirely separate, that he'd needed. But that was childish, he knew, and impossible.

'It's over,' he said.

'Us?'

Tom thought he detected a note of panic in her voice, and despite the circumstances, he was relieved.

'No, not us. Me and her. I'm so sorry. It was a mistake.'

Linda gave a tight nod and when he reached for her hand, she pulled away. They were silent, not touching, the handful of inches between them like a chasm. Tom was trying to think of something more to say, to explain, when Linda spoke again.

'Whatever happens, I want them to have a father in their lives. Promise me?'

'You don't have to ask me for that, Linda. There's no question.'

'Good,' she said.

They were silent for a few long minutes, but Tom sensed that Linda had something more to ask, or say. Eventually, she spoke again.

'Were you with her, the night we lost Phoebe? Did you come home late because you were with her?'

Tom sighed audibly. 'Yes,' he said. 'And I'll never forgive myself.'

Linda met his eyes. 'I'll never forgive you either,' she said.

L inda looked at the calendar, counted back. One hundred and seventy-five days had passed, since that night that Maud had called and asked her to come. Told her that Arthur had had a fall, that he wasn't breathing. One hundred and seventy-five days, and nights, since she'd made the split-second decision to leave the girls alone for a few minutes, while she went next door to help calm her neighbour, her friend. Since she'd rationalised that Tom would be home at any minute, that Esme was seven, old enough – surely? – to watch over her little sister for a handful of minutes.

In a week, it would be six months, and then it would be a year, a decade. Would it hurt less, then? Would she reach a stage where she didn't have to wake up, every morning, and remember all over again? Would she arrive at a place where she could enjoy her remaining children, where she could love them?

Somewhere in the house, Bea was crying. Tom had fed and changed her before leaving for work, dropping Esme off for the first day of a new term on the way. Linda stood in the kitchen, staring at the calendar. What would happen, she wondered, if she didn't go to Bea? As Linda reached for the hidden vodka bottle with shaking hands, her daughter's cries grew louder, more urgent. She took a glass from the cupboard, poured herself a generous measure and tipped it back. And then she did the same thing again. All the while, Bea screamed.

There was a knock at the back door, and Linda moved a couple of inches to the left, hoping she couldn't be seen. Only the family and Maud used that door, and Linda wasn't in the mood for small talk. Wasn't in the mood to pretend that she was doing okay, that she was coping. Maud knocked again, and Linda crouched down, rested her elbows on her knees and covered her face with her hands, like a child who believes she can't be seen if she can't see. When Maud left, Linda stood again, shaking off a feeling of dizziness, and poured herself another drink.

A couple of minutes later, the back door opened. Linda was taken aback.

'Linda!' Maud said. 'I've been knocking. I...'

'What are you doing, letting yourself in?' Linda was furious.

She tightened her grip on the glass in her hand, gritted her teeth. She'd forgotten about the spare key that Maud kept, for emergencies.

Linda saw Maud look from the glass to her eyes, and back again. And then Maud nodded, as though she understood something she'd been struggling with.

'Linda, I'm sorry,' Maud said. 'I could hear Bea crying, and I didn't get an answer when I knocked, so I was worried.'

Linda noticed, then, that Bea's cries hadn't stopped. Somehow, she'd managed to block them out.

'Can I go to her?' Maud asked. 'Do you mind?'

Linda gave a stiff nod, and when Maud had left the kitchen and made for the stairs, she sank to the ground again. She waited there, until Bea went quiet, and in the absence of that sound, there was a slight ringing in her ears. Linda stood, and her instinct was to hide the vodka bottle that was sitting on the kitchen counter, but she knew it was too late. Instead, she poured another glass, and sipped at it.

'I don't know what to say,' Maud said, coming back into the room.

'Then don't say anything.'

'Linda, I'm worried about you. You and Bea. You're not well, and she needs so much attention. I can help more, if you like...'

Linda pulled out one of the kitchen chairs and sat down. She held her drink close to her chest, as though it comforted her.

'I'll put the kettle on,' Maud said, not pausing before filling it up and switching it on.

Linda said nothing, and Maud busied herself getting two matching green mugs out of the cupboard and opening doors, looking for the tea bags and the sugar. The two women were in silence, but it wasn't awkward, not while Maud had something to do. But once she placed the steaming mugs on coasters on the table and pulled out a chair for herself, the quiet engulfed them.

'When I had Karen,' Maud said, eventually, 'I had some trouble, afterwards. The baby blues, I suppose you'd call it. I found it hard to get up in the mornings, and I felt overwhelmed by all the things I needed to do, to look after her. People didn't talk about things then, not the way they do now. But I do know what it's like, to feel like you can't cope. To feel that things are getting out of control.'

Linda drained her glass and placed it on the table, keeping her eyes on Maud.

'Does Tom know?' Maud asked, looking purposefully at the glass.

'Does Tom know what?'

Suddenly, Linda wanted someone to say it. To accuse her of it, rather than skirting around it, being polite.

'Perhaps I'm interfering,' Maud said. 'Perhaps it would be better if I went. Just remember, I'm only next door if you need someone to talk to.' At the door, she paused. 'Would you like me to take Bea for a couple of hours?'

Linda did want that, but she didn't know how to say so. She didn't know how to say that she didn't deserve this kindness, this understanding. Instead, she shook her head, and watched Maud's sad face until she turned and left the house.

Was it just minutes after Maud left that Bea started crying again? It felt like no more than ten or fifteen minutes, but it could have been longer. The light outside had shifted, Linda noticed, as she stood up from her seat at the kitchen table. Some time had passed. This time, she went straight to her daughter, lifted her and held her against her body, rocking back and forwards on her feet. And as she stood there, trying to instil her daughter with a calmness she herself could not feel, she heard Phoebe again. She heard Phoebe say 'Bea'. She looked about the room, wildly, and then she smiled, imagining a world in which Phoebe and Bea both lived. And just as quickly, she collapsed into great wracking sobs that came from deep in her stomach and kept coming. She placed Bea in her cot and clutched at her sides, willing it all to be over. Bea looked up at her, bewildered, and Linda thought she saw an edge of fear in her daughter's enormous, round eyes. Wondered what she would see in her own eyes, if she were to look in a mirror.

Linda went back to the kitchen, gulped from the vodka bottle until she felt calmer. She sat, again, at the kitchen table, trying to empty her mind of all the nagging doubts. Trying to forget that Maud was bound to talk to Tom about what she'd seen, what she knew. That her secret was out, or as good as. When she stood and stretched her legs, she glanced up at the clock on the wall beside the window and saw that Esme had finished school five minutes earlier. Linda stood there for a moment, frozen, picturing her daughter standing at the gates by herself, her face a picture of hurt. And where had the day gone? It was frightening, to have lost all those hours. She dashed upstairs, grabbed a sleeping Bea and, ignoring her daughter's indignant cries, picked up her keys and coat from the hallway.

Outside, it was icy. Linda placed Bea in her car seat and

slipped into the driver's seat, turning on the heaters to clear the windscreen. It took a couple of tries for the car to start. Linda could only see through a small square of clear windscreen, but there wasn't time to wait, so she leaned forward in her seat, fixed her eyes on the road, and began to drive.

There was nobody at the school gates. Linda dashed awkwardly up and down the street, holding Bea against her body, searching for Esme. She felt a familiar fear begin to settle on her, but it was tinged with something else this time. Something Linda didn't want to acknowledge. Something that felt a lot like relief. When she'd established that Esme wasn't nearby, Linda leaned back against the school's iron gates, catching her breath. She looked down at Bea. Somehow, despite the jerking and the dashing about, she had managed to fall asleep. Linda took in her face, a picture of calm, and envied her.

She realised, then, once she started thinking rationally, that Esme was probably inside with a teacher. She went through the side gate, picked her way carefully across the icy playground.

As soon as she entered the school, Linda could hear Esme. She followed the sound, her heart banging in her chest, to Esme's classroom. Esme and Mrs Lewis were sitting on small chairs, playing a game of cards.

'Mum!' Esme called out.

Linda shifted Bea's weight slightly and made her way towards Esme, her eyes on Mrs Lewis.

'I'm so sorry,' she said. 'I've had a difficult day and I completely lost track of time.'

'Not to worry,' Mrs Lewis said. 'I know how it can be, with a newborn.'

'That's my baby sister,' Esme said, with pride in her voice. 'She's called Bea'.

'That's a nice name. Do you help your mum and dad to look after her?'

Esme shrugged. 'Not really,' she said.

Linda reached out a hand for Esme to take. 'Let's go,' she said.

'Just a minute,' Mrs Lewis said. 'Esme, I just want to have a quick chat with your mum before you go. Here, you can play with the cards.'

Linda followed Mrs Lewis to the other end of the classroom, still cradling Bea in her arms. She knew what was coming. More judgement, dressed up as concern. When they were out of Esme's earshot, Mrs Lewis spoke.

'Mrs Sadler, I think perhaps you should leave your car here. I can give you all a lift home.'

Linda blinked a couple of times. She looked at the woman in front of her. She was maybe ten years older than Linda – there were lines around her eyes and slivers of grey in her bobbed hair.

'What are you talking about?' Linda asked, defensive.

Mrs Lewis looked down at her shoes, then back at Linda. Her cheeks were flushed.

'I don't think you should be driving,' she said.

At that moment, Bea awoke. She gazed around her, blinking. Linda looked down at her, reached out to give her cheek a reassuring stroke.

'I'm fine,' Linda said.

She turned and marched out of the room, calling over her shoulder for Esme to follow her. She half expected Mrs Lewis to physically stop her, but she didn't. When they reached the car, Linda took a few deep breaths and blinked back the tears of anger that were waiting behind her eyes, threatening to fall.

'Get in,' she said to Esme, as she manoeuvred Bea into her car seat.

'Why didn't you come?' Esme asked, once they were seated inside the car. 'I thought you weren't going to come at all.'

She sounded hurt, and Linda's heart ached for her.

'I'm sorry,' she said. 'It was just a bad day, Esme, but I'll try really hard not to let it happen again.'

Esme's eyes were serious, and Linda couldn't read them. She

pulled out of the car park slowly, peering forward to see as much of the road as she could through the misted windscreen.

It happened when they were almost home. Esme was chattering about a special project Mrs Lewis had given her and Samantha, something about farm animals and their eating habits. Bea was awake and whimpering slightly, and Linda knew that she only had a couple of minutes, at the most, before the whimpers turned into wails. She was thinking about what Mrs Lewis had said, the way she had looked at her, embarrassed. She was thinking about the fact that almost everyone could see what was happening to her. Everyone except Tom, who was too busy fucking another woman. She was thinking about all of that when she heard Phoebe whisper 'watch the ice, Mum', and then the car was spinning, and the seconds stretched like elastic and somebody started to scream.

Once Linda realised that the screaming was coming from her, she stopped. She looked across at Esme in the passenger seat. She was unhurt, silent, staring straight at Linda with an expression that Linda couldn't quite read. In the back seat, Bea was sobbing, her face a livid red. The car was facing the wrong way. Linda looked in both directions, but there were no other cars in sight. She took a deep breath, and another, closed her eyes and heard Phoebe's voice once more. 'Watch the ice, Mum.'

'Are you all right?' Linda asked Esme.

Esme gave a sharp nod and dropped her gaze.

Linda got out of the car, opened the back door and placed a comforting hand on Bea's head. Instantly, she stopped wailing and arranged her features in a sort of smile. It's okay, Linda told herself. We're all okay. They were just two streets from home. A little shakily, Linda started the car, turned it, and drove them to the house at a crawl.

Esme went upstairs to her room without a word, and Linda took Bea through to the lounge, laid her down on her playmat. She was just starting to become herself, Linda realised. A few weeks of sleeping and eating and then, suddenly, a distinct personality. It was wonderful and heartbreaking for Linda to see, because she knew then, with a rush of clarity, what she needed to do to save her family. And it felt as if she'd known it all along.

'I know you,' she whispered to Bea. 'I knew you first.'

When she heard Esme's footsteps, Linda looked up. Esme's eyes were puffy and red-rimmed. She stood in the doorway with one sock slipped slightly lower than the other and her hair in disarray. Linda really looked at her, made herself think hard about what could have happened.

'I won't tell Dad,' Esme said, her voice a little shaky.

And that just reinforced Linda's decision. Esme was too young to be keeping secrets and holding things together, and Linda's behaviour had forced her to do that.

'Come here,' Linda said.

Esme sat beside her on the sofa, close, and Linda wrapped her arms around her, and whispered an apology into her hair.

13TH JANUARY 1986

182 DAYS AFTER

Tom had meant what he said to Linda at Christmas. It was over with Marianne. And yet he'd put it off, avoided calling her or going to see her for weeks. In the back room of the shop, while it was quiet, he retrieved a small handful of letters and cards she had sent him from a drawer. There, still, was the slip of paper with her name and number, which he'd long since memorised. She sent these things to him at the shop, never intruding on his home life with a phone call or, God forbid, a visit. Tom read through the words she'd written for him, the secrets he'd kept, and he moved to throw them all into the bin. But he couldn't, quite.

He would say goodbye to her, never see her again, because he owed that to Linda. But he would keep hold of these loving words, go to them when things were hard and he needed a boost. He would keep something of her for himself.

She answered on the second ring, as if she'd been poised by the phone, waiting for his call.

'I've missed you,' she said.

Tom ached with the knowledge of everything that could pass between them, but never would. He wanted to tell her he'd missed her too, because he had, almost more than he could bear. But he'd made a promise and he wanted, desperately, to be the kind of man who kept his word, who was faithful to his wife, who did the right thing. And so he didn't return that sentiment, and he didn't tell Marianne how he felt, but he hoped, in his most secret self, that she knew.

'Can I come over?' he asked.

'Yes. Now?'

Tom looked out of the window at the rain that was falling, hard and fast. He wanted to be out in it, just then. He wanted to let it cleanse him.

'Yes,' he said. 'Now.'

She hadn't known his intention on the phone, but when she opened the door to him, Tom saw the realisation hit. Saw her crumple a little, deflate. And he wished that he had two lives, then, and could spend one with her.

'Come inside,' she said, her voice thick.

She led him down the hallway, pausing for just a second outside her bedroom door. The rain had stopped and the kitchen was flooded with winter sun, and when she turned to face him, she looked radiant. He kept his eyes on her, willing his brain to capture this image, to keep it safe.

'I love you,' she said, in a rush. 'And I'm not asking for anything. I'm not asking you to leave her. So why do we have to do this?'

Tom felt heavy, and he pulled out a kitchen chair and sat down. Marianne remained standing, in front of the window, leaning against the kitchen worktop, the light surrounding her.

'Linda knows,' he said. 'It's hurting her. I can't bear to add to her hurt. Not after Phoebe...'

Marianne nodded. She had lost a child, and she understood. Tom was not hers, never had been. And yet maybe, Tom thought, she'd let herself pretend that this would have a different outcome. He stood there, not quite ready to leave.

'You know, when I lost Isaac, I couldn't stand to think about trying to have another child. And yet, these past few weeks, with you, I've begun to imagine it. I know it's ridiculous, I know what the situation is. But I've started to be able to picture it – beginning again.'

'You shouldn't be alone,' Tom said. He crossed the kitchen – just a handful of steps, but it felt like miles – and placed his hands gently on her narrow shoulders. 'You should be with someone, you should have a family. It just can't be with me.'

Marianne shook her head, almost imperceptibly, and he wished he couldn't see the tears in her eyes. He didn't want to let go of her, knowing, as he did, that this touch would be the last. So they stood there for a few moments, his hands on her shoulders, her tears beginning their slow fall.

'I'm sorry,' he said, and it wasn't enough, and the spell they'd been caught in was broken.

'I know,' she said. 'I know you are.'

Tom dropped his hands to his sides, turned and walked out of that kitchen. And although it pained him to keep walking down the hallway, not once looking back, he did it. And when he was outside, in the car, he took a few deep breaths before starting the engine. Just before he pulled away, he dared a glance at her bedroom window, and saw her framed there, standing very still, her face expressionless. His eyes locked with hers for a second, and he tried to pour everything he hadn't said into that look. His sorrow, his shame, his reluctant goodbye.

A handful of hours later, Tom was in the car with Esme.

'Wasn't it cooking today?' he asked. 'What did you make me? Flapjacks?'

'Rock cakes. Some of them are a bit burned at the edges. Samantha's were better.'

Tom twisted in his seat and ran a hand through Esme's hair.

'Samantha's might have looked better, but they wouldn't have won at the British baking championships. The judges there know that burned bits are essential to the perfect rock cake. That's where all the sweetness is stored. Now, how many are there? Because I'm going to eat three, or possibly four, after I've had my tea.'

Esme smiled. 'Twelve,' she said. 'No, eleven. I gave one to Mrs Lewis.'

'Okay, eleven. So that's four for me, one for Mum, one for you, and five for Bea. And I'll have to eat Bea's for her, because she only likes milk. How was the rest of the day?'

It was hard, Tom found, trying to be casual, when he felt like he was breaking apart.

'Okay,' Esme shrugged. 'Samantha had a new coat because her rabbit died.'

'A new coat is the perfect cure for rabbit grief,' Tom said. 'Now, why haven't I seen Samantha for such a long time?'

Esme shrugged again. 'Her mum said no, last time.'

They'd reached the house, and Tom pulled on to the drive, trying to make sense of Esme's words. He turned to face her.

'What do you mean?'

Esme put a hand to her mouth, as if she wanted to push the words back inside. Tom wondered what else there was, that she was keeping from him.

'You can tell me,' he said. 'Nobody will be cross.'

'I asked if Samantha could come for tea, and Mum said yes, but her mum said no.'

'When was this?' Tom asked.

'Ages ago. Before Christmas.'

'Do you know why she said no?'

'No,' Esme said.

Tom pondered this. All of a sudden, he felt that there might be a whole web of secrets that he was locked out of. It was frightening. Esme opened her door and stepped out of the car, and Tom followed her. He rummaged in his pocket for the door keys. Esme stamped her feet against the cold. She was wearing pink earmuffs and her face was pale.

'If I don't find my keys soon, we're going to freeze right here on the spot,' Tom said.

'That wouldn't happen,' Esme said.

Tom felt the edge of his key against his thumb, and wondered when Esme had stopped believing in magic and make-believe.

Later, he was sure that he'd sensed something as soon as he'd opened the door and ushered a shivering Esme inside. It wasn't something he'd been able to put his finger on – nothing as concrete as a smell or a sound. There had been something, though, because as Esme raced down the hallway to the lounge, he'd had a desperate urge to stop her. He hadn't, because it wasn't rational and he didn't trust it. And he'd always have trouble forgiving himself for that.

Esme disappeared into the lounge, dark hair flying. When she screamed, Tom felt the heavy hand of dread pushing down on his shoulders, the way it had the night that Phoebe died. He stood in the hall for a moment, motionless, unwilling to move into the next part of his life, unwilling to face a second tragedy. Was it Bea? No. He felt sure that Bea was safe. It was Linda, of course. It was always going to be Linda. As he made his way to the lounge, stepping ever closer to knowing, Tom cleared his mind and conjured up an image of Linda playing in the garden with Esme and Phoebe. The previous summer, when their grief, and his betrayal, and Linda's spiral into despair couldn't possibly have been foreseen. If someone had told them, then, what was coming, they wouldn't have believed it. They would have laughed, Tom thought. It was the kind of thing that happened to other people. They were the lucky ones.

Esme was sitting on the floor in a corner of the room, her hands covering her face. And on the sofa, Linda lay quite still, a thin line of vomit snaking from one corner of her mouth to her long neck. On the floor, empty bottles. Vodka, sleeping tablets.

'Esme, can you go and find your sister?' Tom asked, his voice cracking slightly.

Already, Tom noticed, Linda's face was no longer her own. He'd seen it with Phoebe, too. Something had changed, something had gone. Tom lifted her dangling arm, tried to find a pulse. He dashed to the hallway, picked up the phone and called an ambulance.

'It's my wife,' he said, amazed at how his voice held. 'She's taken an overdose. There's no pulse.'

After he hung up, Tom turned and saw Esme in the doorway.

'I can't find Bea,' she said.

He went to Esme, lifted her into his arms. She covered her face with her hands again. As if she'd seen too much, and wasn't prepared to see anything else. And she had, of course. Phoebe, and now her mother. As he carried her up the stairs, Tom had a thought. She will never recover from this. She might just have recovered, after Phoebe, but not now. Tom laid his daughter on her bed, gently prised her hands from her face and kissed her forehead. Tears streaked her cheeks, and her eyes were filled with fear.

'I love you,' he said. 'I'm so sorry, baby. I love you.'

Esme curled then, foetal. She pulled her knees into her chest and turned on her side, towards the wall.

Tom found the note before the ambulance arrived. It was tucked in the pocket of Linda's jeans. Torn from the spiral notepad in the kitchen, the words neat and clear. He thought about all the notes she'd scribbled and left for him, over the years. Reminders to collect one or other of the girls, or to pick up bread, or to have a good day. Tom sat on the floor and held her limp hand while he read it.

Dear Tom,

I've been thinking about my mother, lately. I've been wondering whether there's anything in the way I'm raising the girls that is born out of the way she raised me. I've been wondering whether they ever feel alone when I'm sitting beside them, as I used to with her. And they do, I know they do.

I left my mother, and now this. I always thought I'd escaped her, given her up for something better, something wonderful. But perhaps that wasn't it, at all. Perhaps there's just something in me that causes me to give up on things too easily.

Bea is next door, with Maud. I left her there an hour ago and I can still feel the weight of her against my chest. It's the weight of my grief.

Remember when Esme was Bea's age, how we'd stand by her cot, hand in hand, when she was sleeping? Remember how we couldn't believe that she was ours?

Love them, Tom. I know you will.

Phoebe is close by today. I can feel her. And I have to go to her.

Linda

PART II

Bea sat on the edge of the bath with her eyes closed. She felt Julia's cool hand touch hers.

'It's time,' Julia said.

Bea kept her eyes shut. 'Can you see?' she asked. 'Just tell me, if you can see.'

'I'm not looking. It's not right. You have to look.'

Bea opened her eyes and felt dizzy for a moment. She waited until her surroundings came back into focus. Julia's tatty dressing gown hanging on the back of the door, the brightly coloured bottles and jars lining the windowsill, the drooping plant in the corner that neither of them had watered for ages. She looked down at the piece of plastic in her hand.

'It's positive,' she said.

Her voice was level, but her heart was in her throat.

'Fuck,' Julia said.

Bea stood up. All of a sudden, she felt penned in, trapped in the tiny room.

'I need to get some air,' she said.

'Do you want me to come with you?' Julia asked.

'No.'

Almost as soon as she'd pulled the flat's door closed behind her, Bea realised that she should have picked up her coat. It was November, and grey clouds were hanging low in the sky, a bitter wind whistling around corners. Still, she didn't turn back. She walked to the end of the street, turned left by the pub where she and Julia spent a high proportion of their time and wages. She passed the estate, saw a handful of kids kicking a football and a woman sucking hard on a cigarette, her belly swollen and heavy-looking.

Bea folded her arms against the cold, pulled up the neck of her jumper so it covered the lower part of her face. She turned left again, past the corner shop. The owner, a surly Pakistani man who never acknowledged her when she went in for milk, was pulling down the shutters. For once, she was grateful for his unfriendliness. It was one of the things she loved and hated about London: anonymity. Bea turned left twice more and found herself back on her street. It was Sunday afternoon, almost dusk. There was no one around. She could hear strains of reggae music coming from one flat, TV news from another. She looked up at the buildings that were once imposing houses, that had been divided again and again into smaller and smaller units. By every door, a cluster of bells marked with names that had been crossed out and replaced. Nobody stays, Bea thought. Everybody comes to London, but nobody stays.

'Coffee?' Julia asked, when Bea entered the living room.

Bea nodded and sat down on the sagging blue sofa. When Julia joined her, they sat in silence for a couple of minutes, their coffees steaming.

'What are you going to do?' Julia asked, at last.

Bea looked up at her as though she'd forgotten she was there. 'What do you mean?'

'You don't have to keep it, you know.'

'Fuck, Julia,' Bea said. 'I just found out about this. Give me a chance.'

She stood, went next door to her bedroom and slammed the door. She turned the radio on and put the volume up loud, not really hearing the music but keen to drown out the sound of Julia. They'd lived together for several years and most of the time they got along fine, but every so often, Bea longed to have a bit of space that was just hers. Somewhere bigger than this room, which had just about enough space for her bed, her desk, a tiny wardrobe and a chest of drawers.

Lying on her back on the bed, Bea heard her phone buzz over the music and knew without looking at the screen that the message was from Adam. On Sundays, he sold vinyl at Spitalfields Market and he always ended up in the pub with some of the other traders afterwards. Often, she got a call or a text in the evening asking her to join them. Bea pictured him, his sharp features slackened by drink, his speech a little slurred, and his unwashed hair falling in his face. She tried to imagine telling him the news. And then she threw the phone against the wall, watched it drop to the floor, and didn't go over to check whether it was broken.

For half an hour, she lay there running through different scenarios, keen to find one that would fit. And then she returned to the lounge, stood in the doorway.

'Look, I'm sorry,' Julia said. 'I was trying to be helpful.'

She muted the TV and stood to give Bea a hug. Bea let herself be held, her nose in Julia's hair. For the first time since she'd found out, she thought she might cry.

'Listen,' she said, holding Julia at arm's length. 'I can do this, right? I'm twenty-six. People younger and more stupid than me have done it.'

'What about Adam?' Julia asked.

'Fuck Adam. He won't want to know.'

'Are you sure?'

'Yes, why not? I'm going to call my dad and my sister before I can change my mind.'

'I always forget you've got a sister,' Julia said.

Bea conjured up an image of Esme, working in the bookshop with their father, preparing and eating meals with him in the evenings, both of them sleeping alone in the same house. And then she thought about the sister she'd never known, never told anyone about. Phoebe.

Julia had brothers, three of them, all living in London. She was always meeting one or other of them for drinks, and a handful of times, Bea had got up on a Sunday morning to find one of them sprawled out on their sofa. How could she explain to Julia how it was with Esme? The seven years that lay between them like a chasm, the way she'd felt suffocated throughout her childhood, the loneliness that was more acute when she was with her family than when she was away from them. The shroud of silence that surrounded Phoebe's death, and her mother's.

'We haven't spoken for a while. But I'm going to tell them about the baby. Maybe it will make us all closer.' She forced a laugh.

She went back to her room before Julia could say anything else, retrieved her phone from the floor and dialled the familiar number, her heart thudding. She was nervous about telling them her news, but there was something else, too. She was going to have a child and she suddenly had an urgent need to know what had happened to the child she could never quite replace.

'Hello?'

Esme. She sounded distracted, and Bea pictured her in the sunshine-yellow kitchen of her childhood, making coffee or clearing away the dishes from dinner.

'Esme, it's Bea.'

There was a heavy silence, and Bea waited it out, aware that she couldn't expect a typical response. She tried to work out how long it was since she'd been home. More than a year. And in all that time, no phone calls, no emails. The last time she'd seen her sister, Bea had screamed at her to stay out of her life. She'd called Esme an interfering bitch. She remembered the way Esme's face had looked, even now. All that hurt, spoiling Esme's elegant features.

'Bea.'

'Esme, I'm having a baby. I wanted you to know.'

Bea sat down heavily on her bed and waited. She stared at her feet, at her mismatched socks, and when she closed her eyes she could see Esme, sitting at the pine table where they'd eaten their breakfasts as children, which was scratched and marked with felt-tip pen.

'Say something,' Bea said.

'I don't know what to say, Bea. We haven't heard from you for a year, and now this. Are you phoning because you need help, or money?'

Bea was struck by the way Esme referred to herself and their dad. She felt like she was talking to her mother, rather than her sister. And the thought of that, of how she would never break this news to her mother, caused a lump to form in her throat.

'I'm phoning because you're my family, and this is the kind of thing families share.'

Bea wondered whether it would help if she apologised, or whether they'd gone beyond that.

'And,' Bea continued, keen to get the words out before she lost her nerve. 'I want to know about Phoebe, about what happened to her.'

She heard Esme's sharp intake of breath, as if Bea was a child who'd uttered a swear word.

'I know we don't talk about her. But I want to know. It doesn't have to be right now. In fact, can I talk to Dad?' she asked.

'I'll get him,' Esme said.

And then she was gone, and Bea thought that her voice had sounded a little softer on those final words, but she couldn't be sure. Although there was nothing there to see, or feel, she placed a hand on her stomach.

When her dad came on the line, Bea took a quick breath in at the sound of his voice.

'Bea,' he said. 'I'm so pleased you called.'

Bea thought about the journey to her dad's house, about how easy it was. A couple of tubes to Waterloo, then less than two hours on the train to Southampton. And her dad, waiting in the car park to drive her to the house, that grateful look in his eyes. It was hard to justify not doing it. Even harder to justify the calls and messages she'd ignored in her bid to break free from her broken family.

'Hi, Dad.'

'I can't tell you how much I've missed you,' he said. 'Esme too.' His voice was soft and warm, and Bea wished she were beside him. She felt as though she could curl up and fall asleep next to him.

'Dad? I've got something to tell you.'

He was silent, but Bea knew that she had his full attention. She knew that he would be sitting up, his glasses resting on the arm of the chair, his book forgotten. And she thought, then, that it's not always easy, being loved so much. That it sometimes feels like choking.

'I'm going to have a baby,' she said.

'Oh,' he said.

Bea felt tired, suddenly. All her life, she'd been fighting and rebelling. Trying to make Esme and her dad really see her. She didn't want to be angry, or to justify her decisions. She was twenty-six years old, and it was old enough. But then he spoke again.

'Oh Bea, I think that's wonderful. I think that's the most wonderful thing I've ever heard.'

Bea swallowed her surprise. 'Thank you,' she said.

After she'd hung up, Bea realised that neither Esme nor her dad had asked about the father. Her thoughts went back to Adam, who'd sent her three messages now, asking where she was. She imagined getting on the tube and going to find him, letting him fold her in his arms and buy her drinks with the money he'd made that day. Adam was funny and charming and unpredictable. They'd been seeing each other for five or six months and she'd enjoyed it. But he wasn't ready to be a father. And yet, the baby she was carrying tied her life to his forever. Was that what was tugging at her, making her feel uneasy? No, it wasn't that. She was scared of being a bad mother, because she'd never been taught any different.

Bea found Adam's number in her phone and called him. When he answered, she could hear loud music and laughter.

'Bea, are you coming down? Because we've moved to a different bar. We're in that basement place with all the mirrorballs.'

'Not tonight, Adam.'

'Wait, I can't hear you. Did you say you're coming? Hang on, I'll go outside.'

Bea waited. She could picture him moving through the crowd, his messy hair in his face and a short-sleeved T-shirt showing off his tattoos. That's how she'd first seen him, in a bar like that. She knew how girls looked at him, what they wanted. She felt a stab of jealousy, and then she realised that that was ridiculous. Once she'd let him go, she wouldn't have any kind of claim over him.

'Fuck, it's cold. Bea, are you still there?'

'I'm here,' she said.

'So, are you coming? I made a good profit on some of those records I picked up on eBay. Drinks are on me.'

'Sorry Adam, I'm not feeling great. I'm going to get an early night.'

'Shit, sorry to hear that. Anything I can do?'

For a second or two, she considered asking him to come to her, to look after her. She wanted to rest her head on his taut stomach. One more time.

'No, nothing. Enjoy your night. I'll talk to you tomorrow.'

'Night, Bea.'

A few minutes later, Julia knocked on Bea's bedroom door.

'Well?' she said, only her head visible.

Bea was sitting on the edge of her bed, plaiting small sections of her long, thick hair.

'I'm going to do it. I told my family, and it wasn't so bad. I'll tell Adam soon. Don't look at me like that, I'm not expecting him to do anything. Like I said, I'm going to do it.'

'Well, for what it's worth, I think you're mad. Look at how we live.' Julia made a vague gesture that took in the room, the flat.

Bea looked around her, at the mismatched furniture and the yellowed walls. At the piles of unwashed clothes and the scattered mugs. She lived like a student, she realised. Four years after she'd graduated and she was still living like a student. It was time to grow up, make a few changes.

'I don't give a shit what you think,' she said, with a hint of a smile. 'It's not your baby.'

E sme stood in the kitchen, stretching for her morning run. She bent her left leg and caught it behind her with her hand, squinting against the streaks of winter sunlight that were falling through the window.

'How far today?' Tom wandered into the kitchen, opened and closed the fridge door without taking anything out.

'There's tea in the pot,' Esme said. 'And crumpets or wholemeal bread in the breadbin. Or porridge. Not in the breadbin, obviously.' Esme looked at him and he raised his eyebrows, silently reminding her that she hadn't answered his question. 'Five or six miles,' she added.

'Piece of cake,' he said, shrugging his shoulders.

'Dad,' she said. 'Why did we never talk about Phoebe?'

It was an inelegant way to bring it up, she knew. It was shocking and sudden, but it was the only way she knew how to make her mouth form the words, make her say them aloud. She watched his reaction. Not surprise or anger. Just pain, clouding his eyes. Old, heavy pain that was never far away, and that returned in an instant, when summoned. Esme could hear Phoebe's name in the still room, over and over like an echo.

'I don't know, Esme. It was just too painful, I suppose. Especially after we lost your mum.'

Esme wanted to say that not talking about Phoebe had been painful for her, but it seemed childish.

'Bea should know,' she said.

Tom held her gaze. 'She does know,' he said.

'She only knows the bare facts. About Phoebe, and Mum. She should know their stories.'

'I'm not sure that's a good idea, after all these years. Why dredge it all up?'

Esme didn't answer straight away. Although they'd lived together as adults for so long, there were times when Esme was acutely aware of the relationship between them, of the fact that her father still believed that he knew better, and should be obeyed. For years, she'd kept the peace, biting her tongue and going along with his wishes. But this mattered more than any of the other little things they'd disagreed about. This was important. And he was wrong.

'She should know,' Esme said again, struggling to keep her voice firm and even. 'It's her family, her history.'

'Esme,' Tom said, leaning forward in his chair and pushing his glasses back into position. 'Listen to me. It's too late. And it's not your decision. You were just a child, you don't even know half of what went on…'

'I was old enough for Mum to leave me alone with her!'

Esme heard the accusation in her voice and did nothing to disguise it. And she watched Tom's reaction as he floundered, unable to come up with a response. It hurt to see him so unsure. Esme stood and walked out of the room, out of the house.

She started out gently, as she always did, but her body conspired against her. By the time she was a few streets away from home, where the houses got bigger and more spaced out, she was taking longer strides. Her breathing evened and she relaxed into the run, enjoying the feeling of the chilly morning air rushing past her face. That morning, she'd woken from a dream in which she was having a baby. She'd woken up clammy, and sweating, and remembered.

There was a stone sitting in Esme's stomach, and it was made of regret. She regretted the year that she had allowed to slip past since she last saw her sister, and she regretted the way she had spoken to Bea the previous day. Cold, distant. When all she'd really wanted to do was catch her breath at the welcome sound of that familiar voice.

Esme turned a corner and saw the common laid out before her. Despite the cold air biting at her exposed skin, she was starting to feel warmer, the blood pumping freely. She was taking longer and longer strides, feeling a slight burning in her chest. She slowed a little, let herself look around and take in the golden-brown leaves in piles on the grass, the dogs that ran and leapt for sticks, ecstatic to be free of their leads. In the winter, those who weren't serious about their running stayed indoors, and Esme often had the common to herself. That time was coming, and she was pleased. There was nothing quite like the feeling of streaking along, alone. Racing against yourself.

Esme had always struggled to think of Bea as an adult. Those years, when she was a teenager and Bea was a child, had had a powerful effect. In the absences between visits, which were often long, the years dropped away from Bea in Esme's mind, and she retreated into childhood. Esme focused on imagining her sister as she really was – a confident, self-assured woman. Barely a trace of that lost little girl remained. But, pregnant? Esme didn't even know whether Bea was doing this with a partner or going it alone.

Esme slowed a little to let a woman with a double buggy go past in the opposite direction. She took in the two babies – twins, dressed in matching white snow suits, their faces red and their mouths twisted open, crying. And then she looked up at the mother. Took in her puffy eyes, her unwashed hair. Esme smiled, and the woman nodded to acknowledge her. And as Esme picked up her pace again, she hoped that the woman had family nearby, a partner at home. Support.

Was she jealous of her sister? Esme had to consider this. She was seven years older – single, childless. Surely they'd gone out of turn. Surely Esme should have led the way. But she hadn't, Esme reasoned, and perhaps Bea had simply grown tired of waiting.

Perhaps she'd concluded that Esme would never have those things – a relationship, a wedding, a family. After all, that was certainly how it looked.

Esme slowed as she left the common and covered the short distance back to the house. She could feel her heart pounding in her ears. Feel the blood pumping. This was why she ran, for this sensation of being more alive. But was that all there was to it? Was it possible that it was about escaping the past, too? Esme thought about the first psychiatrist she ever saw, when she was eleven or twelve. He would say it was about something more, she knew. He would attack her with silence until she admitted that she was running away from the pain and guilt she carried.

Later, after a slow day in the bookshop, Esme climbed the stairs to her current psychiatrist's office. She'd been coming to Dr Armstrong for almost a year. As she sank into an armchair in the bright, clean waiting room, Esme tried to remember whether they'd ever spoken about Bea. They must have done, she reasoned, but she couldn't remember it. They'd spent long hours dissecting Esme's feelings about her mother. Phoebe. Her dad. Esme felt a pang, then, of remorse. Could it be possible that she'd spent nearly fifty hours talking to this therapist, and never once mentioned her living sister?

A couple of minutes later, Dr Armstrong put her head around the door.

'Come in, Esme'.

Esme moved into Dr Armstrong's small, neat office and sat down opposite the desk.

'How are you, Esme?' Dr Armstrong asked. Her voice was

soothing.

She walked over to the window and pulled it shut. Esme looked at her, took in her dark-grey suit and glossy black heels. When Dr Armstrong sat down behind her desk, she crossed her legs and smiled encouragingly at Esme.

'Good,' Esme said. 'Okay.'

Not for the first time, Esme wondered about the picture frame that sat on Dr Armstrong's desk, its back to the room. She wondered whether it was Dr Armstrong's family, and she imagined a tall, broad husband and three young children. She imagined that they lived in a pristine house, in a village a few miles out of the city, with a dog that they took for long walks in the countryside, that didn't shed hairs on the deep carpets.

'What's been going on, since I saw you last?' Dr Armstrong asked. Her eyes were fixed on Esme's, her gaze intense.

'My sister phoned last night. Bea. We haven't spoken for a year.'

'Why not?'

If Dr Armstrong was surprised at this revelation of a living sister, she didn't show it.

Esme shrugged. 'We argued. She said I smothered her, that I was always interfering in her life.'

'Were you?'

'I don't know. Maybe. The thing is...' Esme paused, not sure how to phrase the next part.

Dr Armstrong nodded, waited. Esme felt warm, suddenly, and wished that Dr Armstrong hadn't closed the window. She shifted in her seat, crossed and uncrossed her legs.

'She was born after Phoebe died, and Mum died when she was a few months old, and we never spoke about either of them. She knows we had another sister, but I'm pretty sure she doesn't know what happened to her. It was just understood, when we were growing up, that you didn't mention it.'

'Does she know that your mother committed suicide?' Dr

Armstrong asked.

'Yes. She asked me about that, when she was a teenager. And then she asked me about Phoebe, too, and I just shut her down, told her it was too hard to talk about it. But now I feel like she should know, about all of it, because it will help her to understand why Mum did what she did. Especially now that she's going to be a mum herself.'

'Your sister's pregnant?' Dr Armstrong asked.

'Yes. That's why she called us.'

For a minute or so, there was silence in the small room. Dr Armstrong picked up her glasses and slid them on to her nose. She offered Esme a half smile.

'If you think she needs to know, then you should tell her,' she said, eventually.

'I don't know how,' Esme said. 'It's hard to know where to start.'

'Yes,' Dr Armstrong said. 'I can see that. Maybe you could write it down? Send her a letter?'

When Esme got home, she went straight upstairs to her room. She sat down at her desk, opened the top drawer and pulled out a few clean sheets of paper, an envelope and a biro. This is where she'd done her homework as a teenager, revised for her exams. If she closed her eyes, she could picture a young Bea standing in the doorway, asking her to play. She could hear her dad moving about downstairs, probably making a pot of coffee. She could go down there, she thought, take her book and sit in that room with him, for company. It would be so much easier than doing what she was planning to do.

Another twenty minutes passed before Esme wrote anything down, and when she did, she found that she wasn't writing to Bea at all. The letter was for Bea, there was no doubt about that. But it was written to Phoebe.

Dear Phoebe,

I lost my first tooth the day you arrived. I was in the garden at playschool, watching pairs of feet thudding against the wet tarmac as the football rolled down the slight incline towards the gates. There were shouts and squeals from the crowd as it bounced, slowed, and finally slipped beneath the iron gates and on to the road beyond. Some of the boys surged forward, pushing one another, prodding, daring. Get it, no you get it.

A car screeched around the corner and there was a collective intake of breath, but it missed the ball entirely, its twin pairs of wheels passing by it on either side, never slowing.

Simon stepped forward. The knees of his trousers were grass-stained and his face was set in a smirk. He slithered through the gates and dashed out into the road without looking left or right and I closed my eyes, expecting another car to skid around the corner and knock him down. I believed what they told me about the Green Cross Code. But no car came, and Simon stood before the errant football, took one step backwards, and gave it a hefty kick.

I watched it sail through the air, closer, closer, and by the time I realised that it would hit me, it was too late to change anything. In the next moment, I was on the ground, gravel pressing into my knees, my mouth salty with blood and my front tooth beside me, gleaming against the tarmac.

One of the ladies there took me to the toilets, washed away the blood, and wrapped the tooth up in a tissue. She watched me looking at myself in the mirror. There was no bruise yet, and my face looked the same until I opened my mouth and the gaping hole in my smile was revealed.

She told me I'd grow a new tooth, and I looked at her, a little wary. She had a son who'd just gone up to real school, and she was plump and kind, like a mum should be. At playschool, she was the kisser of grazed knees and the picker-upper of fallen children. I trusted her, and yet, could she be right about this? How would a new tooth know to appear?

When we emerged from the toilets, everyone had gone back inside. She walked me to my room and I felt important when she opened the door and all those eyes turned to look at me. She passed the wrapped-up tooth to Miss Jameson, who closed it away in her desk drawer. When she saw the look of disappointment on my face, she told me that she was just looking after it until it was time to go home.

I spent the afternoon sticking my finger and my tongue into the new space in my mouth, that secret, cavernous, salty place. When Dad came to pick me up, Miss Jameson pressed the package into my sweaty palm and I closed my fingers around it, protecting my prize. I asked where Mum was, struggling to swallow. Already battling tears. Ready to hear that she was gone, or hurt.

Dad picked me up and swung me high in the air. The wind caught my twin plaits, lifted them the way he was lifting me and I was appeased, giggling. And then he said that the baby was coming.

They'd told me about the baby, of course, about you, and I'd watched Mum's stomach swell. I'd seen her in the bath, that neat mound rising above the bubbles. I'd touched it with careful fingers, amazed by how hard it felt, scared that it might burst if I pressed too hard. But I'd never really believed what they said, when they explained that one day soon Mum would have to go away for a few days and that she would return with a new brother or sister for me. It's not that I thought they were lying. It just seemed so...unlikely. And now, I think of you like that, curled up inside, safe and sleeping, and I wish you could have stayed there forever.

That evening, Mrs Wilson from next door stayed with me while Dad went to the hospital. We played snap and she fed me chicken casserole and, for dessert, a cake she'd made with sticky pink icing. We waited for the phone to ring, and when it did, Mrs Wilson snatched for it. I listened to her side of the conversation, imagining my dad at the other end, pacing the hospital corridor until the phone cord was stretched tight, like he always did at home.

She hung up and turned to me. I was twisted round on one of the kitchen chairs, my legs swinging and my face pressed against the slats, seeing the world in narrow strips. She told me I had a sister, her smile wide.

I didn't really know what it meant. Not until they brought you home.

11TH NOVEMBER 2011

9615 DAYS AFTER

Bea dragged her eyes from the page for a moment. She'd waited a long time for this. All those years, she'd known there was another sister between Esme and herself, and hadn't dared to ask about her. She stood and paced the length of her room a couple of times, opened a window and gulped at the winter air. She felt slightly sick. Instinctively, she put a hand to her flat stomach. Was Esme finally going to tell her? After she'd asked her to, on the phone, she'd waited for a text or a call that never came. And then a few days had passed, and she'd assumed her question was going to go unanswered. Of course it was. How like Esme to just stay silent, to refuse to budge an inch. And then an envelope had dropped on to the mat, with her name written in her sister's handwriting.

Bea didn't open it at first. She knew that finding out about Phoebe was going to change everything. All her life, her dad and Esme had been this impenetrable unit, and she'd been on the outside, never really understanding why they wouldn't – or couldn't – let her in. Before she'd been born, the two of them had been part of a complete family that was nothing to do with her. With her, they'd made a different family, and it had always felt clear that they'd have gone back to the way things were before if they possibly could. Before long, she gave in, ripping open the envelope. Understanding that there was no way back, once she knew.

It seemed as though Mum was gone forever. Dad and I survived on fish finger sandwiches, and every evening Mrs Wilson came over to look after me while he went to visit her, kissing me goodbye on his way out and returning long after I'd gone to sleep. Every evening, I asked if I could go with him, and he reassured me that she'd be home soon.

I was sure that something had happened to my mother, that the truth was being hidden from me. In the mornings, while he buttered my toast and poured me a glass of orange juice, Dad told me that Mum was missing me, that she couldn't wait to be home.

Mrs Wilson brought baked treats in sturdy cake tins. I would lift the lid, letting the sweet scent out into the air. Brownies, scones, fairy cakes. Something different every day. And each night she tucked me into bed and read a story and when her face was hidden behind the book, I pretended that she was Mum. But her voice was croaky and her hands were wrinkled, and when she turned the light out and closed my bedroom door, I cried.

I didn't know, Phoebe. I was too young to know that you would be so tiny and so beautiful. That everything I feared would come true; had already come true, while my back was turned. That I didn't have Mum anymore, not the way I had before. That she was lost to me that day that you forced yourself out into the world, fists curled, ready to fight.

The day you came home, the first thing I heard was your screams. They tore through the house, making it a place I didn't know.

Dad had picked me up from nursery and said there was someone at home for me to meet. There was something in his voice that I didn't recognise. Or perhaps I recognised it too well. It was the voice he used when he talked about me.

Mum was in the kitchen and she swept me up in her arms and covered my face with kisses. 'Baby, I've missed you,' she said. She looked different, smaller. And then I realised. The bump had gone. She was wearing a jumper of Dad's and her face was thin and pale. I wondered for a moment whether she'd been switched, whether they were all trying to trick me. But then she buried her face in my neck and I could smell her. Beneath the layers of hospital soap, I caught a trace of her familiar scent, and I smiled.

I felt safe again, and I'd almost forgotten all about you when that haunting sound started.

Mum said she was hungry, and gestured for me to follow her up the stairs. We followed your cries. Mum first, then Dad, and me, trailing behind. I wanted one of them to turn back and take my hand.

You were lying on your back, your mouth open and your face an angry red. There were no tears and your eyes were screwed up tight. I wanted to put my hands over my ears, or over your mouth. I wanted to make you stop.

Mum picked you up, her hand covering the back of your head, and held you against her chest. She rocked gently on the balls of her feet until you were settled and quiet. Gradually, your face paled to a gentle pink. That's when Dad told me your name. Phoebe.

And then you opened your eyes, and I fell into them. And I was in love.

You were loud and angry and I wondered how someone so small could take charge so swiftly, so completely. All at once, everything was different. You determined when we could eat, and sleep, and make noise. You lay there, unable to do anything for yourself, and you might as well have been marching around those rooms with a whip.

More than once, my bedtime story was abandoned. More than once, I was left alone at the kitchen table while our dinner went cold. I couldn't touch my food, once Mum and Dad had scraped back their chairs and dashed upstairs to be with you. I would push my hand through the slats at the back of the chair until my arm got stuck, and I would wait to be freed.

And then, sometimes, you were quiet and calm and sleepy and Dad sang while Mum and I danced in the kitchen with you in the space between us, your body warm and your skin so soft. I stroked your fine, dark hair, whispered secrets to you. I couldn't remember how it was before you were there. It seemed like we must have been waiting all that time for you to arrive, to make us a family.

Esme

As she finished reading, Bea heard Julia's key turn in the lock, and a minute later, her flatmate appeared in the doorway.

'Coffee?' she asked.

'No.'

'What's that?' Julia strode into the room, gestured towards the letter in Bea's hand. 'Have you been crying?'

'It's nothing,' Bea said. 'Go and get your coffee. I'll be out in a minute.'

Julia shrugged and left the room, pulling the door closed behind her.

Carefully, Bea folded the letter and placed it back in its envelope. She wanted to read it again, and she would, but not straight away. She tucked the envelope underneath her pillow and walked out of her room without looking back.

From the living room, she called through to Julia in the kitchen. 'Good day?'

Bea could hear the kettle boiling, see the steam drifting towards the living room doorway. Without entering the kitchen, she knew that Julia was leaning against the counter, tapping a teaspoon against her hand.

'Awful,' Julia said. 'My feet are killing me.'

Julia was a trainee hairdresser. Like Bea, she had an Honours degree in French and German from King's. After they'd graduated, Bea had spent a couple of years in various administrative roles before securing her current freelance job, which involved translating a seemingly never-ending series of crime novels. Julia had gone straight into hairdressing. She sometimes said that there'd be plenty of time to use her degree later on.

'I don't know how you can stand all day,' Bea said. 'You're an idiot.'

'Thanks. That's nice. Are we doing anything tonight? Shall we go to the pub?'

Bea wondered whether Julia remembered that she couldn't drink. Possibly not. It wasn't her problem, after all.

'I think I'm supposed to be seeing Adam.'

Julia nodded a couple of times before she spoke again. 'You haven't told him yet, have you?'

'I haven't seen him!'

Bea saw that Julia wanted to say more, but she could hear her phone ringing in her room. She knew it would be Adam before she reached it, and for a second, she considered letting it ring out, letting him leave yet another message. But she couldn't ignore him forever. She forced herself to answer.

'Hi Adam,' she said, her voice as normal as she could make it.

'Hey Bea. What are you up to?'

The sound of his voice, low and steady, was soothing.

Bea sat down on her bed, rested her left hand in her lap. Curled around her wrist were the words 'carpe diem'. She closed her eyes momentarily and remembered sitting in the tattoo parlour, nineteen and afraid, wincing with pain as the letters were etched, one by one, on her skin. She'd felt so grown up. She'd thought she was clever, and strong.

'Not much,' she said. 'Do you want to come over?'

Adam was silent for a moment. She lived in Brixton; he was in Hackney. They were continuously bargaining about who should go to whom.

'We could meet somewhere central?' he suggested.

Bea felt tired, like she could lie back and close her eyes right now and sleep until morning. The thought of going out again, in the cold, of battling for a seat on the tube, wasn't appealing. But she knew she needed to see Adam, to tell him the news.

'Upper Street?' she asked. 'In an hour?'

'Perfect. I'll see you in The White Lion.'

AN HOUR and ten minutes later, Bea pulled the door of the pub open against the wind, and stepped inside. Adam was sitting on a stool at the bar, leaning forward to talk to the pretty girl who was drying glasses. She looked around. There were a couple of old men in one of the booths, playing chess, and towards the back, a group of five or six people of around her age. Bea looked at the glasses that filled their table, the way they were talking animatedly to one another, and felt old, suddenly.

She moved forward and touched Adam's shoulder gently.

'Hey,' he said, turning on his stool and wrapping his arms around her clumsily.

Bea took a small step back and then leaned in to kiss him, ignoring the barmaid's eye roll. 'Hey,' she said. And then she looked up and smiled sweetly at the girl. 'Coke, please.'

Adam turned, his eyebrows furrowed. 'You're not drinking?' he asked, draining the last of his pint and gesturing to the girl that he wanted a refill.

'No,' she said. 'I've got a bit of a headache.'

'You should go to the doctor. First Sunday, now tonight. There could be something wrong.'

Bea nodded, thinking that she probably did need to make an appointment to see the doctor. She didn't know how it worked, what the process was like. Would they take her word for it, that she was pregnant? Or would they test her, take a blood or urine sample? Not for the first time, she wished there was someone she could ask. Someone who'd been through it. Bea grabbed hold of Adam's hand and pulled him off the stool, led him towards one of the booths on the empty side of the pub. And then she nipped back to the bar to collect their drinks. Was this really where she'd tell him? She had imagined the two of them in a room somewhere, the light soft and forgiving. Not this. Not sticky floors and torn leatherette benches and indie music from the nineties playing in the background, a little too loudly.

'How was your day?' she asked, once they'd sat down opposite each other and taken off their coats. She reached across the dark wooden table for his hands, placed hers on either side of them.

Adam was a record collector. He scoured eBay and various markets and charity shops for vinyl, and then he sold the records on at a profit. Those he could part with, anyway. It wasn't a steady job, and it didn't pay well, but he loved it. He loved the people who lived in that world, loved the way they valued music.

'Pretty quiet,' he said. 'I spent some time with Dan at Opus listening to the new stuff he's got in, posted some records out. How was yours?'

Bea tilted her head to one side and really looked at him. It wasn't a job, what he did. It wasn't real. 'I got through a couple of chapters.'

'Oh yeah? Did you find out who did it?'

'I know who did it. I always read the whole thing through before I start.'

She felt as though he knew nothing about her, and she knew nothing about him. In the early days, they'd talked for hours, lying in her bed or his, the covers kicked off. She felt as though she was looking at him through a train window, and any second now she would be moving, and he would become a blur and then disappear completely into her past.

'Are you okay?' Adam asked, taking his hands from between hers and placing them on her cheeks.

Bea felt too warm, and shook her head until his hands fell away. 'It's just this headache,' she said. 'Listen, I don't think I should have come. I should go home, go to bed.'

'I feel like I hardly ever see you.' Adam hung his head as he said it.

Bea slid out of the booth and went back in on his side. There was barely room for both of them, and she enjoyed the feeling of being squashed up against him, their legs and hips touching. She said his name and he looked up at her, a smile playing at the corners of his mouth. His hair was in his eyes, and she brushed it away. And then she kissed him again, and it felt like she was saying goodbye.

'I'll call you,' she said. 'Tomorrow. Okay?'

'Yes.'

And all the way home, Bea chided herself for not telling him. But it wasn't easy, she thought, to turn someone's life upside down like that. To end something that has barely begun, when a life has been created.

When she got back to the flat, Julia muted the television and looked up at Bea.

'Well? What did he say?'

'I didn't tell him,' Bea said. 'I just…couldn't tell him.'

And without waiting to hear what Julia thought about it, she went into her room and closed the door.

E sme walked up and down the shop's narrow aisles, straightening books as she went. She ran her finger along a row of travel guides, half-closed her eyes and imagined that she was going to one of those sun-kissed places. The previous day, at dawn, she'd gone for a ten-mile run. She had a half-marathon coming up in a few weeks and she was training hard. Her muscles were tight and aching, and yet she found it hard to sit still. She glanced over at her dad, who was sitting behind the counter, a book propped open before him, his glasses on the end of his nose. He seemed lost in concentration, but he must have felt the weight of her gaze, because he looked up, keeping his place on the page with his finger.

'Is everything okay, Dad?' she asked.

'Fine.'

Esme let him go back to his book. She moved over to the counter, began to tidy the leaflets and gift books that were stacked there. It wasn't long before he looked up again. Esme noticed that he didn't bother to save his place, this time.

'I was hasty the other day, when I said we shouldn't talk to Bea about Phoebe. I still believe it, but I could have been less dictatorial. I'm sorry.'

Esme dropped her eyes. She couldn't look at him, not after sending that letter.

'Anyway, I've been thinking about Bea,' he continued, 'and this baby.'

'Yes?'

'It's such a wonderful thing. Don't you think?'

Esme still didn't know what she thought. 'We don't know anything about the father, about how long they've been together or whether he's supportive.'

'No, we don't. But, you know, if she needs help, financially, I can provide it. I've put some money away, over the years, in case you two ever needed it.'

Esme felt her eyes fill with tears at the thought of her father squirreling money away with her and Bea in mind. The shop wasn't doing too badly, but it was never going to make them rich. She thought of the way her father shopped, for clothes and food and pretty much everything. Carefully.

'The thought of being a grandfather, it's just overwhelming,' Tom said. 'It's just like the way I felt each time your mother told me she was pregnant, but without the worry and the fear.'

Esme forced a smile, hoping she wouldn't have to cast around for something to say. But she didn't have to worry, because Tom was already speaking again.

'You don't seem to feel it, though. And I can't understand why. She's your sister, Esme. This baby will be your niece or nephew. I know you two have had your differences, but surely now's the time to make a fresh start.'

Esme tried to imagine the three of them in the same room again. Tried to imagine a baby among them. Immediately, she thought of Phoebe and the adoration she'd felt for her when she was tiny.

'Think about it,' Tom said. 'I'm going to go out for a bit, get some fresh air. Do you want anything?'

Esme shook her head, watched her dad cross the floor and leave the shop, causing the bell above the door to tinkle. And when he'd gone, she felt hot tears prick behind her eyes, and she covered her face with her hands, trying to keep them inside. Without thinking about what she was doing, Esme reached for a notepad and pen, and started scribbling another letter.

Dear Phoebe,

When I went back to school after that summer when we lost you, everyone knew. Nobody said anything, at first, but people stared at me in assembly and in the playground. For years, I wasn't Esme Sadler. I was the girl whose sister died.

I think that's why I stopped talking about you altogether. That, and the look on Mum's face whenever your name was mentioned. I learned fast, and stopped saying your name, and then we had Bea, so I could always say that I had one sister and it wasn't quite a lie.

Sometimes, when I'm alone in my room, I imagine you there. I imagine you sleeping beside me in my bed, curled in a ball. As a child of three, your hair a shock of darkness on the pillow. I imagine you as you were, a curious mixture of shyness and flamboyance. Your thumb in your mouth, obscuring your speech. Or as a teenager. Fourteen, with a different kind of shyness; the kind that descends like a cloud with adolescence. Your body awkward, hidden by oversized clothes.

I imagine showing you my life. Sharing it. I wonder whether you would still look up to me the way you once did, try to emulate me. Or whether you'd be lost in your own world now, oblivious to mine. When I went to university, I had some control over what people knew of me for the first time. What was known and what stayed hidden. And I tucked you away in a corner of my heart and left you there.

It's not that I want to forget you. It's more that I don't know how to frame you for virtual strangers; don't know what to hold up to show them, what they will understand and what they will judge. I tell myself that I will reveal you once we know each other better; that I will pull you out like a rabbit from a hat. Surprise! More often than not, you stay hidden. It's hard to offer up new information when people have a certain understanding of you. It's hard to say you lied.

I've never spoken any of this aloud, never written it down. Tried hard not to think about it. And I know that this won't change anything, won't bring you back. Of course I know that.

But still, someone should tell your story, shouldn't they? Someone should write about that smile you had when you knew you'd done something wrong but you weren't quite sorry and the way you rubbed Beebee between your thumb and finger, and carried it everywhere. I feel as though I haven't forgotten anything. But what if I do? I'm scared that if I don't write about you now, we'll lose you again.

She was lost in thought when the bell sounded, and it jolted her. She turned around so that her back was to the shop floor, brushed away the tears that had started to fall.

'Excuse me.'

The voice was deep and close, and Esme jumped a little, and then turned, hoping that her face wouldn't give her away. At first, she didn't know him, but she thought she saw a flicker of recognition in his eyes.

'I wonder if you can help me,' he said, half-smiling. 'I'm looking for a book about Italy, but not a guidebook. A travel memoir or a novel, even.'

Esme tilted her head. Perhaps he did look familiar. He was around her age, with short, greying hair and a generous smile.

'That aisle is everything European,' she said. 'Ignore the left side, that's all guidebooks and maps. You should find what you're looking for on the right. They're ordered alphabetically by country.'

And then she realised. It was Simon Treadwell, from primary school. She hadn't seen him since they were eleven, when she went to the local comprehensive and his parents sent him to private school. Esme winced, remembering the horrors that had passed between them when they were children.

'Thank you,' he said.

He followed the instructions she'd given and began surveying the shelves, occasionally glancing back at her. He'd seen her recognise him, she knew. She wondered whether either of them would acknowledge their shared past. A few minutes later, he returned to the counter with a book about an English couple's retirement to Sicily. Esme was puzzled by his interest in it.

'I'll take this please, Esme,' he said.

Esme felt her face change, felt it redden.

'Have it,' she said. 'On me. I definitely owe you some kind of apology.'

Simon looked from the book to her eyes and back again. And then, he removed his coat and pulled at the neck of his grey T-shirt. Esme felt her heart stop for just a second. Surely it was impossible.

'Nope,' he said. 'Teeth marks gone. Is this your shop?'

'It's my father's,' Esme said.

'In that case, I don't think you should give away his stock. I'll pay for the book. But you can take me out for a drink later, if you still want to apologise.'

Time stretched out as Esme grasped for something to say. Was he flirting with her? This man, who she'd shamelessly bullied when he was a boy, who she'd accused of bullying her. Who she'd pinched and teased and…bitten. Stalling for time, she scanned the book and took the ten-pound note that he was holding out, counted out his change and placed it in his outstretched hand. The coins cold, his fingers warm. Out of nowhere, Esme remembered the last time she'd been kissed. It was almost a year ago, outside a Turkish restaurant on a frosty night. His hands had been warm, and he'd held her face with them when he kissed her. But then he'd sent her an email confessing that he was married, and she'd never seen him again.

'I really am sorry for what I did,' Esme said, her voice a little shaky. 'It was unforgivable.'

Simon held one hand up. 'I'll be the judge of that. Come to the pub next door at seven, and you can plead your case.'

And without waiting for her to answer, he turned and walked out of the shop, leaving his book on the counter. She picked it up, knowing he'd left it on purpose, so that she would have to meet him. Still, she slipped it into her bag, which was on the floor beside her chair. She was amazed by how sure he was, how confident. She thought again of him as a seven-year-old boy. He was sure then too, but she'd still managed to belittle and tease him. How much had she hurt him, she wondered? How different was he to how he might have been if he'd never known her?

When Tom strode back into the shop half an hour later, Esme remembered their earlier conversation with a jolt. Tom was whistling, his cheeks flushed from the cold. He approached Esme and held out a steaming container of soup.

'Lunch,' he said. 'You don't eat enough. Careful, it's hot.'

'Dad,' she said, 'I'm going out tonight.'

'Me too.'

'Oh?'

Tom looked at her, his gaze level. 'I'm having dinner with Marianne.'

For a few months now, Tom had been seeing this woman, and Esme had asked very little about who she was, or where she'd come from. She wondered, then, whether her father was in love with Marianne. She wondered whether she would meet her.

Esme opened her mouth to speak, but the door opened and a woman came in trailing two young children. And just like that, the shop was alive with noise and it wasn't the right time to ask more about her father's relationship.

When it was time to go home, Esme wandered across the street to a café she liked and had a sandwich and a coffee. And when it was approaching seven, she walked back past the bookshop to the pub Simon had mentioned. She'd only been inside a couple of times, despite its proximity to the shop. She had to duck her head to go through the door, and inside, it was filled with small wooden tables and stools, with a couple of tatty-looking sofas in the corners. Simon was already there, sitting at a table with a bottle of beer. Esme pulled the Sicily book from the bag and placed it in front of him.

'You know,' she said, sitting down, 'this place isn't exactly the best drinking-hole in town.'

'What can I say? I obviously don't come home very often.'

'So why are you home now?'

Simon cleared his throat, took a long sip of beer. 'My mother's dying,' he said.

'Oh.'

'The book's for her. She went to Italy a few years back, and she's talked about moving out there ever since. It won't happen now, but she can read about it.'

Esme was sorry, then, that she didn't know him better. That she didn't know him well enough to reach across the table and touch his arm, to show her sympathy. And because she didn't feel like she could do that, she changed the subject instead.

'Where do you live?' she asked.

'London, at the moment. But I'm moving back here, to help out.'

Esme nodded. It had often struck her that the options, once you'd grown up, were to stay put or go to London. She rarely heard of people moving anywhere else. So Simon had gone to London, as Bea had. She wondered whether there was a pattern to it, a way to tell which way someone will go. Of the people that had stayed, Esme thought, she was probably the only one who was still living with her dad.

Simon's beer was almost empty, so she went to the bar and ordered two more.

'Here it is,' she said, returning. 'My apology. It doesn't really seem enough.'

'Why did you do it?' Simon asked.

Esme raised her head to meet his eyes, saw that he was serious. That he genuinely wanted to know.

'It's fine,' he said. 'Really. You don't have to feel bad about it. I just want to know. It was so sudden, and so relentless.'

She wanted to apologise again, but she wasn't sure how many times she could say the words when she knew that it was too late for them to make any difference. She'd been cruel, and she hadn't thought, back then, about how he would be affected.

'I'd just lost my sister,' Esme said. 'Everything was a mess. My mum was pregnant, and she wasn't coping, and we were all living in this house, not really communicating with each other. And I just remember feeling that I didn't have any control over anything. I was lashing out.'

She looked at Simon. He was nodding gently, and his eyes were kind.

'I'd forgotten,' he said. 'About your sister. I remember now.'

'None of that excuses it, but does it make some kind of sense?'

'A little. But here's what I always wanted to know. Why me?'

Esme dipped her head and tucked her thick hair behind her left ear. She uncrossed and recrossed her legs, took a long gulp of her beer.

'You were always in trouble,' she said. 'I knew that everyone would believe me if I said that you were the one bullying me.'

'You said that?'

Esme considered the layers of deception, a little amazed by the work her young mind had done.

'Yes. But only because I thought that's what I wanted. I felt like someone should be making fun of me, saying awful things about what happened to Phoebe. I told my dad that you were tormenting me because I believed it should be happening.'

Simon looked at her for a long time, and although it was hard, Esme didn't break eye contact.

'Why?' he asked, at last.

Esme tilted her head, considered the question. It was strange to finally be discussing some of these things with a near-stranger. But it was easier, too. For a moment, she closed her eyes and she was seven years old again. Lying in bed, silently speaking to Phoebe. I'm sorry I'm sorry I'm sorry I'm sorry.

'Because it was my fault that my sister died,' she said.

15TH NOVEMBER 2011

9619 DAYS AFTER

Phoebe, we were never equal. I like to think that we would have been, in later years. As it was, you were young and fragile and I was told, again and again, to be careful with you. The first time I held you, I could sense Mum behind me, holding her breath, ready to catch you. Dad was hovering nearby. Even as a three-year-old, I understood something of the trust they'd placed in me, and its limitations.

I sat back on the sofa, my legs barely reaching the edge, and held out my arms for you. Mum passed you to me gently, showed me how to support your head. There was a heaviness to you that surprised me; you looked so small but you were dense, solid. Within moments, I felt an ache creeping over my arms and I wanted to move them, to be free of you. But there was a warmth, too. Your body wrapped in blankets, your pink toes wriggling free, you looked cosy and content. I lifted you very slightly and pressed my lips to your hot little head.

I wanted to be you, at that moment. I wanted to be closer to you, inside you, looking out at the world from within those carefully wrapped blankets. Warm and safe. I watched your eyes as they moved slowly, tried to imagine what you were seeing, what you understood. When you looked at me, I felt as though you knew everything. As though you'd been sent here, loaded up with aeons of wisdom, to show us how to live.

I will wait, I promised you, silently. I will wait until you can speak and you are ready to share what you know. I will help to raise you and be patient and try to show you what I've learned, so that you can show me everything. It was a belief I held on to, that I wrestle with even now. That you were sent here to show us how to live.

Esme

As soon as she'd finished reading, Bea put the letter to one side and stood, clutching at her stomach. Tears pricked at her eyes as she imagined her sister as a young child, Phoebe as a baby. She reached for her phone and sent a text to Esme.

She didn't expect an immediate response. It was a little after three in the afternoon, and Esme would be at work. But less than a minute later, her phone buzzed.

I need to tell you everything. It's the only way I know how. Give me some time.

Frustrated, Bea threw her phone down on the bed, and then she took a seat at her desk, tried to get her mind back to the novel on her screen. But it was futile. There were things queuing up for her attention. She wanted to reply to Esme, to say that she'd had years and years to tell this story. All the years of Bea's lonely life.

Her thoughts turned, then, to her unborn child. Bea was painfully aware that time was slipping past and she still hadn't told Adam that she was pregnant, or seen a doctor. Was she in denial? The previous night, she'd poured herself a glass of wine, and then another. She knew she needed to take it easy with the alcohol, but weren't there things she shouldn't be eating, too? She didn't have a clue. It was a new, unfamiliar world.

At six o'clock, Bea shut down her laptop, knowing that she'd have to make up ground tomorrow in order to stay on track with the translation. She had tight chapter deadlines to meet, and she'd made little progress since the post had come and she'd picked up the letter. If she was ever going to get back to normal, she decided, she needed to take decisive action. She was going to have to stop holding things inside. Tell Adam, and let him go.

Before she could change her mind, she grabbed her coat and her bag, dropping in her purse, her phone and keys, and headed for the door. If she waited for Julia to get home, they would sit down with a cup of tea and she would talk herself out of it. And if she called him, he might put her off. No, it had to be tonight, it had to be now. As she walked to the tube station and the streets became more and more crowded, Bea took note of the people she was squeezing past. The people her age, heading for the pub, their arms wrapped loosely around each other. The women with children, their eyes tired, their pace slow. Then, she was inside and heading down the steps, the crowds still around her. And more than anything, she wanted a moment of peace to say goodbye to the life she had been leading. To prepare herself for saying goodbye to Adam.

But there was no peace in London; she knew that. It was the place she'd chosen to be. Frantic, eclectic, endlessly noisy. When she'd chosen it, she hadn't been thinking about children. For a brief moment, as she stepped on to the train, she wondered whether she would move away when the baby came. And where she would go, if she did. Was going home an option? Could she ever live there again, after staying away for so long?

Outside Adam's flat, Bea pressed the buzzer for a third time. She could see her breath in the night air, and she pulled her coat a little tighter around her body. She hadn't considered this. She crouched down and brushed the leaves from his stoop with her gloved hand, sat down to consider the options. It was a little after seven and she knew that wherever he was, Adam was unlikely to still be working. But he could be anywhere, really. In a pub with friends or colleagues, at an evening record fair, at a friend's place. She could go home, put this off. Or she could phone him, try to have a conversation with him without losing her nerve.

Bea stood and walked to the pavement, looked up and down

the street. One of the streetlights was flickering, and there was no one in sight. She shivered, suddenly a little afraid to be here, alone. She started walking back the way she'd come, her steps brisk. And then she realised. He was probably in his local, a couple of streets away. She'd met him in there as often as at his flat, and all the bar staff seemed to know him by name. Bea took a right and then a left, hurried up to the pub's front door.

As soon as she was inside, the warmth hit her and she shrugged off her coat. There was a Clash song playing very loudly. Bea looked around the near-empty bar for Adam. And then her eyes landed on him, and she stood very still, just watching.

He was sitting on a low stool at a small, round table, rocking back and forth on the stool's spindly legs. He had his back to her. Opposite him was a girl in her early twenties with messy blonde hair and dark eye makeup. Bea watched as Adam reached across the table and took the girl's face in both hands, pulled her closer to him and kissed her thin lips. She let a small sound escape her lips, but it was lost amid the pounding background music.

Bea turned and slipped out of the door, back into the biting wind that lifted and then dropped her hair. Her heart was beating very fast, as though she'd been running or climbed several flights of stairs. For a few moments, she stood with her back to the pub door, willing it to slow down. And then the possibility of Adam coming outside for a cigarette occurred to her, and she walked away, back to the train station, her steps silent and fast.

She didn't cry. Not while she was on the train or the tube or walking back to her flat. But once she was inside and she'd closed her bedroom door behind her, she allowed herself to wallow for a few minutes. It hadn't been long, but they'd had some good times. A day on Brighton beach with ice creams and sand in their hair. Summer days spent sitting in beer gardens with friends all around them and a constant supply of beer. A couple of times, he'd made her laugh so hard that she'd cried. And the sex. The sex was the best she'd had; sometimes slow and languorous, sometimes fierce.

What now? Nothing had changed, really. She'd expected the relationship to be over, but in her version, there was compassion, and honesty, and sad farewells. Not some other girl, already sitting in Bea's place with wide-set eyes and creamy skin. Bea closed her eyes to the image of the two of them, but it had already crept inside. And then her phone rang, and it was Adam, and before she'd realised that she was going to do it, she had answered and said hello, her voice thick.

'Hey you.'

Bea could hear Adam's intake of breath as he inhaled on a cigarette, could see him squinting his eyes against the smoke.

'Hey, what's going on?' she asked.

'Nothing much. I had drinks with a mate after work. Just got home.'

Bea wondered whether he was lying about where he was. And if he was at home, was that girl with him? Had he snuck out of the room to make this call? She had no idea whether she wanted to confront him or not, whether she wanted him to know what she knew.

'I miss you,' Adam said.

Bea felt as though her heart had dropped a few inches inside her chest. She closed her eyes, and her mind was empty. White, and peaceful.

'I need to go, now,' she said. 'I came to see you. I saw you, with that girl.'

There was silence. Bea considered hanging up, but part of her wanted to know what he would say, whether he would try to make excuses or talk her round.

'Oh.'

She cried, then. She made sure there was no sound, that he would not hear.

'Look, Bea, I don't know what to say. We've had fun, but I'm not really looking for something serious. I'm only twenty-seven.

It wasn't fair, though, seeing her behind your back. I should have told you.'

Bea wondered what he would say, or how he would feel, if he knew what she knew. She didn't think it would make much difference.

'Goodbye, Adam.'

'Wait, Bea. Is that it?'

'What do you want?'

There was a long pause before Adam spoke again. 'Nothing.'

After she'd ended the call, he sent her messages. Apologies, rationalisations, regrets. She read a few and then she turned her phone off and crossed the room to her record player. She slipped a Leonard Cohen record from its sleeve, trying not to remember the way Adam always told her to handle her vinyl more carefully, to hold it by the edges with the very tips of her fingers. She sank on to her bed as the opening bars of 'Suzanne' filled the room, and tried to think about nothing but the story, the tea and the oranges from China, the garbage and the flowers. Tried to be empty.

Bea didn't remember falling asleep, but she woke up cold, lying on top of her bed in her clothes. The room was dark and she waited, looking at the big clock on her wall, as her eyes adjusted. It was a little before four in the morning. A lonely time. She stripped to her underwear and crawled under the covers, curled into a tight ball. And before she went back to sleep, her final thought was that she would be a mother in a few months, and she would be alone. She reached for her phone, turned it back on and sent a message to her sister. *If I come home this weekend, can we talk?*

E sme heard the key turn in the door and laid her book down on the arm of the chair. She couldn't say why, but she'd missed her dad's company that evening. Over the years, they'd both led their own lives, to a limited extent. His dinners with friends and occasional trips to the theatre, her running, and her infrequent attendance at weddings and birthday gatherings. Esme was a master of solitude, but that night something in her craved companionship. She stood and walked through to the kitchen, flicked the switch on the kettle.

'Esme,' Tom said, entering the kitchen. 'I'm glad you're still up.'

Esme had just reached for two cups in the top cupboard. She turned and smiled at her dad, and then she froze, seeing the woman standing a few steps behind him. She was petite, with cropped blonde hair and high cheekbones. Beautiful.

'This is Marianne,' Tom said, stepping to one side to reveal her. 'Marianne, this is my eldest daughter, Esme.'

Marianne was dressed head to toe in black. Woollen trousers, a silk blouse and a well-cut blazer. She took a step forward, tried out a smile. And she held out a small hand to Esme.

'It's nice to meet you.'

There was something in her voice, some trace of foreignness. Esme waited for her to speak again, keen to identify it. She took Marianne's hand in her own, felt the woman's fine bones and papery skin.

'Coffee, Marianne?' Tom asked. 'Esme, get another cup, will you?'

And just like that, the introductions were over and her father was behaving as though this kind of thing happened every day.

There had been no one, since her mother's death. At least as far as Esme knew. And then in the last few months, her father had mentioned this woman, this Marianne. Had had dinner with her, travelled to London for a day to see the art galleries. Esme had wondered whether it was a romantic relationship, had even hoped that it might be. He deserved a bit of happiness, after all these years. But now that Marianne was standing in their kitchen, Esme wasn't so sure, and it was when she was pouring the milk that it came to her. With her small frame and her elfin haircut, her fair hair and skin, this woman was the antithesis of Esme's mother.

When she'd made the three coffees, Esme put them on a tray and carried them through to the lounge, where her dad and Marianne were sitting on the sofa, his arm around her in what seemed to be a protective gesture.

'How did you meet?' Esme asked, placing their cups on the coffee table in front of them and taking hers over to the armchair where she'd spent most of the evening.

'We were at school together,' Marianne said, looking at Tom and not at Esme.

Was she French? Esme thought she could detect the faintest hint of a French accent. And then she processed what Marianne had said. At school together? That meant they'd known one another before her parents met.

'We hadn't seen each other for years,' Tom said. 'And then back in the spring, I bumped into Marianne in the supermarket. She had a basket full of vodka and gin.'

'I was having a cocktail party that night,' Marianne said, picking up the story quite naturally. 'I invited your father, but he didn't come. And then he phoned me a few days later, and we arranged to meet up.'

Esme sipped at her coffee. Who was this woman, who threw cocktail parties and dressed so elegantly? Who was her father when he was with her? For a minute or two, the three of them sat together in silence. Esme noticed her father's hand hovering over Marianne's hair, and she felt angry with him, but also confused by that anger. Surely she didn't want him to be lonely for the rest of his life. Her mother had committed suicide more than two decades ago, and he had brought up her and Bea alone, never complaining. Surely it was time for him to have a little happiness.

When they'd finished their coffees, Esme stood and put the cups back on the tray, carried them through to the kitchen. She was stacking them in the dishwasher when she felt another presence in the room. And she turned, hoping that it was her father, but knowing it was Marianne. She was standing in the doorway, her arms folded across her chest, her right hip resting gently against the frame.

'I could never really imagine you,' she said. 'Tom talks about you so often. And I wanted to meet you all those years ago, after Phoebe died, but then...'

Marianne's voice trailed off and Esme saw in her face that she realised what she had revealed. Esme said nothing, watched Marianne stumble to recover the situation.

'I've had too much wine,' she said. 'Forgive me.'

Esme sat down at the kitchen table, watched Marianne go back into the living room. A couple of minutes later, she heard the click of the front door and waited for her father to appear before her.

'Who is she?' Esme shouted, when Tom walked into the kitchen, his face a little red.

'Esme, calm down. She's an old friend, like I said. An old girlfriend, from school. I've run into her a few times over the years; she moved down here when you were little.'

Esme stood up and walked towards her father, didn't stop until their faces were no more than a foot apart. She cast her mind back to those days, between losing Phoebe and Bea's birth. Her mum, broken and so full of pain that there were days when she could hardly bear to look at Esme or Tom, when they were nothing more than reminders of what she'd lost. And the memories began to surface, of how distracted her dad had often seemed in that time. She'd always assumed it had been because of Phoebe.

'You had an affair!'

Not a question. She'd never considered it before, but just then, she knew for certain, and she fixed her eyes on her dad's, willing him to tell her the truth.

'Yes,' he said. 'I did.'

Esme felt the tears rise up in her throat. They were tears of anger, and loss. This man standing before her, he wasn't the man she'd always thought he was.

'How could you?' she spat. 'While Mum was grieving...'

'It was a terrible thing to do, but it happened.'

Esme looked up at her dad through her tears. He looked tired and a little older than usual. There was a small part of her that would forgive him instantly for everything, but she held it in check.

'I'm not perfect, Esme. I never claimed to be.'

There was a rage inside Esme that she'd felt for most of her life. Occasionally, she had let it out, like the times she had been cruel to Simon. But mostly, it had remained curled up inside her, like a coiled spring.

There was a bottle of red wine on the kitchen worktop, and Esme reached for it and threw it against the wall, watching it shatter and fall, the liquid fanning out and splashing against the wall, the door, the tiled floor.

Tom didn't move an inch.

'It changes everything,' Esme sobbed, her shoulders heaving. 'It makes you someone else.'

'No,' he said. 'It doesn't.'

He moved to the sink and opened the cupboard beneath it, pulled out a wad of newspaper. And then he crossed the room again and crouched down, picking up shards of glass with his fingers. Esme wanted to tell him to be careful, to sit down and let her do it, but she didn't. She walked past his stooped figure and out of the room. In her bedroom, Esme closed the door heavily, firmly.

There were adjustments to be made, to all of her memories. In a few days, Bea would arrive. Esme had thought she had the past straight in her mind, had thought that Bea was the only one who'd been kept in the dark. Now, she didn't know what she would say to her sister. Didn't know how she would frame her childhood in a way that would be easy for Bea to understand.

Esme went to the bathroom to wash her puffy face and clean her teeth, and then she undressed and got into bed. It was late, almost midnight, and she hadn't heard her dad come upstairs. She wondered whether he'd finished cleaning up the broken glass and whether he'd tried to lift the wine stain from the kitchen's yellow walls. She pictured him, still there on his hands and knees, trying to clear the mess she'd made. She lay back and closed her eyes, but she knew sleep wouldn't come. There was too much to think about. Too much to say. After half an hour, wide awake, Esme propped herself up with pillows and pulled out the notepad and pen that she kept just under her bed.

Dear Phoebe,

You never had Mum to yourself: not like I did in those years before you were born. But, oh, how she loved you. Her whole body smiled when you were here, and the way she grieved for you was like nothing I've ever known. At your funeral, I couldn't look at her. I held her hand and Dad's and I looked at the ground and pretended it was a game, or a dream.

A part of her never came home that afternoon. Secretly, quietly, she closed herself off to further hurt. You couldn't notice, by looking at her, that something was missing. She still looked whole. Only Dad and I knew. I wanted to fix her, to gather up the pieces and stitch them together until she was real again.

I never asked her to forgive me. Never dared, in case she couldn't.

Just before our first Christmas without you, there was a heavy snowfall overnight and I woke up, looked out of my window, and saw everything covered in a thick white sheet.

I was ready to let go of the sadness that morning, ready to play and laugh again. I ran to Mum and Dad's room. Dad had left for the shop already, and Mum was lying on her back, ignoring Bea, who was softly crying in the Moses basket beside the bed. There was a cold cup of tea on the bedside table.

I shook her, Phoebe. I shook her and begged her to get dressed and play, and she just looked at me with those blank eyes and waved me away. When I left the room, my eyes were brimming with tears. I didn't understand. If I was ready, why wasn't she? How long would we be locked in these never-ending days of sorrow?

I asked Dad that evening. He was easier to approach. He took my small hand in his and led me into the lounge. Away from Mum. Out of earshot. Still, he spoke in a whisper. He told me Mum was very sad about Phoebe. That she needed lots of time. I wanted to ask how much time, but I sensed I shouldn't. So I just nodded, and he told me I was a good girl.

I wasn't. I was the worst girl.

There had been times when I was so jealous of you that it was hard to speak. We were an isolated group, our little family – Dad's parents had retired to Spain and Mum's mum was all those miles away in Lancashire – never visited and not forgiven for the loneliness of Mum's own childhood. No one else. And I'd got used to it being the three of us, of course I had. Without knowing anything different, I'd got used to that abundance of attention and focus, that concentration of love.

When they told me you were coming, I didn't know I'd feel jealousy like that. I was three years old, full of wonder and excitement at the prospect of a brand new person, a brother or a sister to spend my time with. I didn't know that you'd stay. That you'd change everything. That you'd come complete with your own personality, and curiosity, and will.

In your first months, I adored and resented you in equal measure. Sometimes, when I woke in the morning, I'd make deals with myself. That if I got out of bed the minute that Mum called me, if I brushed my teeth for three full minutes like I was supposed to, if I got through breakfast without spilling anything on my clean shirt. If I managed all of that, you'd be gone. I wasn't clear about how, about where you'd go, or whether you would ever have existed at all. Usually I faltered, and you remained, and I could never be sure whether you'd have kept up your end of the bargain if I'd kept up mine.

By your first birthday, I understood that you were a permanent fixture. And then I went too far the other way, of course. I began to depend on you, to expect certain things of you, and never once considered that you'd be taken. That one day, you just wouldn't be there. That we'd live to see your body without you inside it.

Bea was rattled by the letter's mention of her, as a baby. Lying beside her mother's bed, her cries ignored. She closed her eyes and tried to summon up a memory of it, but she knew it was futile. Over the years, she'd stared at photographs of her mum and tried desperately to remember her, but the memories just weren't there. She'd been too young. Bea opened her eyes and returned them to the page before her.

On your first birthday, we had a party with cake and games and presents. Some of the neighbours came, and a few mothers and children that Mum had picked up as friends. I felt sick with envy when I saw the presents, brightly coloured and stacked high on the table, just out of reach.

I wanted to tell them all that you didn't even know, or understand. You didn't care that it was your birthday. You liked the shiny wrapping paper and you'd like the way it felt and how it sounded when you tore it, but the presents were wasted on you. You weren't quite walking, then. People exclaimed as you crawled across the floor, reaching down to lift you into their arms, holding you tightly and covering you with kisses. Mum wore an expression that I didn't quite understand. Her eyes watery, her lips pursed. I can see it now when I close my eyes. I can recognise it, now. It's pride, and love, and that happiness so pure it's almost painful. I got to know it well during those years that we had you, and I never once saw it after you'd gone.

When everyone went home and left the four of us alone, the house felt strangely quiet. Empty. Dad turned the music off and started to clear away the bowls of crisps and biscuits. I remember sitting on the sofa in the lounge while Mum and Dad moved around me. I asked Mum to turn on the TV, and she said no, that it was almost time to have a bath and get into bed. I'd eaten too much sugar and I was wide awake. I whinged and moaned until Dad knelt before me and told me, in his warning voice, not to ruin the day.

I watched you cross the floor, your face heavy with concentration, your hands and knees moving in perfect coordination. You were heading towards me. And when you reached me, you sat back on your heels and raised your arms high. I knew the signal. You wanted me to lift you and hold you, place you beside me on the sofa.

I said no and your face fell. You dropped your arms to your sides, then lifted them again a moment later, hopeful that I would have changed my mind. I said it again, a little louder.

Mum and Dad were in the kitchen and I could hear the taps running. I watched your face collapse into tears and I felt warm inside. I felt justified, and happy, and warm. You cried there on the floor until Mum heard you, and came in. She scowled at me and swept you up, stroked your hair until you were quiet and calm again. And that night I wished, for the first time in a long time, that you weren't there. That you weren't a part of our lives, of our family.

It was partly about those presents I wanted, I know, even though they were less enticing when the wrapping was gone and I could see how babyish they were. It was partly about that. But it was mostly about Mum. About that look. About the love I now had to share.

For years after we lost you, I wished for you to come back. I lay in bed every night with my head underneath the pillow, Beebee clenched in my fist, and I closed my eyes and emptied my head of thoughts. And once

you were there, clear and still, I talked to you, inwardly. I told you about
my day and about Mum and Dad, about Bea. I begged you to return. I
remembered – but tried not to remember – all the times I was cruel, all
the times I did the wrong thing when I was supposed to be being your big
sister.

And I was so empty without you that I couldn't even cry. That's what
I couldn't have imagined, in the early days and months of you, when I
wished you were gone. That you'd infiltrate everything so deeply that
your loss would leave a hole we could never fill.

Esme

Bea had just finished reading the letter when her name was called. She folded it and slipped it back into its envelope, and then she took a deep breath and walked down the corridor to the doctor's office.

'How can I help you today?' the doctor asked.

She was female, a handful of years older than Bea. Bea tried to determine whether she'd been to see this doctor before, but she came so infrequently, and she'd moved around a few different surgeries in the time that she'd lived in London. For a moment, she longed for the doctor her dad had always taken her to when she was a child. He was a kindly man whose face crinkled around his eyes when he smiled, and he knew Bea's medical history and that she was allergic to some antibiotics and scared of needles.

'I'm pregnant,' Bea said. 'At least, I did a test and it was positive.'

'I see. Please have a seat, Beatrice.'

'It's Bea.'

She sat down on a green plastic chair, took her coat off and laid it across her lap.

'And have you decided whether you want to have the baby?' the doctor asked, gently.

'Yes,' said Bea. 'Yes, I'm going to have the baby.'

'Are you in a relationship with the father?'

'No.'

Adam was still sending messages, but she wasn't sure why. He didn't seem desperate for the two of them to get back together, and he wasn't trying to deny that he'd been cheating on her. Often, he said that he missed her and she felt herself softening, considered calling him. But then she remembered that everything had changed, and she told herself that she didn't have space in her life for someone like that. It was just her, now, just her and the baby.

'Well,' the doctor said, 'I don't need to do a test or anything, as the home tests are so accurate these days. I will give you some leaflets to read through and contact the hospital to get your ante-natal care under way.'

Bea nodded as the doctor carried on, talked to her about the damage alcohol and nicotine could do, ran through the list of foods she should avoid. She tried to stay focused, but she found herself drifting in and out. For the first time, having this baby felt like a reality, and she wasn't sure it was feasible. How would she support the two of them, financially? Where would they live? How would she cope with it all?

'Are you okay? I'm sure it's all very daunting.'

Bea fixed her eyes on the doctor's and wondered what had given her away. And then she became aware that there were tears running down her cheeks, dripping from her chin.

'I don't know what the fuck I'm doing,' she said. 'It wasn't planned. I had a boyfriend, but then I found out he was cheating on me. I've got a job but it doesn't pay well, and I can't do it once I've had the baby…'

Once she'd started listing the problems, Bea realised that they were endless. She wanted to keep saying them, to stop them from crowding her brain and get them out into the space in the room, but the doctor smiled and cut her off.

'Try not to worry,' she said. 'There's help available. I can give you some numbers. But…'

'What?' Bea knew what the woman was going to say, and she looked at her without blinking, almost daring her to say it.

'I think you should think long and hard about whether or not having this baby is the right thing for you.'

And Bea thought that she was going to launch into a tirade about how her decision was made and it was none of the doctor's business, but she didn't in the end. She just hung her head, and nodded.

LATER, on the train back to Southampton, Bea thought again about her options. She knew girls who'd had abortions; friends who'd found themselves pregnant at the wrong time, to the wrong men. She didn't oppose it. She believed in a woman's right to choose. And yet, now that it was her, and it was happening, she knew she couldn't bear the thought of checking into one of those clinics and leaving with the baby gone. She knew it wasn't for her.

Bea saw her dad as soon as she came out of the station building. He was standing beside his car, his arms wrapped around him for warmth, looking around for her. For those few seconds before he spotted her, Bea enjoyed watching him. She'd always felt calmed by his presence, this man who was the only parent she'd ever known. Despite feeling lonely as a child, despite feeling that her dad and Esme were part of a group she didn't belong to, she loved him fiercely. Now that she was an adult, she understood what he must have sacrificed to raise his children alone. And for the life of her, she couldn't believe she had let a year slip past without seeing him. She'd always been stubborn, but that was wrong, she realised now. When their eyes met, Bea picked up her pace to a run and headed straight for his arms. And when her head was against his chest, she could feel his heart pounding, and she was reminded of all the times she'd curled up against him like this. Safe and warm.

He held her at arm's length and she saw the tears in his eyes.

'Dad,' she said. 'I'm sorry. I'm so sorry.'

'It doesn't matter. You're here now.'

They spoke very little in the car. It was a ten-minute drive from the station to the house, and Bea was eager to get there, after so long away.

'I've made a chicken casserole,' Tom said, as he pulled onto the driveway. 'Are you hungry?'

'I'm always hungry at the moment,' Bea said. Tom turned to her and smiled. Neither of them reached for their door handles.

'I've missed you,' Tom said. 'So much. Esme too. We're glad you're home.'

Bea felt her cheeks flush red, and she looked down at her feet. What had they done, her sister and her dad, to deserve her year of silence? They had loved her so much that she felt suffocated, that was all. And they'd never talked to her about her lost sister, and it had hurt, knowing that they had something that she was locked out of. But all those times during that year that they'd tried to reach her, she'd closed herself off to them. She was ashamed. Because the more she read about Phoebe, the more Bea felt that she could understand their overprotective instincts.

'Let's go inside,' she said.

As Bea stepped into the familiar hallway and took in the aroma of chicken cooking in the oven, she felt an overwhelming sense of belonging. Esme came out of the lounge to greet her, and they hugged a little awkwardly.

'I'm sorry,' Bea whispered into her sister's hair. When she pulled away, Esme looked a little surprised, and Bea realised that she hadn't done much in the way of apologising over the years.

OVER DINNER, Bea tried to determine what was going on between Esme and their dad. There was a palpable tension, and Bea wondered what could have caused it. Selfishly, she was cross. She'd thought that once she was home, and she'd apologised for staying away for so long, everything would be fine. Not once had she imagined that there could be an entirely different rift in the family.

And almost immediately after they'd eaten and had a cup of coffee, Tom announced that he was going to bed.

'I'll take the cups through and then I'm going to head upstairs,' he said. 'Sorry, Bea. I've had a long day. But it's wonderful to have you home.'

Bea stood and kissed his cheek, taking the coffee cups from his hand and telling him to go straight up to bed, if he was tired. That she was perfectly capable of clearing up. She took the cups through to the kitchen, knowing that Esme would follow her.

'What's going on between you two?' she asked, turning as soon as she heard Esme's footsteps.

Esme shook her head. 'It's complicated. Do you want another coffee?'

'No, I shouldn't. Too much caffeine's bad for the baby, apparently.'

Esme smiled, pulled one of the chairs out from under the kitchen table and sat down. 'I still can't believe it,' she said.

'You and me both.'

They were silent while Bea loaded the dishwasher, and Bea rehearsed the things she needed to ask, a little fearful about the answers she would hear.

'Tell me,' she said, finally, sitting down across from her sister. 'About Phoebe.'

Esme closed her eyes, as if she were reaching out for her own memories. 'She was so funny,' she said, after a pause. 'Hardly like a little girl at all. She used to copy me, but always in a bigger and more dramatic way. She was always at the centre of things.'

Bea wanted to ask Esme to elaborate, wanted to ask her exactly what she meant, but she remained quiet, hoping that her sister would go on.

'Mum adored her. It was so obvious that Phoebe was her

favourite, and I didn't mind, mostly. Dad and I were always close. And even as a child, I could see that Mum couldn't really help it, adoring Phoebe the way she did. She made you love her.'

'Does Dad know that you've told me?' Bea asked

Esme pulled her hair away from her face and wrapped it into a bun, securing it with a band. 'No,' she said.

'Why did you do it, do you think? Why did you all make her life a secret?'

Esme sighed audibly. 'I don't know, Bea. Maybe Dad thought you could escape it if you never really knew.'

'Escape the grief?' Bea felt her throat start to swell and swallowed back tears.

'The grief, the awful sorrow of it all. We were so broken, afterwards. And then you came, and perhaps he thought it could be a fresh start.'

'What happened, Es? How did she die?'

Bea watched Esme closely, saw her sister shake her head as if to dislodge a memory. And as much as she wanted to know, she understood, in that moment, that Esme was unable to say it out loud.

'You'll tell me, though?' she pressed. 'In a letter?'

Esme nodded.

Bea stood and walked to the kitchen door, pushed it closed. Behind it, on the wall, there were pencil lines marking the heights of her and Esme at various points. Bea bent down, studied her dad's neat handwriting. Esme, September 1987. Bea, April 1995. Esme, June 1989. Bea, September 1998. She crouched lower, then, and saw the markings from when they were much smaller. Esme, March 1979. Esme, May 1980. The handwriting was different. Bea reached out and touched the wall.

'Did Mum do some of these?' she asked.

Esme stood and then crouched down beside Bea, gazing at the wall. 'Yes,' she said. 'It always used to be her that measured us.'

'Where are Phoebe's marks?'

Esme stood again, then, but Bea remained where she was, captivated by the sight of her mother's looping handwriting. Why had she never noticed, before?

'She rubbed them off. After Phoebe died, it was like Mum erased her. She took down all the pictures, cleared her bedroom.'

Bea stared harder at the wall, trying to see where Phoebe's marks had once been. But they were gone. And although she had a head full of other questions, Bea realised then how tired she was.

'I'm going to go up to bed,' she said.

'Me too.'

And so, for the first time in as long as she could remember, Bea followed her big sister up the stairs, and they took it in turns to use the bathroom. When they were both settled in bed, Bea closed her eyes and tried to clear her mind. And then she heard it. Quiet, from across the hallway.

'Goodnight, Bea.'

And she smiled at the sudden memory of her sister calling across to her like that every night when they were children. It was something that had made her feel safe, something she'd missed when she first left home. It's going to be all right, she thought. It's all going to be all right.

20TH NOVEMBER 2011

9624 DAYS AFTER

E sme lay awake for a long time after she called goodnight to Bea. She was thinking about those marks on the kitchen wall, remembering her mum's sweet breath on her face as she drew each new line, her furrowed brow of concentration. Each time, Esme was astonished by how much she'd grown. Each time, Phoebe was disappointed that she hadn't caught up with her big sister. Esme remembered Phoebe reaching for her hand and telling their mum, 'One day, I'm going to be as big as Es.' Her fingers were clammy. Her expression stoic. Her love pure.

And then, that day in September, after Phoebe's death, when Esme asked her dad to measure her. She'd stopped asking her mum for things. She was elsewhere, Esme knew. No longer really with them. There was a disengaged look in her eyes that frightened Esme. She still believed her mum was coming back, though. She was giving her the space and time she needed, so that she could come home. That September afternoon, as soon as Esme led her dad into the kitchen, towards the drawer where the pencils were kept, she saw. All her marks intact. Phoebe's, gone. Esme pictured her mum, armed with a rubber, on one of the nights that she roamed around, unable to sleep. She pictured her mum on her knees, taking away Phoebe's name and her dates, and she hated her.

THAT NIGHT, Esme's sleep was fitful, her dreams scattered and uneasy. At dawn, she got out of bed and dressed quietly, slipped out of the house and began to run. The streets were deserted, the light dim. Most of the houses were in darkness, but behind a few of the upstairs windows, a light was on. Esme liked the feeling that she was almost, but not quite, alone in the world. As her muscles loosened, she thought back over the previous evening, from the way it had felt to hold Bea in her arms and inhale her familiar scent to the small stabs of pain she'd felt when she saw the adoration in her father's eyes. It was easier to love someone who was mostly absent, Esme thought. Was that why they all idolised Phoebe?

As Esme ran, steadily putting mile after mile between herself and her home, she tried to empty her mind. Tried to focus solely on the pounding of her feet on the tarmac, the pleasant ache in her thighs. But Bea broke through, and Esme eventually tired of trying to keep her out. When it was Phoebe demanding attention, Esme worked harder to banish the thoughts, but she was exhausted from it, ready to give up and let her mind go wherever it wished.

When Bea was a baby, Esme had sometimes looked into the cot with half-closed eyes and pretended that she was Phoebe. She wondered whether her mum or dad had ever done the same thing – whether they ever saw Bea as a replacement, a second chance to get it right. When Bea started talking, though, it became impossible to pretend. She was unique, and nothing at all like Phoebe. She was all stubborn silences and quiet thoughtfulness, a world away from Phoebe's attention-seeking whining and boundless affection. Of course, by then, their mother was gone, so she couldn't make those comparisons. What was going through her mind, Esme wondered, when she swallowed all those pills, washed them down with a bottle of vodka? It was a question she kept coming back to, futile though it was. And every time she settled on an answer, it was a different one, and it was about Phoebe and unstoppable grief and Bea, but never about Esme.

By the light of the rising sun, Esme ran on, her pace steady, her stride long. Aware, now, that she couldn't outrun her own thoughts. Her breathing heavy but calm, Esme tried to picture adult Bea alongside their mother. They would speak French together, Esme reasoned, and they would laugh that rich laugh they shared. The laugh Esme had entirely forgotten until she heard it from Bea, one late summer day when Bea was about fifteen, and thought, for a sweet second, that her mother was behind her.

As the city woke up, Esme ran past a children's playground. She noticed that one swing was moving slightly in the winter wind and there was a cream bobble-hat abandoned on the bench. Esme tried to picture Bea in that place, a child by her side. But it was too alien, too early. Bea's pregnancy was still invisible. A little later in the run, an ambulance drove past Esme, its sirens blaring. The sound was bleak and too loud in the still of the early morning, and Esme tried not to wonder where it was heading. Tried not to think about the fact that somewhere, there was a family in crisis. She was close to home and although she'd planned to do another lap of the route she'd already taken, Esme decided to cut her run short. Outside the front door, she did some stretches, and then she let herself back in to the house, wondering whether she would find anyone up.

The house was silent, so she went upstairs for a shower. For years, she'd hated using that bathroom. Had used the downstairs toilet and avoided brushing her teeth whenever she could get away with it. But five or six years ago, she'd suggested ripping it out and starting again, and her dad had nodded, gratefully, as if he'd simply been waiting for her to suggest it. Now, it was almost unrecognisable: the toilet and sink where the bath had once been, and a new, double-sized shower cubicle in one corner. Esme peeled off her sweaty clothes and stepped into the shower, keeping the water cool at first, then turning it up and up, as hot as she could take. To Bea, this room had always been just a room. She was lucky, in some ways.

When Esme returned to her room, she heard a beep from her phone and picked it up. It was Simon. He'd sent her a few text messages and emails since they'd had that drink together. Without saying why, he'd started to fill her in on things that were happening in his life, and ask her about hers. It felt good, Esme realised. It felt good to be the person that someone went to, when they wanted to share something that had happened. *I'm coming home tomorrow. Can I see you?* Esme sat down on the edge of her bed, a little cold in her towel. She typed a reply, quickly, before she could change her mind. *Yes, tomorrow night?* Just then, there was a knock on her door and Bea stuck her head around it.

'I forgot to bring shampoo,' she said. 'Can I use yours?'

'Help yourself. It's in the shower.'

Esme's phone buzzed again and both sisters turned towards it. *Perfect.* Esme smiled to herself, and Bea left the room. As Esme dressed and dried her hair, she could hear Bea singing in the shower, her voice full and clear, and she felt happier than she remembered feeling in a long time.

That afternoon, Tom made roast lamb. He shooed away Esme and Bea's offers of help, and so Bea suggested that she and Esme should leave him to it and go for a walk. They headed to the common. It was a cold but bright day, and the bare trees looked beautiful with the sun shining through them, making patterns on the grass.

'What's it like?' Esme asked. 'Being pregnant, I mean.'

Bea was quiet for a moment, and Esme looked at her, and saw that she was thinking about how to respond.

'For the first week, it was a real mind-fuck. I couldn't think about anything else. And I couldn't believe that it wasn't obvious to everyone around me, and that everyone was just going about like everything was the same as before. And now, I forget sometimes, for a few minutes, and when I remember it seems ridiculous, impossible. I'm always hungry and I get very tired all of a sudden. It feels good, though. I wouldn't change it.'

Esme wasn't sure whether to ask her next question, but she knew it would have to be broached at some point, so she went ahead, hoping that Bea wouldn't clam up, or be angry, or sad.

'Who's the father?'

'His name's Adam.'

Esme said nothing, confident that Bea would continue if she just gave her time.

'We're not seeing each other anymore, and he doesn't know about the baby,' Bea said, after a long silence. 'We were together for a while, and it was good, but we didn't plan this. I'm going to do it by myself.'

Esme admired Bea's courage and conviction. She wasn't sure that she would be so brave in her sister's situation. She wondered about this man, Adam, and she hoped that he hadn't hurt Bea, or given her cause to worry.

'Dad did it by himself,' she said, eventually.

'Yes, and look how we turned out.'

Bea's voice was flat, and Esme wasn't sure what she meant by that. She pulled her scarf a little tighter around her neck, and walked on in silence.

When Bea packed up to leave the following afternoon, Esme was sorry. Her mind was on the evening ahead with Simon, and a girlish part of her wanted to tell her little sister all about it, to have Bea there, waiting to ask questions, when she came home. She didn't tell Bea those things. Instead, she hugged her tightly, and asked her to come again, soon.

'I will,' said Bea. 'Promise.'

Tom was driving Bea to the station and he'd already slipped past them and out of the door to start the car.

'Will there be more letters?' Bea asked. She kept her voice low, even though it was only the two of them in the house.

'If you want to read them,' Esme said.

'Please.'

Esme nodded, and then Bea smiled and Esme saw a flash of their mother in her for the first time in years.

'Come on, Bea,' said Tom, suddenly back in the doorway. 'You'll miss the train.'

And then she was gone, and it was almost like she'd never been there.

ESME AND SIMON had arranged to meet in the same pub as last time. She arrived first and she sat at a table in a corner with a glass of wine, her eyes on the door. While she waited, she chastised herself. Did she really think this was going to be the romance that had evaded her? They didn't live in the same city, and she'd spent a year tormenting him when they were children. He might say he could forgive her, but was it possible to put something like that behind you entirely? No, she thought. It wasn't. She'd burned her bridges with this man when she was seven years old.

When Simon arrived, he stood in the middle of the floor, surveying the room. Esme moved to wave, to alert him, but she stopped with her arm half-raised, enjoying seeing him put off his stride. When he saw her, his face broke into an easy smile. He walked over and leaned down to kiss her cheek.

'It's good to see you,' he said. He gestured at her wine glass. 'Should I get us a bottle?'

Esme nodded. There was a kindness in his face, she realised, which drew her to him. She watched him while he stood at the bar, waiting to be served. She looked forward to him coming back.

'Tell me about yourself,' she said, when he came back. 'What's happened since you were eleven?'

Simon poured himself a glass of wine and topped up hers. 'Well, I finished school, went to university, got a job, married, divorced...'

Esme's head snapped up. 'I didn't know you were married,' she said.

'I was. It was a disaster. Although, she never bit me.'

Esme smiled a little. How was it that she'd got so left behind? While she'd stayed at home, living and working with her dad, other people her age had gone out and got real jobs, had real relationships. They'd failed at things, and broken vows, and got things wrong, but at least they'd done something. At least they'd tried.

While they shared the wine, Simon spoke openly about his marriage and subsequent divorce. Esme could see that it was raw, still, even though two years had passed, and she was careful about what she asked and what she left alone. They talked about his life now, in London, his job, his mother's illness.

At ten o'clock, Esme said that she should get home. They stood, and as they crossed the pub, he placed one hand on the small of her back. Outside, she pointed in the direction she was going and he dipped his head and said that he was going the other way.

'Well,' she said, 'I'll see you soon.'

It was cold, and she felt foolish and unsure.

Simon took a step forward and she thought he was going to hug her, and she was ready for that, her body crying out for a little comfort. But she wasn't ready for him to kiss her, so although she didn't really want to, she stopped him.

'I'm sorry,' she said.

She expected him to avert his eyes, but he didn't. He looked straight at her, daring her to look away.

'It wasn't your fault,' he said. 'And even if it was, you don't have to pay with your life. If anything, you should live your life to the full, because she can't.'

He was holding on to one of her hands, and she didn't realise it until he let go, and she would have given almost anything for him to touch her again. The touch of someone who knows the whole truth, and wants to hold on anyway.

Esme turned, her eyes full. She would not say goodbye. It was just one more thing to add to the list of times when she'd said or done the wrong thing. Just one more situation she'd misjudged. That she'd look back on, with regret.

When she got home, she couldn't sleep. So to stop herself from running through the date over and over again, she turned the light on and pulled out her notebook, and started another letter to Phoebe.

Dear Phoebe,

I was there when you took your first steps. I was sulking. It was a Sunday afternoon, and all weekend Mum had been promising that we'd go to the park, but there were jobs to be done on Sunday morning. So while the sun was flooding through the windows and creeping across the lounge carpet, she was dusting and we were helping to tidy up. By the time we'd had lunch, grey clouds had gathered and rain was starting. Mum and you and I were in the lounge, unsure what to do next and waiting for a break in the clouds when you grabbed hold of the coffee table with your chubby fingers and hoisted yourself up. You'd been doing that for a while, and I didn't understand why Mum cried out and made exclamations every time. I looked over, the picture I was colouring in momentarily forgotten, and we locked eyes for a second or two. And then you looked away from me, looked straight ahead, and you let go of the table with both hands and took a faltering step, and another, slightly more confident, and then a third.

Mum called for Dad and the spell was broken, and you fell backwards, on your bum, and looked my way again. You gave me that look I was so familiar with, the one you wore when you weren't sure whether or not to cry. As if you were silently asking my permission. And I shook my head and went back to my colouring. But out of the corner of my eye, I saw Mum make her way over to you on her knees, like she was forgetting how to walk, just as you were learning. She scooped you up in her arms and covered you in kisses. I watched, covertly, as they fussed over you and set you on your feet, again and again, encouraging you to repeat it. And I felt a little cold, and left out, and I didn't understand why nothing that I did seemed to create that same level of excitement, and I thought that maybe I hated you.

We didn't go to the park that afternoon, and I was annoyed. I didn't care about this breakthrough you'd made, didn't realise what it would mean for me. Didn't realise that our relationship would change, now that you could walk alongside me. I don't remember anything else of that learning process, after those first few steps on that rainy Sunday afternoon. It seems to me that, from that day on, you were by my side, or running slightly behind, following me.

I didn't realise that I'd been lonely until we started playing together. I didn't realise that I'd been waiting for you. That your ability to walk would have a much bigger impact on me than it would have on Mum and Dad, despite their excitement. That was the day when you truly became my sister.

The next summer, we spent a week in a cottage by the sea. I don't know where it was, or what it looked like, but I remember running with you through the sand, our feet bare and the sun on our naked backs. Mum and Dad far behind us and forgotten. I dodged other families, weaved in and out of spread towels and sandcastles, and you followed me, blindly, trusting me not to lead you too far or too fast. I could hear you shrieking with joy, could smell the salty sea air, and I wanted to run forever, to never go back to Mum and Dad, our house, my school. I wanted to stay on that beach, in the sunshine, and run with you until we collapsed.

I heard Dad's voice, calling us back. We'd gone too far. He'd made us promise to stay close, to go nowhere near the sea and to only play on our part of the beach, where he could keep an eye on us. I stopped abruptly, my breathing heavy, and you stopped a second later, almost colliding with me on the soft sand. I looked back at Dad, saw that he was standing and gesturing for us to come back to where he and Mum had set up our things. And I looked at you, watched the breeze lifting your fine hair and took in your eyes, questioning, waiting for me to tell you what came next. And without really thinking about the consequences, I started running again, further away from our parents, and without hesitating, you followed.

I knew that Dad would give chase, then. I knew that it wouldn't take him long to gain ground, that he would catch us in a matter of seconds. My heart thudded as I ran, too scared to sneak a look back, unsure of everything other than my need to keep moving forward and to have you with me. Dad was furious when he caught us. He passed you and grabbed hold of my arm, gripping it tight enough to leave an angry red mark. Knowing, as I knew, that I was the one to be stopped, that you were just following my lead, that you wouldn't go on alone.

I looked at you as he crouched down in front of me, his face twisted with anger, his hand still clinging to my arm as though he thought that, even now, I might try to wriggle free, to escape. You had that look that was always a precursor to tears, and I was sorry, as I watched your face crumple, that I'd made this happen.

There are so many memories like this one, of me leading the two of us into potential danger, into trouble. And now, of course, I understand the fear that our parents lived with – the fear that all parents live with. But back then, all I knew was that the punishments we suffered were inconsequential. I would run off again, and take you with me, because anything that might happen afterwards was nothing compared to the pure joy of running, with you, along the sand.

I rarely misbehaved with Bea. I didn't dare. I'd learned, by then, that the terrible things parents lectured about were real. That life was fragile, not to be taken lightly. And so, once I had a new sister, I was careful with her, and I kept her close and safe. But it makes me sad that Bea and I have never run alongside one another, away from our parents, for the sheer joy of running. That has cost us something too.

Esme

Bea looked back to the start of the letter – Phoebe's name, in Esme's handwriting. It was hard to know where she fitted in. It took a while for her to realise she was crying. There were tears streaming down her face, dropping from her chin on to the letter in her hand. She closed her eyes and pictured herself and Esme running across an imaginary sandy beach in the sunshine.

Pictured, for the first time, another girl running between them. A girl who looked like them, who existed in the seven-year gap between them. A girl called Phoebe.

She'd worked hard that day, the letter propped up against a stack of paper at the far right side of her desk. Taunting her, like a reward. She hadn't allowed herself to open it until she'd caught up. There had been too many days, recently, when she'd finished early or taken a long nap at lunch. But that day, she'd remembered why she mostly loved what she did. Her mind was alive, her brain working as fast as her fingers could type, and she was caught up in the story, her heart beating a little faster every time the heroine was in danger. In the next week or so, she would finish the book, do a final check and send her translation off for proofreading. She was back on schedule.

And it felt good, because it was one thing she could control. These letters from Esme, this secret history, were beyond her grasp. And the life that was growing inside her – that was unstoppable, and terrifying. Bea gulped down her water and went to the tap to refill her glass. She pulled herself up so that she was sitting on the kitchen worktop, tapped her heels gently against the pine cupboard doors.

'Hello,' said Julia, entering the kitchen.

Bea jumped a little. She hadn't heard Julia come in. 'Hi,' she said.

Things were a little strained between the two friends. Bea knew that she would have to move out, when the baby came. She didn't have any idea where she would go, but she knew that she'd have to go somewhere. Julia hadn't signed up for sleepless nights and childcare. And although they hadn't had a conversation about it yet, Bea knew that this looming change was on Julia's mind too. She felt that, in a covert, silent way, Julia was holding it against her. There hadn't been much laughter in the flat, since that day in the bathroom with the pregnancy test. There hadn't been much closeness.

'Can I make you some dinner?' Bea asked.

She opened the fridge door, saw that there was plenty of veg for a stir fry.

'Shouldn't I be the one offering to do things for you?' Julia asked.

'Later,' Bea said. 'When I'm too fat to get out of bed without assistance and I can't see my feet.'

Julia smiled and reached over Bea's shoulder to take a bottle of beer from the fridge. 'Does it scare you, all that?'

Bea assembled beansprouts and mushrooms and peppers on the worktop, hunted in the low cupboards for a chopping board. Did it scare her? She'd always been slim, no matter what she ate, and she'd noted with interest the careful way some women dealt with food. Julia was one of those women. If she went a few weeks without going to the gym, or went through a break-up and drank more than usual, it showed on her waist and thighs.

'Not really,' she said, holding each mushroom and slicing it thinly. 'I mean, it's just my body. I can try to change it, afterwards.'

'I think I'd be terrified,' Julia said, tapping the glass beer bottle against her teeth.

Bea saw this as an opportunity to tell the truth, to be honest with her best friend about how she was feeling. But it was hard. She took a deep breath, scraped the chopped mushrooms into the wok, drizzled them with oil.

'I am terrified. Not about that, just about all of it. I mean, how do you know whether you'll be a good mum?'

Bea stole a look at Julia and saw her friend's uncomfortable expression. Was it because this wasn't a normal concern, just the lonely territory of those who've suffered at the hand of their own mothers? Or was it just because Julia didn't know the answer? All the time they'd known each other, Bea and Julia had faced similar problems. Workload stress at university, unemployment and poor job prospects after. Unsuitable boyfriends, arguments with friends and relatives. But now Bea was facing something that was wholly alien to Julia, and she could feel the thread of their friendship stretching and tightening, and that terrified her, too.

'My mum once told me that she always felt like she was making it up as she went along,' Julia said, at last.

Bea kept her eyes on the wok, letting the vegetables sizzle and steam. She wanted Julia to continue, and she felt that they were treading a delicate path.

'With me, more than with my brothers. Because I was the oldest. And she said that she was always scared that I'd be hurt or snatched away or lost somehow. She didn't know whether she felt differently about the boys because they were boys, or just because she was more used to it by the time she had them.'

'When did she tell you that?' Bea asked. She turned the heat down and looked over at Julia, slowly, carefully.

'I don't remember,' Julia said.

Something in her face shut down, and Bea knew that the conversation was over.

A little later, when they'd finished eating and Julia was washing the dishes quickly and sloppily, Bea's phone rang. It was her father. She slipped out of the kitchen, stepped into her bedroom before answering.

'Hello?'

'Bea,' he said, his voice all relief.

'What's wrong? Is something wrong?'

'Nothing to worry about. I'm just glad to hear your voice.'

Bea sat down on her bed and then dropped her head back so that she was lying down, her hair fanned out around her.

'How are you? How's Esme?'

Bea heard her dad's heavy sigh and thought back to that tension she'd noticed when she was at home. It was disconcerting, knowing that there was a problem between the two of them. It was something Bea hadn't known before. If anything, they'd always been a little too close, leaving Bea feeling left out.

'What's wrong?' she asked. 'Are you not getting on?'

'I've fallen in love with someone.'

Bea felt a little lift in her heart as his words sunk in. All through her childhood, she had hoped that he would meet someone. She'd looked around, at her friends' mothers, at women in shops, noticing anyone who looked fondly at her dad. She couldn't understand why he was alone. But as the years had passed, and he'd remained single, Bea had given up hope of this. And now, out of the blue, he was telling her that he'd met someone. That he was in love. It was wonderful news.

'Bea, there are some things you don't know. You were so young, and some things are difficult to talk to your children about...'

Bea wondered what he was talking about, whether he was alluding to Phoebe.

'It's okay, Dad. I'm pleased for you. Isn't Esme?'

He sighed again, and Bea felt a flash of anger towards her sister. Why was she ruining this for him? What possible reason could she have? Was it because she was frightened of things changing?

'I need to tell you something, and it's hard. It might make you feel differently about me.'

'No,' Bea said. 'It won't. It couldn't.'

She was sure. She sat up, twisted her hair into a tight knot and then let it go, enjoying the weight of it on her shoulders.

'I had an affair, Bea. When you were just a baby.'

Bea said nothing. She listened, while he told her about being with Marianne at school, meeting her again all those years later. She wondered whether he would mention Phoebe, hold her death up as an excuse. But he didn't. While he spoke, she thought briefly about Adam, about seeing him there with that other girl, when she'd needed him most. She thought about shouting, telling him that he'd let them down, but her heart wasn't in it. Bea hadn't known her mum, and she couldn't bring herself to feel enraged on her behalf. And, despite all of it, she was pleased for him. Pleased that he'd found someone to love.

'I want her to move in here,' he said. 'But I don't know what Esme will say. I don't want her to feel pushed out.'

There was a pause, a silence, and then he spoke again.

'What are you thinking, Bea?'

'Just tell her, Dad. You've been on your own for a long time. You deserve this.'

And then she heard a sound from him that could have been a sob, and she swallowed back her own tears.

'Everything's changing,' she said. 'I'm having a baby, you've fallen in love. It's a good thing.'

'Thank you.'

After they'd said their goodbyes and she'd ended the call, Bea tried to imagine what it must be like for Esme. She'd always been alone, and yet she'd never seemed particularly lonely. Perhaps that was because she and their dad had always had each other, for companionship. It did make sense that Esme might feel pushed out by this new relationship. Betrayed, too, by the affair that happened so many years ago. Esme was older. She had memories of that time. Bea wondered whether the two of them would ever talk about it. It seemed unlikely, somehow. But things were changing, in their family. Secrets were being uncovered, difficult conversations were being faced. Things were getting better.

E sme arrived at the restaurant five minutes early, and a thin, harassed-looking waiter showed her to a small, round table in the corner. She looked around her. She'd passed this place countless times, but she'd never been inside. Simon had suggested it, said that it was one of his favourites, and it made Esme think about how rarely she ate out. How rarely, over the years, she'd had someone to eat out with.

It was early, not quite half past seven, and yet the restaurant was buzzing with conversation and laughter. There were bright, bold paintings on the walls, and large mirrors hanging everywhere. As she took in her surroundings, Esme was confronted again and again by her reflection, and there was no getting away from the fact that she looked scared.

She hadn't seen Simon since that night that he'd tried to kiss her. For a few days, he hadn't contacted her, but then they'd gone back to their routine of regular texts and emails, and she'd tucked away her embarrassment. But seeing him again was different. Esme closed her eyes momentarily, pictured him crossing the room towards her, willed her cheeks not to flush. And when she opened her eyes, he was standing beside the table, and Esme flinched.

'Having a nap?' he asked, smiling.

'I was just...' Esme had no idea how to end the sentence she'd started. In the silence that followed, Simon sat down, rested his elbows on the table and propped up his chin with his hands.

'I missed you,' he said. 'There, I said it. I told myself I wouldn't. But why not? It's the truth.'

Esme dropped her chin and smiled a little, said nothing.

'So, now that's out in the open. Let's get some wine, shall we?'

When they'd just finished eating their main courses, Simon reached across the table and took hold of Esme's hand. His touch was gentle, warm. Esme was grateful for it.

'There's something wrong,' he said.

Not a question.

'Sorry,' she said. 'I'm not getting on so well with my dad. He's got this girlfriend now, and he's talking about her moving in with us. I feel like everything's changing all of a sudden.'

Simon nodded. 'They've given my mum two months,' he said, after a pause.

Esme's hand flew to her mouth and when she returned it to the table, she couldn't quite bring herself to touch him again.

'I'm so sorry,' she said.

She was selfish, that's what he was telling her. Her dad was healthy, and she was making a fuss about his relationship, which was really none of her business. She looked closely at Simon, daring him to meet her eye. He looked like he might cry. When the waitress came over with dessert menus, Esme waved her away. She refilled Simon's wine glass, and he lifted it, swirled the burgundy liquid.

'Do the right thing,' he said, at last. 'That's my advice. I haven't always been the best son in the world. I didn't always make it home for birthdays and parties. I wasted a lot of time.'

Esme nodded, bit her lip. And out of nowhere, she wondered

whether this diagnosis would mean that he'd stay in London, instead of moving home as planned. And then she felt terrible, again, for turning the situation around to what it meant for her. A woman was dying. The most important woman in Simon's life was dying. From nowhere, Esme dredged up a memory of her mother and Simon's mother at the primary school gates. Her mother, accusing and fierce. Simon's mother, indignant and full of bluster. Both women had seemed to loom larger than life, to Esme. Both women were strong and unstoppable. And in a few months, they would both be gone. Esme and Simon were the grown-ups, now. It was their turn to be brave and strong.

'I remember her. Your mum,' Esme said.

'I remember yours. I thought she was beautiful.'

Esme opened her palm, turned her hand over on the white tablecloth, stretched it forward a little until she reached Simon's long fingers. Before she could change her mind, she touched them, folded Simon's hand into hers. And they sat there, quite still, for a few minutes, while the noise and the laughter exploded around them.

'Come on,' said Esme. 'Let's pay the bill on the way out and go for a walk.'

Simon looked puzzled, but he stood and followed Esme to the counter, where she insisted on paying for dinner.

Outside, it was cold but very still. They pulled on their coats and scarves, their eyes adjusting to the sudden change in light.

'Where are we going?' Simon asked.

'I'm not sure. I just felt we needed to be out in the open.'

To Esme, the cold and the darkness felt fitting. There was a streetlight flickering on and off to their left, and Esme turned in that direction and started to walk, knowing that Simon would follow her.

'Show me your Southampton,' he said, once he'd caught her up.

'What do you mean?'

'Well, you've always lived here. There must be things that keep you here. I want to see the city from your perspective.'

Esme thought hard. 'A lot of the things I love aren't here, in the city centre. I love the common, that's where I run. I love the street I live on. But give me a minute, I'm sure I can think of something.'

They walked on, in silence, her gloved hand a few inches from his ungloved one. She wondered whether it would feel cold to touch, if she reached for it. She took a right turn, away from the smells and sounds of the high street and towards the sea. And a memory was there, waiting.

'My mum used to bring me and Phoebe here,' she said. 'Phoebe was in the pushchair, I was walking. She used to let me stand on the railings and watch the sea. Phoebe always cried because she wasn't big enough to see very much. At night, Dad would ask what we'd done that day and whenever I told him we'd been to see the sea, he'd make up a story on the spot about a sea monster called Luigi.'

Simon laughed, throaty and deep. 'What else?'

They walked on for a couple of minutes, and then Esme made a couple of quick turns and they were standing at the gate to a small park.

'Bea and her friends used to spend all their time here, when she was about fourteen. Dad was terrified that they were injecting heroin or having sex, so he used to send me down here to spy on them. I had to walk here from the bookshop at least three times each Saturday, and then get close enough to see what Bea was doing but without her being able to spot me.'

'And?'

Esme turned to face Simon, and was surprised to find that their faces were only a few inches apart.

'And what?'

'What was Bea doing?'

Esme shrugged. 'Nothing much. It was just a place for them to be. It's pretty horrible, being a teenager. Didn't you think?'

Simon nodded, but he didn't speak. And Esme knew that he was going to try to kiss her again, and she resolved that she wouldn't push him away. They stood, face to face, the still night air heavy between them, and she noticed that there were flecks of grey in his blue eyes and that his lips were a little dry. And she saw that he had a narrow, silvery scar just above his lip, and that was the last thing, because then he kissed her, and her eyes were closed and she finally stopped thinking entirely.

When he pulled back, Esme felt dizzy. She could still feel the pressure of his lips on hers, the warmth of his tongue. His hands were in her hair and hers were on his back, and she turned her head to one side and rested it, for a moment, against his chest. She could hear his heartbeat, fast and steady, and more than anything, she wanted to take him home, take him to bed. And she wished she had a place of her own, a little privacy.

'You're getting cold,' he said, at last. 'I think it's time we went home.'

There was a tiny crack in his voice, but then he cleared his throat and it was gone. Esme looked up at him, tried to read his face. She didn't see anything there that worried her. As they walked towards the taxi rank, their hands interlinked easily now, Esme thought about asking him to come back with her, or asking him to take her back with him. But no, she decided, she'd rather wait until they could be properly alone, not sneaking around in their parents' houses like teenagers.

'Goodnight,' Esme said.

There was a queue of taxis and they were standing at the front of it, shivering slightly. There was no one else around.

'You know, it's like you had two childhoods,' Simon said.

'What do you mean?'

'You had one with Phoebe and your parents, and then another one with your dad and Bea. And the second one was steeped in sadness, but it sounds like it had some great moments too.'

Esme smiled. 'It was a bit like that.'

'It's interesting that your dad's the only constant in the two. Don't push him away.'

Esme raised herself up on her tiptoes and placed her hands on the back of Simon's neck. She leaned in and kissed him lightly on the lips.

'Thank you,' she said.

When Esme got home, she didn't mind so much that Marianne was in the living room with her dad. She gave them a quick wave and went straight to her room, but when she heard the front door close a few minutes later, she descended the stairs again, put her head around the living room door.

'Do you love her?' she asked.

Her dad looked up, startled. 'I do,' he said.

'Do you want to tell me about her?'

It was hard to say the words, but she was glad she had. She saw her dad's face relax.

'What can I say? She was my first love. And then we reconnected, in that time after Phoebe died. And everything was collapsing around me. Your mum wouldn't get out of bed. I didn't know what to do.'

'Did Mum know?' Esme asked.

'Yes. In the end, she knew.'

Esme nodded, paused. She tried to find the right words to ask her next question. And then she just asked it anyway. It wasn't the right time for caution.

'Do you think that's why she...?'

Her dad interrupted her question, knowing that she wouldn't be able to finish it, and she was grateful. 'I don't think so. Not really. In a way, your mum was gone from the day that Phoebe died. She was never really ours after that.'

Esme recognised the truth in his answer. It wouldn't have mattered what she and her dad did in those months – good or bad. They'd already lost her.

'There's something else,' he said, after a long silence.

Something else? Wasn't this enough? Esme wanted to silence him, to beg him to leave it there. But she was curious too.

'The night Marianne came back into my life, that was the night...'

He broke off and Esme waited for him to pick up the thread again. And when he didn't, and she looked up at him, she saw that he was crying. His clenched fist pressed against his mouth, as if it might force the words, and the truth, back inside.

'It was the night that I was late home, the night your mum left you alone with Phoebe.'

'The night she died?' Esme gasped.

'That's why I was late. Nothing happened. She came into the shop, and I talked to her while I was locking up. And...'

Esme didn't go to him, or reach out to touch him, or give him an encouraging look.

'And just before she left, she wrote down her phone number and gave it to me, and I kissed her cheek. I've always wondered, whether Phoebe gave up the fight before or after that kiss. I've always wondered that.'

For Esme, it was the final piece of the puzzle. She'd spent years blaming herself for Phoebe's death, and she knew her mum blamed herself too. But now she saw that there was a third contender for blame. That all three of them carried some of the weight of responsibility. It didn't make things any easier, any lighter. It just made her sad to think of the three of them, living under the same roof with their secrets and their guilt. All of them alone with their self-reproach.

Esme watched as her dad stood and started to cross the room, unwilling to let her see his raw emotion. Instead of staying where she was and looking away as he passed, she stood, causing him to stop. And she put her arms around him, and held him, as he cried. She felt his tears on her neck, in her hair. She thought about all the things this man had done for his family. How none of them had been easy. How he'd done them anyway. And she didn't move, or speak, or let go, until his tears stopped.

When she finally went to bed, Esme was exhausted. But she reached for her notepad and pen anyway, because her head was full of what Simon had described as her first childhood. She was ready to share a little more of it.

Dear Phoebe,

Time passed quickly. At least it seems that way now. Sometimes, I swear I could see a change in you from morning to evening. There was always something new. You learned to smile, to grab your feet, to roll over, to crawl. Before bed, while I was brushing my hair, I stared hard at myself in the mirror, wondering why I wasn't changing at the same rate. It seemed to me that I never grew, or altered, or learned new things.

When I asked Mum about it, she said that I was changing every day too, but that it was more obvious with babies. She said that almost every day, she heard me use a new word, and that my hair was getting lighter in the sun and I was getting closer to being able to write my name. She told me that some of the clothes you wore were once mine, and I closed my eyes and tried to imagine myself, as small as you, unable to talk or walk or do anything for myself.

You never stopped growing and changing, Phoebe. You never even slowed down. You learned to walk by following my footsteps. You strained to copy the sounds that came out of my mouth. I always knew that you wanted to be me, and I wondered why. Everyone loved you so much. Your smile reached into strangers' chests and pulled their hearts towards you. You were a human magnet. I had nothing of your power. Yes, I could read and write my name and tie my shoelaces. But who was watching?

Sometimes, I wondered whether Mum would have another baby. I wondered how far she could try to stretch out her love, when I was already feeling the loss. Sometimes, she'd say she wanted to talk to me, and I would watch her stomach for signs of another new life. And then she would tell me something trivial and slight and I would break out in nervous laughter, temporarily relieved. But I was always waiting to hear it, on some level, always perched on the cliff edge of that anticipated news I was so desperate not to hear.

I was a restless child, never still. Always running around on my skinny legs, finding things to occupy me wherever I went. Mum said I wouldn't sit still for long enough to have a haircut, so my hair grew long and wild. I pulled out the plaits that Mum tied every morning and let it follow me, covering my shoulders and back like a cape. And there you were, always a heartbeat behind, no matter how fast or far I went. Most times, I didn't look back.

I thought we'd always have you. Of course I did. I didn't realise that every mean thing I did – shutting a door with you on the other side or tricking you or running away from you – would live with me, so many years later. And it's only because we don't have you now. It's only because we'd give anything, now, to open a door and see you there, waiting, on the other side.

29TH NOVEMBER 2011

9633 DAYS AFTER

B ea was crying, but she kept brushing away her tears and reading on, because she had to know what had happened. Esme had written down her innermost thoughts and memories, her most painful recollections, and entrusted them to Bea. If her sister could write this down, she owed it to her to read it.

I talk to you, Phoebe. I tell you the things I keep hidden from everyone else. Make up your responses. And there's an emptiness in me, a gaping hole. A sister-shaped gap.

I dreamed of you last night. It was your fourth birthday, the first of all the birthdays you never had. Mum and Dad weren't there; it was just you and me. And I was an adult, and you were mine. I'd baked you a cake and I clapped while you blew out the candles, your cheeks puffed out and your eyes closed, wishing.

As the years have crept by, the dreams have been the best and worst thing. Back then, just after it happened, I woke again and again with a gasp and a sense of you that was so strong that I'd throw back my covers and go into your bedroom, truly believing that you'd be there, tucked up and sleeping. I never told Mum and Dad. Those nights, I just crawled

back into bed and shut my eyes tight and tried to recapture that lost state where you were still with us.

In later years, I caught brief glimpses of you in dreams, and I chased you, trying to pull you back into life. Sometimes you were wet and gasping. And I would wake, breathless and terrified, have to layer on clothes to keep out the cold. You would take on different shapes, be different ages, and your face wasn't always your own. And yet, I always knew it was you. Sometimes, when I reached out and touched you, your skin was cold.

Oh, but there have been happy dreams too. Ones in which you're animated and chatty, childlike and beautiful. Once, when I was sixteen, we met in my subconscious and we were both seven or eight. We were at the beach, our hair windswept and our bare feet sandy. Mum and Dad were lying on towels with their eyes closed, their books propped open on their chests. We ran through the sand, the sun warm on our backs and our minds blissfully empty, until we reached the sea. And then we kicked water at one another and let the waves lap at our legs. For once, I wasn't chasing you. We were side by side.

There was another one this year. You were a baby, kicking and howling in your cot, and I was a child. We were alone in the house and I was the only one who could comfort you. I reached out, lifted you and held you against my chest. And you were heavy and warm, and you resisted me for a few moments, pushing at my face with your tiny hands and gulping out sobs. I rocked you, stroked your fine hair and whispered soothing words in your ears. Within a minute or two, you were still, and I watched your eyelids droop and close. There was no sound, and I stopped moving and just held you, inhaling the scent of sleep and washing powder. And when I woke up, my arms felt empty.

Esme

Bea put the letter to one side and picked up her ringing phone. It was Adam. He'd been calling, on and off, and she never answered. On a sudden whim, she accepted the call, held the phone to her ear. But she didn't say anything.

'Bea, are you there?' There was a pause, and Bea listened to him breathing. There was a hum of noise in the background, and she imagined him, sitting in a bar somewhere, deciding to give her a call after a few drinks.

'Bea, it's Adam. I want to see you. Fuck, I miss you.'

She strained to hear signs of drunkenness in his voice, but he just sounded weary. Lonely.

'Are you there, Bea?'

'I'm here.'

Bea hadn't intended to speak, and the words surprised her. Adam sighed, long and hard.

'It's so good to hear your voice.'

'What do you want, Adam?'

'I've told you. I want to see you.'

Bea stood up and began pacing the short length of her bedroom. She thought about going to him, about letting him kiss her and touch her. She missed him, too. She missed the solidness of his body, and the heat of it, and the way she could go to sleep in the crook of his arm and stay perfectly still until morning.

'Where are you?' she asked.

'I'm in a pub. But are you coming? If you're coming, I'll go home.'

'I'll meet you at your place,' she said.

Before Adam could respond, Bea ended the call. And then she threw her phone on her bed, furious with herself. It wasn't too late to call him back, call it off. But she didn't want to. She stood still in the centre of her bedroom, stared hard at the words tattooed on the skin of her wrist. Carpe diem. When she'd chosen those words, she'd felt so sure of herself, so certain. But what did they really mean? And what did her teenage-self know about the situations she would find herself in, and how she would react?

Hastily, Bea showered and dressed. She looked at herself in the mirror from every angle, trying to determine whether or not her pregnancy was showing. It was so early, of course, but she felt as though she'd put on a couple of pounds, as though she'd thickened, slightly, around the middle. In preparation. But it was nothing Adam would notice, she decided. It was barely perceptible.

On the tube, she sat still with no book and quieted her doubts as they appeared. It was like playing one of those games at the fairground, where things pop up and you have to hit them with a hammer. And she was good at it, she discovered.

Opposite Bea sat a young couple. Nineteen or twenty at most. Their fingers were interlaced and their faces were pale, and they didn't speak. Every so often, he would lift his hand and stroke her hair, and she wouldn't smile, but she would tilt her head towards him in acceptance of the comforting gesture. Bea tried to guess at what had happened to them. It was a game she liked to play. One or both of them had had bad news, she decided, but it wasn't clear whether the news had come from the other one or from outside the relationship. Suddenly sentimental, Bea hoped that neither of the young lovers had let the other one down. She hoped that the tragedy had come from outside – an illness in one of their families, an academic or career disappointment, a betrayal by a friend. As the train lurched into Bea's stop and she stood, she cast one final look at the couple, at the matching sadness in their eyes, and she hoped that they would make it through this time.

The walk to Adam's flat was short, and Bea was grateful because the wind was biting and the streets were dark, with a couple of streetlamps along the way flashing on and off or out of use completely. Bea listened out for footsteps behind her, but there was nothing. Everyone was inside, safe behind their windows, the curtains drawn. An image came to mind of Adam, then. It was from a couple of months ago and he was standing, naked, in her bedroom, peering out from behind the curtain, trying to see what the weather was like. Bea had watched him from the bed, admiring the straight lines and sharp angles of his body, taking in the contrast between the creamy skin and the black ink that covered so much of it. She'd felt, in that moment, that she was falling in love with him. And now two months had passed, and everything had changed. But nevertheless, she was heading towards him, making her way to the familiarity of that body.

At the door, Bea took a moment to collect herself. She took a deep breath and ran her fingers through her hair. And then, just before she reached up to ring the buzzer for Adam's second-floor flat, the door opened and he was there in front of her. He must have been looking out for her from his window, must have watched her walking down the street towards him.

'Bea,' he said.

There was something broken in his voice. He stepped forwards, stepped out on to the path with his bare feet, and pulled her into his arms. And Bea concentrated on breathing, on inhaling his earthy scent, on how good it felt to be held. When he kissed her, she didn't resist, and when he pulled her inside, she followed. She followed him up two flights of stairs, her breathing quick, and into his bedroom, where he pushed her gently against the door, as it closed, and kissed her hard.

'I want you,' Bea said.

She had doubts, but she ignored them. She wanted to let herself believe, for an hour or so, that everything was all right. This man was the father of the baby she was carrying, and he was undressing her in his room, and everything was as it should be. When Bea was naked, Adam laid her down on his narrow bed and she propped herself up with one elbow while he looked at her. She wasn't ashamed of her body, and she liked the feeling of his eyes on her. Standing at the side of the bed, Adam pulled his white T-shirt over his head, unbuttoned his jeans and let them fall to the ground. And then he took his place beside her, and pulled her into his arms again.

They kissed, fiercely, and their hands were everywhere, and finally, he was inside her and Bea sighed, long and hard. Part of her wanted to bite him, to hurt him, because she knew this was the last time and she wanted to be sure that he felt something, that he would remember. Instead, she dug her nails into his back as he came, and when he cried out, she turned her head to one side, and smiled.

They fell asleep for an hour or so with their limbs tangled. When Bea woke, her head was in the crook of Adam's arm, but it was no longer comfortable. Her neck was at an awkward angle, stiff and painful. She sat up, and her movement woke him. He shifted a little in the bed, placed his hands under the back of his head, and smiled up at her.

'Okay?' he asked.

'I should go.'

Already, Bea was standing, bending down to pick her clothes from the messy pile on the floor.

'Stay,' Adam said.

He rose and caught her arms from behind, pulled her back on the bed. They fell awkwardly, him on his back and her on top of him, and she wriggled into a more comfortable position at his side, but she didn't get up again immediately. Bea looked around the room. She'd always liked Adam's flat, but now, in near darkness, his room looked grubby and worn. The carpet was almost threadbare, and all the furniture was heavy and imposing and didn't match. Along one wall, his precious music collection. Boxes and boxes of old records. And here and there, untidy piles of books. Bea wanted to be at home, suddenly. Not at her flat but at her father's house, where everything was clean and tidy. It was an unexpected, sudden impulse, but it was a strong one. She was tired of being in rooms like this. She was ready to make a change.

'Adam,' she said. 'I'm going home.'

'Why?' He sat up, grabbed a packet of cigarettes from his bedside table and offered one to Bea before lighting his own.

'Nothing's changed,' she said. 'I shouldn't have come.'

'You wanted to come, I wanted you to come. Where's the harm?'

It was then that Bea realised that she had to tell him. It was his baby, after all. But the idea of him being a father was laughable. He wasn't ready, really, to be a boyfriend.

'I'm pregnant,' she said. 'Almost ten weeks. The baby's yours. I've decided to keep it. But...'

Adam was looking at her, the shock clear to read on his face. Bea almost laughed. He was like a child, she thought. He was going around town, having sex whenever and with whomever he wanted to, rarely using contraception. And yet he was astonished when there were consequences.

'But I don't expect anything from you,' she finished. 'I don't expect you to be a dad.'

'I can't,' he said. 'I can't be a dad. I'm just not ready.'

Adam leaned down, crushed his cigarette out in a glass ashtray on the floor beside the bed. And then he stood, pulled on his boxer shorts and went to the window. He folded his arms across his chest, and then he pulled up the blinds and opened a window. Bea felt cold almost instantly and pulled the covers around her. Suddenly, she felt exposed and stupid. She moved to the edge of the bed, the duvet still wrapped around her, and reached for her underwear.

'Look,' Adam said. 'Are you sure?'

'Am I sure about what?' Bea asked, angry now.

'About all of it. That you're pregnant, that I'm the father, that you want to keep it?'

Bea dressed quickly with her back to him. 'I don't know what I expected,' she said. 'I never asked you to be a part of this.'

'You came here,' he said. 'I asked you to come over and you came.'

Bea felt tears beginning to form behind her eyes, and she willed herself to get out of this flat before they fell.

'Fuck you,' she said. She left the room and slammed the door behind her, did the same thing at the entrance to the flat. She took the stairs two at a time, the tears starting to fall, her vision blurry. On the second flight, she almost tripped, and she let out a sob as she caught herself and jumped down the last few steps. Outside, she breathed deeply, suddenly aware of the flat's smoky, musty odour now that she was gone from it. And then she started walking, back to the train, letting the tears fall freely and not caring who looked at her. She wished again that she were going home, to Southampton, to her family.

'Esme, I need to talk to you,' Tom said.

Esme looked up. She was sitting at the kitchen table with a cup of coffee and a newspaper. All day, they'd been together in the shop and they'd worked and chatted as usual. And now, when they'd been home for less than an hour, her dad had come to her with a worried look on his face. He was wringing his hands. She watched him as he walked to the window, turned his back on it, returned to the table and rested his hands on the back of the chair opposite her.

'What is it, Dad?'

Esme felt a cold flash of fear, then. Was he ill? As a child, after they lost her mother, Esme always worried that her dad would fall ill and die, that she and Bea would be left entirely alone. For a few years, the thought hadn't crossed her mind. But he was getting older, of course. Nearing sixty. Weren't there all kinds of cancers and heart problems that became more likely at that age? Wasn't that the kind of thing you read about, all the time? Esme's mind flickered briefly and landed on Simon's mum, a similar age and dying of cancer. Of course, Esme knew that people could die at any age. If her life had taught her anything, it was that.

'Dad, I'm scared,' she said. 'Please tell me.'

He frowned and finally sat down. 'Scared?' he said. And then he seemed to understand. 'Oh, I'm sorry. There's nothing wrong, really.'

Esme sighed deeply, smiled a shaky smile. It was unthinkable, really, losing him. And yet she would have to face it one day. Esme pushed that thought as far back in her mind as she could and tilted her head, ready to hear whatever her father had to say.

'I've been thinking, lately,' he said, his voice low.

Esme had to lean in to catch his words, but she didn't ask him to speak up.

'About you and me, and Marianne, and Bea and her baby, and the shop. I've been trying to work out what's best for everyone. And I don't think I'm quite there yet. But I have decided one thing. I'm ready to retire.'

Esme was surprised, but she hid it as best she could. All her life, her father had loved that shop. Loved the fact that it gave him freedom, meant he didn't have to work for anyone else, that he could be his own boss and determine his own hours. He'd used it as his escape when things were difficult, hidden away there. Esme had learned to do the same thing. It was a place of shelter, of comfort, of safety. She'd never really considered that this day might come.

'I don't want you to worry,' Tom said. 'I know how much you love the place. I'm happy for you to go on running it, if that's what you want. And in time, you could buy it from me, really make it your own.'

Esme considered this. Going on standing behind that counter, but with one big difference. She would be in charge. It would be her shop, her decisions, her books. It was tempting. But she also knew that sales were falling, that online shopping was killing businesses like theirs every day. Her dad had always dealt with the accounts, but she knew enough.

'Let me think about it,' she said.

'Are you angry? About me giving up?' Tom looked directly at her, his eyes pleading.

'Of course not,' she said. 'You've worked hard. It's time you had a break.'

Esme thought back to her original fears, about his health. Neither of them knew how long he had, of course, and the last thing Esme wanted was for him to go on working and working until he was old and weak. She did have worries, though, about what this decision meant for her. She would end up working at the bookshop alone, or leaving and doing something else entirely. And she'd never done anything else. She didn't know what else she might possibly do. Carefully, she kept all of her questions and concerns inside, and reached across the table to take her father's hand.

'Thanks, Es,' he said. 'I'd never want to do anything to upset you. You know that, don't you?'

Esme nodded. She did know that. She had a sudden memory of the day she found her mother's body. It was one her mind brought up often, and she'd stopped trying to fight it. Her dad had carried her up the stairs, and she remembered sinking her weight against his body, feeling that it would be impossible to ever carry her own weight again. She looked over his shoulder as he negotiated the steps, carefully and slowly. Through the open lounge door, she could still see her mother's pale, bare legs against the floral sofa. And she knew that that would be the last she saw of her. Knew, too, that her dad would do anything in his power, for the rest of their lives, to make her happy. Because she'd lost everyone else, and he was all that remained. Him and baby Bea.

Shivering slightly, Esme shook off the memory and stood up.

'Thanks for telling me, Dad,' she said. 'It's fine, really. I'm just going upstairs to make a phone call, and then maybe I could make dinner? Spaghetti Bolognese?'

It was one of her dad's favourites, and they hadn't had it for a while. Esme smiled at him, wanting him to nod and say yes. She wanted him to be happy, she realised. It was all she'd ever wanted for him. Just as it was all he'd ever wanted for her. And so they'd stuck together, at home and at work, both desperate to make things as easy as possible for the other one.

'Lovely,' he said. 'I'll give you a hand.'

Esme went up to her room and closed the door before dialling Simon's number. When he answered, the sound of his voice made her smile, and she thought back to the kiss they'd shared the previous weekend. And she wished that he were there, in person, rather than at the end of the phone line. But really, she was glad he was there at all.

'How's your mum?' she asked.

Simon sighed and didn't say anything for a long minute.

'She seems comfortable,' he said, at last. 'And she's excited that it's finally December. She wants to live beyond Christmas. I'll be home again next weekend. Perhaps the two of you could meet?'

Esme had to hide her surprise for a second time. 'Me?' she said, stupidly.

'Yes, you. It's good for her to see new faces, keeps her going. She remembers you, too. I mentioned you to her last time.'

'Did you tell her about … what happened?' Esme asked.

Simon was quiet again, and when he spoke, he sounded confused. 'About us kissing?' he asked.

'No! About when we were children.'

'Oh! No, of course not.'

'Okay then,' said Esme. 'I'd like that.'

And then she told Simon about the conversation she'd just had with her father. About the possibility of him selling the shop, and her having to find another job.

'I think it's a great opportunity, to be honest,' Simon said, when she'd explained it all. 'I think you only ended up working there because you didn't want him to be on his own. Now you're free to do whatever you want. What did you want to do, when you were younger?'

Esme thought back, tried to conjure up her childhood self. But all she could see was two images – her, biting into Simon's neck and being carried up the stairs by her father after her mother's death.

'I don't know.'

'Well, start thinking. You could do some training, or more education. You could do anything.'

Esme considered this. When she was doing her degree, she'd toyed with the idea of becoming an English teacher. A love of books was in her blood, and she'd thought it would be wonderful to be able to share that with young people, the way some of her favourite teachers had shared it with her. And then later, as she'd talked her problems through with one psychiatrist after another, she'd considered training to be a counsellor. Learning how to help people like her, who were broken. Somehow putting her own brokenness to good use.

'Thanks Simon,' she said. 'I have to go now.'

'Okay, I'll call you tomorrow.'

She wasn't sure when they'd crossed over into speaking every day, but she liked it. She liked knowing that whatever happened, he would be available in the evening to hear about it. Esme glanced at her watch and saw that it was still only a little after six. Dinner could wait for a little while, she decided. First, she would write another letter for Bea.

Dear Phoebe,

That summer, your last summer, there was a holiday in a cottage in Wales. The car journey felt like days, your bony elbows poking into my ribs and the rain streaking the windows. Mum drove, leaning forward in her seat to concentrate, and Dad sat with his head twisted round to face us, stories on his lips.

He told us to imagine a sky full of stars, to the left and right, above and all around. So many stars that if you started counting them that day, you wouldn't have finished in a hundred years. There was wonder in your eyes. But me, I'd heard this one before. I was disappointed when he started it, hoping for something new, but watching you hear it for the first time was the next best thing.

He told us that every night, the stars went to work, that shining to light up the dark sky was their job. One night, one little star didn't feel like shining. He was young and he wanted to do something else, something more fun. So he went off to play and he didn't shine at all that night. But the next morning, when the stars all stopped shining and were ready to go home, the chief star called them all together and made a very serious speech. The chief star said that one of the stars hadn't shone that night, and because of that, a little boy in Sweden had had a nightmare. He said that it might sometimes feel like no one is watching, but that each and every star was shining to protect the sleep of a little boy or little girl somewhere in the world. The little star hadn't known that. He started crying and admitted that it had been him who didn't shine. And from then on, he took his job very seriously, so that little boy in Sweden never had a nightmare again.

You giggled, and Dad reached back to run his hand through your hair. I watched you squirm from his touch, smiling. When Dad stopped talking, I saw Mum take her eyes off the road, just for a second, to look at him. I didn't recognise it then, but I can still picture that look now. It was happiness. It was love.

You asked how you know which star is yours, and Dad said that you can never know for sure, but that if you look at a star very carefully, and it's yours, it might wink at you. Mum laughed, and a few minutes later, she pulled up outside the cottage and we piled inside, holding bags over our heads to keep ourselves dry.

7TH DECEMBER 2011

9641 DAYS AFTER

It rained all week. We splashed through puddles in our wellies whenever we went out, but mostly, we stayed indoors, playing cards and made-up games. Mum and Dad read their books while we played round after round of snap, because you were too little to understand any of the other games I knew. When we got bored, we tugged at Dad's sleeve until he groaned, closed his book and agreed to tell us a story, or bring us some juice and biscuits.

If I had to pinpoint a time when we were happiest, I think I'd choose that holiday. I remember moments, frozen in time like photographs. Mum, plaiting your hair beside the window in the bedroom you and I shared. Dad, dashing out to pick up something for lunch, his head down to shield himself from the driving rain. You, sitting cross-legged before the small television as bright cartoons flashed before your eyes. Mum, bent double with laughter, clutching at her stomach as though in pain. I can't remember what caused it. Just the sound. The joyous ring of it. The unleashed happiness. It was you, I think. It was you who caused it.

Esme

Bea paced the room, summoning up memories of holidays. It felt strange, in early December, to be thinking about sunshine. A fortnight in the sun in the south of France, odd weeks in Devon and Cornwall. Her and Esme, and their dad. Buckets and spades and beach towels flung to free them of sand. Candyfloss and kids' clubs, finger paints and a jellyfish sting that had made her cry out in pain. She'd enjoyed them, hadn't she? Hadn't she been pleased to get away from home and play in the sun and swim in the sea with her family? She had. And she'd never felt like something was missing from those trips, until now.

Bea closed her laptop, deciding that work could wait for a while. She went into the kitchen, flicked on the kettle. And it was then that she felt it. A sharp, stabbing pain in her lower abdomen. Instinctively, she curled forward, wrapped her arms around her stomach. And then again, even sharper this time. Slowly, Bea went back into her bedroom and lay down on the bed on her left side, her body curled, almost foetal. She closed her eyes. If she went to sleep, she thought, it wouldn't be happening. She wouldn't be losing the baby.

An hour passed and Bea didn't move. She was fairly sure that she was bleeding, and she was too scared to go to the bathroom to check. She thought of her father and Esme, of the way their faces would change when she told them the news. That there was no longer a baby. Her dad would wince as though in pain, she knew. And with Esme, there would be a fast flicker, a flash of sorrow, before she was back in control. This baby was the first really good thing that had happened to their family for a long time, she realised. If it was gone, where would that leave them?

For a time, Bea drifted in and out of sleep. She dreamed rapid, sharp-focus dreams, about Adam, about herself as a mother, about hospitals with white walls and noisy wards, about Phoebe. And then she was awake, the dream of Phoebe still tugging at the corners of her brain, demanding attention. Somehow, at some point, her brain had confused things, had mixed up the baby she was carrying with the sister she'd never known. If the baby lives, she resolved, silently, and if she's a girl, I will call her Phoebe.

She wasn't sure how much later it was when she stood, a little shakily, and made her way to the bathroom. There was a little blood in her underwear, but less than she'd feared. Suddenly cold, she sank to the floor beside the radiator and pulled her phone from her pocket. If she called Julia, she had no doubt that she would come home and look after her. If she called her dad or Esme, they would get on a train, if she asked them to. What about Adam? Would he pick up the phone? And if he did, would he be sympathetic? Something was tugging at her, and it was while she was thinking about Adam that she realised what it was. There was a chance that people might say that this was a good thing, really. That it was a blessing in disguise.

Bea pulled herself up and went back to her bedroom. Full of purpose, she leafed through the papers on her desk, the letters from Esme and the unopened bank statements, until she found the list of contact numbers the doctor had given her. In bold at the top of the list, there was a number to call if you wanted to speak to a midwife. Bea tapped it into her phone and sat down with her elbows on the desk while she waited for someone to pick up.

'Community midwife, hello?'

'Hi,' Bea said. 'My name's Bea Sadler. I'm eleven weeks pregnant. I'm having pains, and bleeding a little, and I don't know what to do.'

Bea was surprised by how calm she sounded. She could have been talking about someone else, or something trivial. She took a deep breath, let it out shakily, and listened to the midwife's soothing voice.

'Bea, I'm Jessica. Try not to worry. Can you describe what the pains are like?'

'Like period cramps, but a bit sharper.'

'Okay, and is there a lot of blood or just a few spots?'

Bea closed her eyes. 'Not a lot, but more than just spotting.'

'Okay, here's what we're going to do. Call your doctor and ask for an emergency appointment. The doctor will take a look at you and ask you some questions and if they think it's necessary, they'll send you to the early pregnancy unit at your nearest hospital. Now, do you have someone with you?'

'No.'

'Okay. Do you think you can get to your doctor's on your own?'

'Yes, it's not far.'

Bea felt a single tear slide down the left side of her face. 'Do you think I'm losing the baby?' she asked.

There was a pause, and she thought for a minute that Jessica had gone, and she wanted to take back the question she'd asked and go back to those clear, straightforward questions and instructions.

'I can't answer that, Bea. But there's every chance that it's nothing to worry about. We just need to be sure.'

Bea nodded helplessly, and then she ended the call. After-wards, when she'd called the doctor and was making her way there, she realised that she hadn't said thank you. And she was sorry, because the woman on the end of the phone had been kind, and patient, and just what she'd needed.

The doctor was none of those things. 'It's probably nothing,' he said, with a slight shrug of his shoulders. 'Let's take a look. Could you go behind that curtain, take off your jeans and underwear and put on a gown?'

Bea nodded weakly and tried to let his words repeat over and over in her head, because she was worried that she was going to forget something he'd asked of her. It was a little cold in the room, and she shivered slightly as she pulled her jeans off. She closed her eyes when she lay back on the stiff bed, tried to think about other things as the doctor examined her, answering his questions with fast monosyllables.

'Okay,' he said, after a minute or two. 'You can get dressed now. And then we'll have a chat.'

He left the room and Bea returned to the clothes that she'd carelessly thrown onto the blue plastic chair that sat beside the bed. If it was nothing, she thought, he would have said so. She felt tired, suddenly, too tired to talk about the ways in which her body might be failing her and the things that might be wrong with her baby that would cause it to self-destruct. When the doctor returned to the room, she was sitting beside his desk with her hands clasped together, ready to hear the worst. For the first time, she looked at him closely. He was in his mid-forties, she guessed, with greying hair and a slight paunch. She wondered how many women had come to him like this, in ruins? She wondered how many times he'd had to say these words.

'Right,' he said, pulling out his wheeled chair and sitting down. 'Have you got your scan booked in?'

'Next Friday,' Bea said.

'Great. Well, I don't really think there's anything to worry about here. A bit of bleeding isn't too unusual, and often we don't really know what's caused it. Of course, it can be an early sign of miscarriage, but if that is the case, there's really nothing we can do to prevent it. I suggest you go home, take it easy and wait for your scan. And all being well, you'll see then that everything is fine.'

Bea felt as if she was underwater. She couldn't quite make out what he was saying, or the meaning of it.

'So I might not lose the baby?'

The doctor tilted his head to one side. 'No guarantees, but I don't think it will come to that. But call the surgery or your midwife if the bleeding gets any heavier, or if the blood is a brighter red.'

'What about the cramps?'

He shrugged, and Bea saw, then, that there were tiny flecks of dandruff on the shoulders of his navy-blue jumper. She wanted to shake him, to tell him that this news was the most important of her life. That she needed him to at least pretend to care. 'Again, keep an eye on them. Let us know if they get worse. Take a couple of Paracetamol and they might just stop altogether.'

Back at home, Bea changed into a pair of flannel pyjamas and took a hot water bottle to bed. She thought about the day she'd done the pregnancy test, about how unsure she'd felt. A month had passed, but it felt more like a year. In that time, she'd accepted the fact that she was having a baby, lost Adam and that morning she'd been convinced that it was all over. It was impossible to believe that that day, sitting on the edge of the bathtub, she'd wished for the test result to be negative. And now, the thought of losing the baby was enough to undo her.

She reached out of the side of her bed for her phone, dialled her dad and Esme's number.

'Hello?' Esme's voice was soft, a little hesitant.

'It's Bea.' Bea felt that she might cry, then, and she wasn't sure why. All she knew was that it was good to hear her sister's voice at the end of the telephone line.

'Hi Bea, how are things?'

Bea considered telling Esme about her day. She'd intended to, when she picked up the phone, but now she wasn't so sure. There was still a chance, after all, that it could all fall apart. The doctor had said that she could miscarry. He didn't think that she would, but it was a possibility.

'I wanted to ask you a favour,' she said, hardly thinking about the words before she said them. 'It's my twelve-week scan next Friday. I don't want to go on my own. Will you come with me?'

'Of course,' Esme said. 'Bea, you don't have to do any of this on your own, okay? Just let me know where and when, and I'll be there.'

Bea propped herself up a little with her pillows and closed her eyes against the hot tears that were brimming. 'Thank you,' she said, swallowing hard.

And as if Esme knew that it was difficult for Bea to speak, she led the conversation from there, filling Bea in on their dad's retirement plans and her own thoughts about running the shop or making a change of career. She talked about how she wanted to do something that would help people. And Bea held the phone to her ear, only half listening, but grateful, nonetheless, for the comforting sound of her sister's voice.

12TH DECEMBER 2011

9646 DAYS AFTER

I t was Monday afternoon, and Esme was alone in the shop. That morning, when her dad had asked whether she minded him taking the day off, she'd felt a little annoyed, but as the day wore on she became grateful for the solitude. There was a steady stream of customers, mostly looking for Christmas gifts, and in the gaps between them, she thought about her plans for the future.

She'd spent much of the weekend with Simon, and on a long walk around the common, he had let her talk and talk about the things she might do. And after she'd finished talking, and asked him what he thought, he had taken her hand and kissed her and told her that he thought she already knew what she wanted, deep down. That night in bed, she'd wondered what he meant, a little frustrated at his lack of input. But when she woke on Monday morning, everything seemed a little clearer, and by mid-afternoon, she was certain.

Esme pulled her phone from her pocket and sent Simon a text. *I'm going to be a counsellor. And I'm going to get my own place.* A few minutes later, she felt the buzzing that signified his reply. *I know.* Now that she'd decided, she was anxious to get started. She searched on the computer for counselling courses in the area. Most of them didn't start for months, but she read about things she could do in the meantime to strengthen her application. Volunteering in a centre or on a phoneline for vulnerable people – victims of domestic abuse, people who were grieving, those who were considering suicide. Esme looked away from the computer, out over the rows and rows of books, and thought of her mother. How she'd needed help, and no one had known.

Just then, the bell above the door jangled and Esme looked up to see her dad entering the shop. He was wearing his heavy coat and reaching back outside to shake his dripping umbrella. Esme noticed that his scarf was looking old and tatty, and made a mental note to buy him a new one. He walked up to the counter, placed his hands on the edge. They were red from the cold and wind.

'Anything happening?' he asked.

'It's been fairly quiet,' Esme said. 'It's this weather.'

'Let's close up.'

Esme looked at him in surprise. Over the years, there had been busy periods and slack ones, times when everyone seemed to just want to browse, times when the bell didn't ring for hours on end. But they were patient, Esme and her dad. They tidied the shelves, made up imaginative displays, invited authors in to read and sign copies of their books. They plucked titles from the shelves and read them, sitting at the counter or in the back room. They didn't close up. But if this was all coming to an end, Esme thought, then why not? If the shop was going to be sold, then what difference did one afternoon make?

When they'd locked up and were sitting in the car, Tom made no move to start the engine. Esme looked at him, knowing that he was trying to find the best way to say something. She didn't rush him. The rain fell in fat drops against the windscreen, and Esme waited.

'There's somewhere I want to take you,' he said, at last.

'Okay.'

He drove, his eyes on the road, his expression giving nothing away. Esme looked out of the window at the streets she knew, and barely noticed. And then they were heading out of the city, and the streets were less familiar, and Esme felt a knot starting to form in her stomach, and she didn't know why.

But of course she knew why. It was obvious, wasn't it? As soon as her dad pulled up outside the crematorium, Esme was seven years old again. She was wearing an itchy black dress and a heavy cardigan that she never saw again, afterwards. She was with both of her parents, and she was more sorry than either of them knew. Esme sighed a deep sigh.

'I've never been here, since that day,' her dad said. 'Have you?'

Esme shook her head from side to side, not caring whether the tears spilled.

'It's time,' he said.

He opened his door and stepped out of the car, into the driving rain. Esme did the same. She had an umbrella in her bag but she didn't stop to take it out and open it. She just let the rain fall on her, as she walked up the side of the car to meet her dad at the front. He reached for her hand, and she let him take it, surprised by the warmth of his skin. Together, they walked around the back of the building, to the small, neat plots behind it. Esme felt her father tug at her hand as he led the way. She was amazed that he could go straight to Phoebe's plot, after so many years. And at the same time, she wasn't amazed at all. He was seeking out his daughter. Of course he knew where to find her.

'Bea knows,' Esme said. 'About Phoebe. I've told her every-thing. I really think it's the right thing.'

Her dad said nothing, just stopped and looked straight ahead. Esme followed his eyes with her own. Some of the plots were adorned with fresh flowers. Phoebe's was bare, just a stark white cross and a sign with her name and the dates of her birth and death. Esme stared at those dates, with not quite four years between them. She imagined other people coming to visit their relatives, pointing out the tragedy of the little girl who died when she was three years old. For a time that could have been a minute or an hour, Esme and her dad stood shoulder to shoulder in the rain. When he broke into sobs, she took both of her cold hands and wrapped them around his.

'Let's go,' she said.

It was enough. It was too much. When they got home, they went their separate ways. Esme to her room, her dad to his. She pulled off her wet clothes and put on a pair of old pyjamas, sat down at her desk. And before she knew it, she was writing. She was writing the things she'd been putting off, the things she'd stayed silent about for twenty-six years. The final pieces of the puzzle.

Dear Phoebe,

I've heard there's a peacefulness to drowning, if you don't thrash or struggle, once the water has filled your lungs. But I can't know whether that's what it was like for you.

I loved and hated you in equal measure. And now all that hate is turned in on myself and I don't know what to do with it. And the love? That went with you, I suppose. We sent it off and set it on fire on that sultry summer day.

The night before your funeral, I couldn't sleep. I lay with my eyes closed, rubbing Beebee through my fingers, wondering what it would take to bring you back. What if I was the one who was buried instead? Could they have you back, if they gave me up? I didn't know how it worked, didn't know what the rules were or whether there was a way to cheat them. I didn't know who to ask.

I'd been talking to you every day since it happened. Dad said that you were gone and we'd never be able to see you again but he didn't say anything about talking. I was starting to lose the sound of your voice and the kind of things you used to say. And so I talked, inside my head, understanding, somehow, that Mum and Dad wouldn't approve. I told you everything I could think to tell you: what we'd been doing and how sorry I was and that we missed you. Despite what Dad had said, I asked you to please come back, if you could.

It was my fault that you were gone and I knew that nothing short of bringing you back would make up for it. So I promised you things – my possessions, my time. I promised you everything, and I waited a little impatiently for you to answer.

Now that I'm telling these truths, I have to tell them all. Phoebe, there was a small, awful part of me that was glad. I tried not to give it any space, terrified that it would take root and grow, but it was there. I hated it, that ugly part of me that thought I'd got my mother back. That believed, naïvely, that she would come back.

That night before, it felt late and sleep wouldn't come. I tried to guess how much time had passed since I came upstairs. It felt like hours. It felt like too many hours to count. And yet, when I got out of bed and pulled back the curtains, there was no sign of morning. And then I heard it. Movement and voices from downstairs. So it was still night. Mum and Dad were still up.

I knew that the next day was an important one, had heard the word funeral in countless solemn conversations, but I didn't know quite what it meant and I didn't dare to ask. Quietly, I crept down the stairs and sat on the bottom step, resting my head against the wall. The lounge door was open and, from that spot, I couldn't see them and they couldn't see me, but if I strained, I could just about make out what they were saying.

They were talking about the funeral. Mum thought I shouldn't go; Dad insisted I should. He thought they might regret it later, if they left me at home. Thought it was a stage of grief that you had to go through. But Mum kept repeating that I was seven, that I didn't understand.

I must have fallen asleep on the step, because when I woke up it was morning, and I was in my bed, the covers tucked neatly around me. And I tried to remember being carried up the stairs, thought I could. Dad, his arms strong and his breath hot in my ear. But it's impossible to know whether it was a real memory or one I created, cobbled together from all the other times he'd held me, carried me. I tried to take comfort from the fact that they hadn't just left me there, stepped over me and made their way upstairs. I tried to take comfort from the way someone had laid me down and covered me up.

Breakfast was silent. I wanted to know who had won and cursed myself for having fallen asleep. Were they leaving me at home, or was I going with them? I didn't know which option I dreaded more.

Mum and Dad barely touched their food, and I felt guilty for being hungry. While they bit half-heartedly at the corners of their toast, I tried to eat without making a sound. And I pushed my bowl away with a few flakes of cereal and some milk left in there, to show that I was affected too.

Dad asked if I understood that it was the day of Phoebe's funeral. I jumped, a little, at the sound of his voice. And then nodded. Mum left the room and I heard her padding her way up the stairs. Knew, from that, that it was Dad who'd got his way. So I was going with them. I wondered what that meant. He explained that we were going to say goodbye to her, and that it would be very sad. I swallowed tears and grief and more guilt than there should ever be in a seven-year-old's body.

16TH DECEMBER 2011

9650 DAYS AFTER

In the back of the car, I sat between Mum and Dad and neither of them touched me, and they didn't touch each other. I wanted to take their hands, but I couldn't. How could I try to comfort them when it was all my fault? We stayed locked in our individual sorrow, and I tried not to look at the car in front, where your tiny coffin lay.

I couldn't quite make myself believe that you were inside it. I wanted to know what you were wearing, and if anyone had brushed your hair. Because only Mum could brush it without making you cry when it was all tangled up from running outside. It was too small a space, would be too dark with the lid closed. I wanted to ask them to stop the cars, to open the lid so that I could see you, help you get out. And I had a memory, then, and although I fought it, it played out behind my eyelids.

Phoebe, you were three. I was six. Mum had told us to play upstairs while she started making dinner, and we were going through the dressing-up box, pulling out dresses and wigs and trying on old pairs of Mum's shoes. There was a shimmering blue dress we both wanted to wear, and you snatched it from my hands. And I felt it tear and was overtaken with rage for you.

I told you I hated you. I said it slowly and deliberately. You began to cry, loud sobs left over from your time as a baby and Mum called up the

244

stairs, asked what had happened. I shouted that we were just playing, glared at you, letting you know there'd be a price to pay if you contradicted me. You were silent.

I scooped armfuls of clothes out of the old wooden chest, scattered them on the floor until it was empty. Ordered you to get inside.

You shook your head, dark hair fanning out around your face and tears still falling from your chin and plopping on to the carpet.

I pulled a clown mask from the top of the pile on the floor, put it on. I made my voice low and menacing, and told you to get inside again.

This time, you obeyed. You climbed in, and I knew how scared you were, your heart thudding, and it made me feel powerful. And I loved it.

I watched your face as I closed the lid, slowly. Neither of us said a word but you didn't close your eyes. You watched me, made sure I knew how cruel I was being, saw how I enjoyed it. I counted to ten before I let you out and when I did, you bolted past me and down the stairs to Mum. And I waited for a call and a punishment that never came. Phoebe, even when I was at my worst, you were loyal to me.

I'll never know how scared you were that day. Whether I damaged you, somehow. Or why it made me feel so good to see you terrified, to have that control over you. That day, your funeral, I thought back over it all and decided I must be bad. Like the eggs that Mum discards without a thought when she's baking.

And now? I still believe it, sometimes. I still believe that it should have been me, lying trapped in that small coffin, and you, sitting between Mum and Dad, giving them a reason to carry on.

The room was packed full of people and it had that sticky feeling you get when everyone has come in from the rain and started to warm up. Umbrellas dripped and coats were shaken off. Everyone stared at us when we walked in. Their eyes said that they were sorry for what had happened to us, but when they looked at me, their eyes said that they knew, too. Their eyes confirmed what I already knew. It should have been me.

The minister talked about you as if he knew you, and I looked to Dad, confused. I'd never seen this man. How did he know you? But Dad wouldn't look at me. He was sitting very still and holding my hand very tight. Too tight. It hurt a little, but it didn't hurt enough. My chair was uncomfortable and I was too warm in my heavy cardigan, but I sat still throughout the service. It was the least I could do.

And then, like magic, your coffin disappeared and nobody seemed surprised but me. Where were you going, now? Wasn't it bad enough that we couldn't see you anymore? Did you really have to keep leaving us, over and over again?

There was some music then, and I wondered why they weren't playing one of the songs you loved. The ones you'd sing along to whenever they came on in the kitchen or the car. Your voice was high and sweet and clear and I couldn't believe – just couldn't – that I'd never hear it again. It seemed impossible. I thought that getting a sister was like a promise, that you'd have a sister forever, then. That it wasn't right, or possible, to have to go back to being alone. And I know now that I was right. I've had a sister forever.

I didn't realise that it was over, or that I was crying, until Dad scooped me up and held me close to his chest and I felt my tears starting to seep through his dark shirt. I glanced over his shoulder at Mum, then, and she was almost unrecognisable. Stiff, white, broken. Hardly a mum at all.

Phoebe, we went to a hotel and there was food and people drank and talked about you, and I wished every minute that you were there with me. Everyone wanted to take their turn with Mum and Dad, and me, and all I wanted to do was grab your hand and lead you to a hidden corner, make up a game for us to play to pass the time. I wanted us to pass those triangular sandwiches back and forth between us – no fish for you, no cucumber for me – and grab handfuls of crisps and nuts to eat beneath the tables when no one was looking. But of course, if we could have done that, if you'd been here, we wouldn't have been there at all.

Later, when we got home, Mum settled on the sofa and cried as though she'd never stop. Whenever I cried, she would kiss the tip of my nose or stroke my hair with her warm hand and it would always make me feel better. But I knew that I couldn't make her feel better that way.

Not now. I was tainted. Why weren't they punishing me? I thought that
perhaps, if they did, the ache would start to lessen.
   Esme

B ea read the letter on the bus on her way to the hospital.
When she had finished, she read it again. She tried to
itemise the things she knew. Phoebe had drowned, and both of
her parents and Esme seemed to blame themselves, somehow, for
that fact. She didn't know the hows and whys of it all. But she was
on her way to meet Esme, and if she felt up to it, and if everything
was all right with her own baby, she would ask her sister about it.

Bea had woken up that morning feeling stronger, more positive. Every day since the cramps and the bleeding and the visit to
the doctor, she had woken up with a cold stone of dread sitting on
her chest. But there had been no more signs of anything being
wrong, no more bleeding, and that morning, when her alarm
sounded, she'd sat up and placed a hand on her stomach and
wished. The day had finally arrived, when she would know one
way or the other. She would see her baby on the screen, and the
sonographer would be able to tell her whether its tiny heart was
still beating.

Seeing the hospital loom large in the distance, Bea rang the
bell and made her way to the front of the bus. She called thank
you over her shoulder to the driver as she stepped down on to the
pavement. As planned, Esme was waiting in the small coffee shop
next to the reception desk. Bea glanced at her watch. They had
half an hour. She watched her sister for a few moments from the
café's entrance, which was decorated with a flimsy piece of tinsel.
Esme had her elbows on the table, her chin resting gently in the
cup of her hands. A mug of coffee sat in front of her, but she
didn't reach for it. She looked different, Bea thought. Content.
And then she approached her, and Esme saw her and stood to give
her a hug.

'Do you want anything?' Esme asked.

Bea shook her head. 'Thanks for coming. Did Dad mind?'

Esme tilted her head to one side. 'Of course not. Bea, is everything okay?'

'I'm just really nervous. This is a really big deal.'

Part of her wanted to tell Esme everything. That she was terrified of what was going to happen in the next hour. That she didn't want to see her baby on the screen, if it was dead or dying. That she couldn't bear to listen out for a heartbeat that might not be there. She wished she had an older sister who had been through all this, who could reassure her and tell her what to expect and not to worry. But that was unfair, because Esme had travelled here to be by her side, and she was doing the best she could.

'Let's talk about something else,' Bea said. 'How are things at home?'

Esme smiled, then, full and genuine, and Bea thought back to the contented look she'd seen on her sister's face a few minutes before, and knew that something had changed.

'I've made a few decisions,' Esme said. 'I'm moving out, finally, and I'm going to train to be a counsellor. And I've met someone.'

Bea raised her eyebrows. 'Wow, that's a lot to take in. Are things all right, with you and Dad?'

'They're fine. Better, really. I feel like I know what I want for the first time in years. I feel like a cloud has passed.' Esme sipped her coffee, poured in a little more milk. Her movements were precise and sure. She looked like someone who'd had a heavy weight lifted. And Bea was genuinely pleased for her. She saw, now, that Esme had spent years in a kind of limbo. She wondered how big a part revealing the truth about Phoebe had played in Esme's transformation.

For the first time that day, Bea smiled, wide and easy. 'I'm pleased.'

'Me too,' Esme said, draining her coffee. 'Now, it's probably time we made a move. Come on.'

They both stood simultaneously, and Bea let Esme take her

arm, take charge. They followed the signs to the Early Pregnancy Unit and announced themselves at the reception desk. Bea had to go for a blood test, and when she returned, she took the plastic chair next to Esme's in the waiting area. But two minutes after she'd sat down, her name was called, and they were walking down an empty corridor, and Bea felt a weakness in her legs. But she kept on walking, regardless, with her sister at her side.

'Everything looks good here,' the sonographer said. 'Strong heartbeat. Listen.'

Bea held her breath while she waited. And then the sound was there in the room, loud and fast and strong. It sounded like galloping horses. And she felt Esme's hand reach for hers and there was a smile spreading over her face, tears in her eyes. And after that, she didn't take in anything the sonographer said. She lay there, half-hearing things about the risks of Down's Syndrome and the baby's measurements. When it was time to get up from the bed, Esme passed her a wad of tissue paper and she wiped the sticky fluid from her stomach, fastened her jeans.

'It's amazing, isn't it?' Esme said, a big smile on her face. They were back at the reception desk, waiting to book in the next appointment and pay for the photos Bea was clutching.

'I feel like I know the baby,' Bea said, her voice low. 'It's so strange, I don't even know if it's a boy or a girl. But I love it. I feel so protective. Fuck, does that make any sense?'

Esme reached out one hand and stroked Bea's hair. It was a gentle, caring touch, and a motherly one. Bea wished, briefly, that it could have always been like this between them. When they were outside, in the fresh air, Bea took a deep breath.

'Are you going straight back, or have you got a bit of time?' she asked.

'There's no rush. Shall we walk for a bit?'

Bea nodded and they set off. She didn't know the area very well, and the roads were busy, cars whipping past them in a blur of noise and speed. Perhaps that was better, Bea decided, for what she needed to bring up. Perhaps silence would make it too hard.

'I read your letter this morning,' she said.

Esme was walking slightly ahead of her sister, and she turned, then, her head tilted to one side. 'Sorry? I couldn't hear you.'

Bea reached out and grabbed Esme's hand, forced her to stop walking for a minute. 'I said I read your letter, about Phoebe's funeral.'

'Oh.'

'It was awful to read that you thought it should have been you,' Bea said. 'Do you still think that?'

Esme grimaced, turned her head this way and that, anything to avoid looking directly at her sister. 'I try not to,' she said, at last.

Bea didn't know how to respond to that, but she kept hold of her sister's hand as they started walking again.

'It was just incredible,' Esme said, beaming.

Simon looked at her quizzically. This is the happiest he's seen me, she thought. She couldn't get the events of the previous day out of her head. Seeing her sister's baby on that screen had made it all so real, at last, so immediate. It had made Esme realise that she hadn't fully believed in Bea's pregnancy until she saw the evidence with her own eyes. It wasn't that she thought Bea was lying. It just seemed so unlikely, somehow. And now it was concrete and true, and miraculous.

'Do you think you'll ever have children?' Simon asked. 'I mean, would you like to?'

'I don't know. I never thought I would, but now, I really don't know.'

Simon smiled a tight smile and reached for her hand. 'I think this is the place,' he said.

They were looking at flats. This was the fourth one and Esme was starting to get them mixed up. There was something samey about every place they went into. Neat, square boxes with neutral walls and simple furniture. Simon kept insisting that they would look more homely once she'd filled them with her belongings –

her books on the shelves and her pictures on the walls. But Esme knew that her reluctance was more than that. She'd lived in the same house her entire life. It was where she'd known her mother, and Phoebe.

But it was also where both of them had died. Esme looked at the house in front of her. The others had all been in purpose-built blocks, but this one was a house conversion. It was close to town, and it had a garden.

The estate agent, Jenny, arrived a few minutes later and let them in. Esme was sick of their sales patter, but this woman left them to it, standing in the hallway while they stuck their heads around the various doors.

'This is the best one, I think,' Simon said.

They were standing in the small garden, under the tree that had obviously been planted to provide a bit of privacy. It had rained earlier, and as they stood there, the odd drop of rain fell from the bare branches and on to their heads and shoulders. Esme closed her eyes and ran back through the flat in her mind. It was perfect. Small, cosy rooms with splashes of colour on the walls and in the curtains. The galley kitchen was painted yellow, just like the kitchen at home, and Esme had made up her mind as soon as she saw that. It felt like a sign.

'I'm going to take it,' she whispered, letting her smile creep into her voice. 'I love it.'

'That's great!' Simon held out his arms and Esme folded herself into him, buried her face in his chest. He smelled earthy and clean. Safe. She wished that this was something they were doing together, that they'd found this place for the two of them to share. It was big enough, with two double bedrooms and a tiny third bedroom that she hadn't quite decided what to do with. But no, it was too soon for that. And Simon was based in London, for the time being. It was enough that they would have somewhere to spend time together when he was home.

Esme told the estate agent that she'd take the flat and they talked about the forms she would have to fill in and the identification she'd have to provide, and then Jenny walked off to her car without looking back, and Esme and Simon stood rooted to the spot, outside the front of Esme's new flat.

'Listen,' Simon said, 'we're only a few minutes from my mum's. Do you fancy going over for a cup of tea?'

Simon had mentioned introducing Esme to his mother a couple of times, but somehow it had never happened. Esme was anxious about it, but she was on the spot and she couldn't think of a good reason to say no.

'Why not?' she said.

Simon smiled, and she could see that he was grateful to her for agreeing, and she felt bad, then, for not making the effort before. They walked to his car hand in hand, Esme's mind still full of the flat and the scan and how well everything seemed to be working out. The drive took less than five minutes, and the same song was still playing on the car radio that had been playing when Simon started the engine and the car sputtered to life. Esme got out of the car and looked up and down the street. She'd run here, she was sure, but then she'd run up and down almost every street in this part of the city over the years. The houses were 1930s semis, uniform and unattractive.

'So this is where you grew up,' she said.

Simon locked the car and joined her on the pavement, looking up at the house in front of them. 'That's right,' he said. 'This is where I spent all those hours crying about what you were going to do to me the next day.'

Esme turned her head to look at him, and saw that he was smiling.

'Let's go in,' he said.

Simon's mum was smaller than Esme remembered, and she wondered whether it was the illness, or just age, that had shrunk her. When they were at school, Esme had remembered her looming way above them all, even above the other mums. She was one of those women who wore too much makeup and looked like she'd always spent a long time doing her hair. Now, she was lying in a bed that had been brought down to what had once been the dining room. Her face was plain, pale, and her hair was cut short and looked lifeless and drab.

'Mum,' Simon said, 'this is Esme.'

Esme thought she heard a slight crack in his voice, but she wasn't sure. How awful, she thought, to see one of your parents waste away, bit by bit, like this. For the first time in her life, she felt grateful that her mother had just gone, when she was still young and beautiful. That she hadn't had to live through a transformation as complete as this one.

'Hello,' said Esme. 'It's nice to meet you again.'

She felt like a child, unsure of herself.

'Esme,' Ellen Treadwell said, reaching out a thin hand and pulling Esme a couple of inches closer to her bedside. 'He always had a thing for you.'

Esme felt her cheeks redden, and when she looked at Simon, she saw that he looked a bit flustered too.

'I'll go and put the kettle on,' he said.

When he'd left the room, Esme shifted her weight from foot to foot, not knowing what to say next.

'Sit down,' Ellen said.

She looked around the room. The double bed was taking up most of the space, and there were no chairs. She was about to kneel on the floor when Ellen's hand appeared again and grabbed hers, pulled her towards the bed until she had no choice but to sit down on the edge of it. Esme was uncomfortable, and she realised it was because death was hovering in the room. It was clear that Simon's mum didn't have long, and there was something in the air, some aroma of decay or emptiness, that Esme hadn't felt for many years. Since Phoebe, since her own mother.

'He loves you,' Ellen said.

Esme dipped her head. It was too intimate, too personal.

'He's a good man, and he loves you. Don't forget that.'

AN HOUR OR SO LATER, Esme made her excuses and left. Simon kissed her at the door and she felt her stomach drop away just like it had the first time.

'Do you have to go?' he asked.

'Sorry, I do. I've got an appointment.'

'On a Saturday?'

Esme shrugged, said nothing.

'Well, what are you doing tonight? Can I see you? We could celebrate you finding your new home.'

Esme was about to say yes, but something was tugging at her, making her feel uncomfortable. It was time.

'Sorry, I can't tonight. I need to do something for Bea.'

She walked to Dr Armstrong's office, a large part of her wishing she'd just told Simon that she was going to see her psychiatrist. She was fairly sure he wouldn't judge her, that it wouldn't change things between them. But still, she wasn't quite ready for it. And yet, she was fairly confident that she would be, soon.

'How are things between you and your sister?' Dr Armstrong asked. She leaned forward in her chair, looking Esme straight in the eye.

'Good. I've been writing her letters, like you suggested, telling her what happened to Phoebe.'

'And?'

'And, it's almost done. I just have to write one more. To tell her how it actually happened, how Phoebe died.'

'And you're worried about what she'll think of you afterwards?' Dr Armstrong suggested.

'I was, when I started this. I was worried that she'd blame me, the way Mum did. But now I'm pretty sure she won't. I feel ready.'

It was something she'd talked over and over with every new

psychiatrist. It was what they all came back to. The maternal love that changed to blame. And had she imagined it? The psychiatrists thought so, she could tell. Despite all the sorry stories they heard, they couldn't quite believe that Esme's mother would have given up on her entirely. And it didn't matter how many stories she recounted, about the cold looks and the hard words her mother gave her after Phoebe's death. They thought she'd imagined or exaggerated them all. But Esme knew better, because even now, in her mid-thirties, she could still close her eyes and feel her mother slapping her face on the day that she cleared away Phoebe's things. That slap had said it all. That slap had told Esme that her mother wished it was her, instead.

But Esme was determined to see this thing through. And so, as soon as her time with Dr Armstrong was over, she took a bus home, and went upstairs to write the words she'd been avoiding since she was seven years old.

Dear Phoebe,

There were no signs, that morning, when we woke. I looked back afterwards to check for things we might have missed. I wrote everything down in a blue notebook I kept hidden beneath my mattress, adding to it daily, never crossing anything out, searching my memory for seemingly insignificant details. But it was just like any day.

At breakfast, you found a toy in the cereal packet. It was a plastic dog on a skateboard, and you wheeled it across the table towards me, stood up and leaned across to grab it back, though I made no attempt to take it. You did it again. Again. After the third time, I kicked you underneath the table and you paused, looked a little hurt, but then you pushed your hair behind your ears and began again. After the fifth time, Dad reached out and snatched the toy as it came past his plate of toast. He didn't say anything, he just put it in his pocket and went on eating. I smiled, and you saw. You gave me a weak slap on the hand and I kicked you again, a little harder.

There was a small puddle of spilled orange juice on the mat in the centre of the table. Mum was wearing a pale yellow dress with a brown belt. Dad's shoes needed cleaning. This is what I remember.

Dad dropped me off at school on his way to the shop. I don't know what you and Mum did after we'd gone. You might have taken a picnic to the park or walked to the shops or played in the garden. It was a beautiful day, and I hope you were outside. I hope you got to draw a picture or read a story or make up a game.

If we'd known, we would have stayed together that day. We would have made it one of the best, like the days we ran on the beach or the day when one of Mum's friends from work looked after us and she let us watch cartoons and eat sweets all day long. I would have given you something. I don't know what. I would have given you anything you asked for. I would have let you roll that toy across the table as many times as you wanted.

But if we'd known, of course, that knowledge would have hung over us, and we wouldn't have been able to make it one of those days. It would have been more like the days when we were looked after by Mrs Wilson next door, trapped inside her stifling house with its thick layer of dust, hearing other children playing outside. If we'd known, I'm not sure how we would have acted, how we could have put one foot in front of the other.

Mum was making dinner when the phone rang. Dad was due home in ten minutes and we were watching for him at the lounge window. We didn't hear Mum's side of the conversation. You were telling me about a story you'd heard about a girl who could close her eyes and make time spin backwards, but it didn't make any sense and when I asked you what you were talking about, you stamped your foot in frustration.

Mum appeared at the door, her face white. She rushed to the window, joined us in the search for Dad's red car. I wanted to tell her that you were being annoying but I knew, somehow, that it wasn't the time. That something had happened to stop this day from being ordinary, that we'd stumbled into dangerous territory.

She said that Mr Wilson next door had had a fall, that she was going round there. I looked at her and nodded. I thought we were going with her. That's what we did. Mum knelt in front of me, gripping my hands. She told me to look after Phoebe. Dad would be home any minute. Until then, I was in charge.

I nodded again, and you giggled. 'Look after Phoebe, look after Phoebe, look after Phoebe,' you said.

I heard the door slam shut and I stayed by the window, watching for Dad. When you wandered away, I just let you. I'm not sure I even noticed.

There were so many points at which it could have taken another turn, and gone differently. This was the first, I think. You, wandering away. Me, not even turning to see where you were going, so anxious was I to see Dad. Look after Phoebe. It was the first time it had been asked of me. The first time I was trusted with you, and the very worst thing happened.

When you came back, I heard your footsteps and turned. As I spun around, I saw the redness on your face and my heart stopped for a second. Paused. I remember thinking first about the trouble I'd get into if you were hurt while I was supposed to be looking after you, second that you were hurt, that you looked like you might be bleeding. And then I saw the lipstick in your hand, saw that the streaks on your face and arms were too bright to be blood. You swiped at me with the lipstick, leaving a thick line across the back of my hand, and you laughed.

I took the lipstick from your chubby hand and pulled you into the downstairs toilet. But it wouldn't come off you, with water. It just smeared and faded, and felt greasy on my hands as they held yours.

I looked at you, thought about Mum and what she'd say. I left you there, by the sink, and took one last glance out of the window for Dad, but he was nowhere to be seen. 'You'll have to have a bath,' I said, chasing you out of the room and up the stairs as you squealed with laughter. How many times had I seen Mum do the same thing, when you were dirty from the garden or the park? I was doing what I'd learned. And you were still okay, still you. But on the landing, I stopped, shocked. A wavy red trail ran along the wall, angry against the cream paint behind it. That's when I knew it was really bad. I called up a memory of

Mum and Dad standing at the top of the stairs, Mum with a roller, covering the wall in quick, effortless strokes, Dad carefully handling the edges and corners.

As we walked past, I rubbed at the red line with my fingers, watched with dismay as it smeared and spread. I looked at you, to see whether you knew what you'd done, and I saw a tear fall, trickle down your cheek.

It was unusual for you to be the one to lead us into trouble. I didn't think about all the times I'd taken you along with me when I knew we'd be punished for whatever we were doing. I was furious. I remember the anger descending, settling over me until I could barely see for it. I marched you into the bathroom, dropped the plug into the bath and turned both taps as far as they'd go. I ordered you to take your clothes off, ignoring the tears that were flowing freely now. I crouched down, looking you in the eye as you lifted one leg at a time to pull off your socks.

I told you that you were bad, said that Mum and Dad were going to kill you. But even in my rage, I checked the temperature of the water before I lifted you over the edge and into the bath. Nobody ever asked about that, because it didn't matter, but I did check that that water wouldn't burn you.

And then I left you, sobbing in the bath, ordered you to wash off the lipstick and left the room without looking back. Mum and Dad are going to kill you. It was the last thing I said to you. I've never told anyone that.

I ran down the stairs to the kitchen and grabbed the dishcloth that was hanging on the tap. And then I took it upstairs, dripping, and began to scrub at the angry stain you'd left. I remember hearing you, crying. I don't remember when you stopped.

It wasn't long after that that I heard a key in the door. I hoped it was Dad, felt sure that Mum's anger would be worse. I was crying, too, by then, in anticipation of the punishment we would be dealt. I heard footsteps on the stairs and I didn't turn. I just kept on smearing that lipstick mark, desperate to show that even though I'd let this happen, I was at least trying to fix it.

*Mum must have seen what I was doing, but her voice was calm when
she spoke, and she didn't mention the mark on her newly painted wall.
She just asked where Phoebe was.*

*My face was streaked with tears and my shoulders were slumped. I
said she was in the bath, that she'd got lipstick everywhere.*

*Mum pushed past me, and it was only then that I noticed the silence
and wondered why you'd gone so quiet. For a second, I thought you
might have got out of the bath and done something else, just as terrible,
that I'd be blamed for.*

*And so I stood, leaving the stained cloth on the floor, and followed
Mum to the bathroom. But I never got there, because when she reached
the doorway, she let out an animal sound that I'd never heard before and
haven't heard since, and I knew exactly what had happened in that
moment. And I knew, at once, that those minutes we'd been left alone
had changed everything, and that it was my fault.*

Esme

W hen she'd finished reading, Bea got up and closed the
window in her bedroom. She felt terribly cold. So that's
it, she thought. That's all of it. She wanted to reach back through
time, to stop it happening, or at least to comfort the younger
Esme. It was excruciating to think that her sister had been
irreparably damaged on that day, and there was nothing she could
do about it. That, when her sister needed her the most, she hadn't
even been born. Bea found that she was weeping, for the sister she
would never know, and the sister who remained.

For the first time, she could see her mother as a real person,
could feel sorry for her. She pictured her, pregnant and struck
dumb with sorrow. One daughter tugging at her, full of need.
Another daughter gone. A third daughter growing inside her,
unwanted. Bea hadn't noticed the wall of anger that had built
inside her chest until it started to fall, brick by brick. And when it
was gone, or going, she felt that she could breathe a little easier.

At last, she understood everyone's guilt. The crushing weight and the excruciating pain of it. Her mum, who had left her two girls together, her dad, who hadn't arrived home on time. Her sister, who hadn't known that Phoebe was too young to be left alone in the bath. Everyone in her family had made small, understandable mistakes that day, and those mistakes had come together to create something dreadful, something none of them had ever got over.

Bea sat still, the letter in her hand, her mind playing out different scenarios, imagining how things might have been if Phoebe had lived. If her mother had lived. If she'd had two older sisters, instead of one, and neither of them had been trapped by the weight of sorrow and guilt. They could have been an ordinary family. They might have been a happy one.

Bea walked to the window and looked out on the bleak December afternoon. She could have done with opening the window to a sunny summer day, just then. There was enough darkness in the letters she'd read to last a lifetime. And that's what they represented, of course. A lifetime of darkness. Not Phoebe's, whose life, though short, had been happy. Esme's darkness. Bea wondered, sat on her bed with her sister's words scattered around her, whether she could be the one to lift it.

On a whim, she wrapped up in her coat and scarf and left the flat. She needed some air, some perspective. It was the middle of the day, and she should have been working, but things were winding down for Christmas, and no one seemed in too much of a hurry. She walked towards Brixton's high street, happy for once to be in the middle of a jostling crowd. There were Christmas decorations in every window and people laden down with bags. Bea realised that next year, she would have a baby, and the thought amazed her. Everything would be so different. Could she see herself as one of these mothers, steering a pushchair down packed streets, manoeuvring herself and her baby on to city buses? Every time she thought about it, the idea seemed more alien. Perhaps if she weren't going to be doing it alone, things would be different. But these women she saw around her, they looked tired and anxious and irritable, and she didn't want to be one of them.

Bea turned around, made her way back to the flat. And once she was out of the throng, she took her phone from her bag and dialled her sister's mobile number. Esme didn't answer until the fifth ring, when Bea was about to give up.

'Hello?' Esme sounded breathless, a little harassed.

'It's Bea. Are you too busy to talk?'

'It's okay, Dad's here. I'll go in the back.'

Bea pictured her sister moving through the shop and into the back room. Of course they'd be busy, so close to Christmas. She resolved not to keep Esme for long. But she thought she'd made a decision, and she wanted to share it with someone before she changed her mind.

'What's up, Bea?'

'I've been thinking, about what I'm going to do when the baby's born. Where we're going to live.'

She paused as a gust of wind blew her hair across her face and she couldn't see for a moment. And then she reached up, cleared her face and tucked her hair behind her ear, and she could see again. Bare trees, litter, broken paving stones.

'I want to come home,' she said. 'To Southampton, to live.'

'Oh,' said Esme. 'Well, that's fantastic.'

Bea smiled. 'I can do my job from anywhere, and I want to be close to you and Dad. I'm going to need some help, I think. I'll call Dad tonight, ask if I can move home for a while. What do you think he'll say? Do you think he'll mind, if Marianne's moving in? Shit, I only just thought of that.'

'I don't think he'll mind at all,' Esme said.

'That's good.' Bea stopped. She'd reached her front door. She rummaged in her bag for her keys with one hand, and then let herself in. She'd just stepped into the hallway when Esme spoke again.

'I don't think he'll mind,' Esme said, 'but, would you think about living with me instead? I've found a place, and there's room. A bedroom for you and a small room that we could turn into a nursery. I'd love to have you both there.'

Bea couldn't face the stairs. She leaned against the cold wall of the communal hallway, sank down until she was sitting on the floor. There were tears in her eyes. She didn't brush them away. She just let them track their way down her face. Slowly, steadily.

'Bea? Are you still there?'

'Yes,' she said. 'I'm here. I'm here.'

Bea got back to work after the call, but her head was full of plans. Esme had emailed her some photos of the new flat, and it looked homely and clean. Bea could imagine bringing up her baby there, with Esme on hand to help out and her dad a few minutes down the road. She could picture summer afternoons in her dad's garden, walks with the pushchair on the common, trips to the seaside. She hadn't realised it until the pregnancy had put things in perspective, but she was tired of London. It was something she was glad she'd done, and she'd loved spending a few years in the thick of it, close to the museums and theatres, at the centre of everything. And now, she was ready to go home.

When Bea heard Julia's key turn in the lock, she closed her laptop and tried to swallow the lump in her throat. Telling Julia she was leaving was the only thing standing in her way, the only thing she was dreading. She opened her bedroom door just as Julia was walking past it.

'Shit, you scared me,' Julia said, raising one hand to her chest.

'Sorry. Good day?'

'Same old.'

They went through to the kitchen, via the lounge, where Julia dropped her bag, coat and scarf on the armchair. Julia took a bottle of beer from the fridge, hunted in the drawers for a bottle opener.

'Do you want a drink?' she asked.

Bea shook her head. 'Julia,' she said.

'What?' Julia opened her bottle and took a long swig of beer. She leaned back against the sink, opposite Bea, and they looked at one another. Something was ending. Bea could feel it. She wondered whether Julia could.

'I'm going to move out,' she said. 'Not immediately, but before the baby comes. I'm going to move back to Southampton.'

Julia tilted her head to one side, set down her bottle of beer on the worktop at her side. 'Are you sure?'

'Yes. I spoke to Esme today. We're going to live together. Me, her and the baby. I want to be near my family.'

'It's not just about getting away from Adam?'

Bea laughed. She realised with a jolt that she hadn't thought about Adam for a few days. He certainly hadn't been a factor in this decision. She was moving on as well as moving away. 'No. It's just the right thing to do. But I'm sorry to leave you in the lurch. And I'll miss you. I hope you'll visit.'

Julia took a couple of steps forward into the middle of the room, and Bea did the same. When they were standing an arm's length from one another, Julia reached out and pulled Bea into a close hug.

'You're not angry?' Bea asked, speaking into Julia's hair.

'What?'

Bea pulled away, looked closely at Julia's eyes so that she'd know if her friend was lying. 'You're not angry?'

'Of course I'm not angry, you silly cow. You're doing the right thing. I'm almost jealous. I don't even know what the right thing is.'

'You won't be jealous in a few months, when I haven't slept in weeks and all my clothes smell of baby sick.'

'You're right,' Julia said. 'I won't.'

A LITTLE LATER THAT EVENING, Bea was lying on her bed, listening to music when there was a soft knock at the door.

'I'm going home for Christmas in the morning,' Julia said, sticking her head around the doorframe. 'I wanted to give you this.'

She stepped into the room and threw a soft, bulky package in Bea's direction. Bea reached out and caught it in both hands.

Because they never had any money, and they both loved reading, Bea and Julia always bought each other a book. Every birthday and every Christmas. This was the first present she remembered receiving from Julia that wasn't small and rectangular.

'What's this?' she asked.

Julia shrugged. 'The woman in the shop said you'd need loads of these. Happy Christmas, Bea.'

When Julia had closed the door, Bea pulled at the neat ribbon and tore the glittery sliver paper. Inside, she found a packet of sleepsuits and one of muslin squares, both in bright, cheerful colours. She pulled one of the muslins out of the plastic and unrolled it. She had no idea what it was for, and she knew Julia didn't either. She pictured her friend, standing in the middle of a baby shop, with no idea what to buy. It made her smile.

Underneath, of course, there was a book. *The Catcher in the Rye*. She was surprised. She'd had this iconic red volume on her bookshelves since she was a teenager. Julia knew she'd read it. The first night they'd met, Bea had told Julia that she and Esme were named after J. D. Salinger characters.

Confused, Bea began to flick through the slim paperback. And there it was: Phoebe, Holden Caulfield's little sister. How had she failed to realise it before? Esme, Bea, and Phoebe. She tucked the knowledge away with the growing list of things she knew about her lost sister, and went to throw the ripped paper in the bin.

Esme and Bea stood by the sink, side by side, peeling and chopping vegetables. Tom was on the other side of the small kitchen, checking on the turkey. He opened the oven and a wave of heat gushed out, steaming his glasses. Nobody had said anything for a while, but it was a companionable silence. The radio was on low, playing Christmas songs. Her family was complete, Esme thought. As complete as it was ever going to be.

'What time is Marianne coming?' Bea asked. 'And Simon?'

Tom turned. 'Marianne will be here in a couple of hours.'

'Simon's just calling in this evening,' Esme said. 'He's having dinner with his mum.'

Bea nodded, then let out a small laugh.

'What?' Esme asked.

'I just think it's funny, that you've both been on your own for so long. And now, I'm pregnant and single and you've both found someone.'

Esme sneaked a sideways look at Bea. Her sister often covered up her real emotions with humour. She wondered how scared Bea was, to be going it alone. But then she would be on hand to help, every day. Bea's body had changed, slightly. She wasn't exactly

267

showing, but her sharp angles had softened. She'd said that she would move down in the springtime. Esme thought about how she would look then, couldn't help picturing the way their mother had looked when she was carrying Bea. Esme had always thought she was at her most beautiful then, her belly curved and her long hair falling around her shoulders. But there had been that terrible sadness in her eyes, which Esme could do nothing to alter. Bea's pregnancy would be different. It would be all anticipation and excitement.

When Marianne arrived, Esme watched as Bea hugged her warmly. It was the first time they'd met. Esme was ashamed to think about the way she'd reacted to the relationship at first. But it was different for Bea. She knew about the affair, but it had all started before she was born, and how could you be angry about something from so long ago? Esme stepped forward and kissed Marianne on both cheeks. Her perfume was sweet and subtle, her clothing, as always, immaculate.

'Let's eat,' Tom said, shooing everyone out of the kitchen so that he could serve the dinner.

Christmas dinner had always been his meal. Esme and Bea had helped with bits of it, but he was the one who made sure everything went smoothly. That was what he was good at.

'So Dad,' Bea said, once they were all seated with a heaped plate of food in front of them. 'When are you retiring?'

Tom looked at Esme, as if asking for her permission. She smiled at him, nodded. 'I'm going to put the shop up for sale in January, and then we'll see what happens. I'd like to retire by spring. Esme has offered to keep things ticking over if it takes a while to sell.'

'I can't believe it won't be your shop,' Bea said.

Tom shrugged. 'It's time.'

He stole a look at Marianne, and then spoke again.

'Speaking of which, there's something else we wanted to tell you. Marianne's house is on the market. She'll be moving in as soon as it sells.'

Esme wasn't surprised. They were happy, she could see that. Once she'd stopped being angry, her dad had told her a little about the three stages of their relationship: at school, after Phoebe died, and now. They were bound by something, he said, that kept bringing them back together. It didn't change the way he'd felt about her mum, but he was getting older and he didn't want to let her go for a third time.

'Congratulations,' she said, raising her glass of red wine. 'I hope you'll both be happy here.'

Not long after dinner, Marianne made her excuses and went home. Esme could see that she was trying to be considerate, to give them some time as a family, and she was grateful. Everything was moving so fast, after years of stagnation. Marianne moving in, her moving out, Bea coming back to Southampton. Selling the shop, the baby, starting her counselling course. There wouldn't be many times ahead when it was just the three of them, and she wanted to cherish it.

Bea made them all a coffee, and they went through to the lounge and settled down, Tom in his usual armchair, the girls on the sofa, their legs curled beneath them.

'Tell us a story,' Bea said, looking at her dad.

Tom looked back at her, amused. 'A story? It's a long time since you've asked me that.'

'Tell us the story of how you met Mum,' she said.

'Oh, that story.'

Tom was silent for so long, his eyes on the wall, fixed on nothing, that Esme began to wish Bea hadn't spoken. But there was hope, too. Hope that things hadn't always been so tragic.

'I was twenty-two,' he said. 'So young. I didn't feel it, then, but I only have to look at you now to know just how young I was. And she was even younger. Twenty. Two years into a French degree and trying to work out who she was and who she wanted to be.

She was so clever, and her tutors had these big plans for her. A Masters, maybe a PhD. She felt strangled by it, all those years laid out in front of her, already mapped out and decided, fixed. No one asked her whether it was what she wanted. That's what made her fall in love with me, she said. I asked her.

'That first day, she came into the café where I was working and ordered a coffee. It was a quiet afternoon and we got talking a bit, and when she said that she was going back to university in September, I sensed her reluctance. And I asked her what she wanted. She told me she wanted to run away. She laughed when she said it, and I saw her eyes change. I'd already seen that she was beautiful, but when she laughed, then, it was like a veil had been lifted and she'd been lit up from the inside.

'And we did run away. You know, I wonder about that, sometimes, whether it was the right thing. It was wonderful, in its way, the life we had together, and it's really all I ever wanted, but I hope she never felt like she missed out on anything. I hope I didn't take her away from what could have been a better life.'

Esme searched her memory for those happy days, that wonderful life he spoke of. It was all still there. But Bea had never seen it.

'Did you ask her out on a date that day?' Bea asked.

'Not that day. I was too scared that she'd say no. But then she came back the next day, and the next, and she'd sit at the counter with her coffee, always alone, and I wondered whether she could possibly be coming back to see me. She talked to me about the books she was reading, about films she'd seen, and she talked about her family. She let me into her life, a little, and I wanted to stay, to become tangled up in it all so that, one day, she might mention me when talking to someone else about the things and people in her life.

'On that third day, she came in half an hour before the end of my shift, and those final minutes seemed to last a lifetime. I'd decided to ask her out, but I was terrified that she'd finish her coffee and go before I had a chance. When I finally finished, I asked her if I could join her for a few minutes, and she smiled and I saw her all lit up again, and I remember thinking that I might be in love.

'We ended up sitting there for three hours or more, that afternoon. Swapping stories and laughing, doing that fast exchange of information you do when you're learning about someone new. And when we finally left, it was dark outside, and we were both surprised. It didn't seem like enough time had passed. I kissed her on the cheek, and she smelled of coffee and fresh flowers, and I knew that I had to see her again. See her every day, if I could. So I just asked her, and she said yes. She said I could see her every day.'

He stopped and Esme wanted to ask him what happened next, but she knew, of course. They fell in love, they ran away, they had her, then Phoebe, then Bea. And then their lives fell apart, and they washed up here.

A LITTLE LATER, Bea disappeared upstairs for a nap and Esme and Tom stayed in the lounge together, feeling full and content.

'Can I ask you something?' Tom asked.

'Yes.'

'Why did you want to tell her, about what happened with Phoebe?'

Esme had thought about that a lot, while she'd been writing and posting off the letters. She'd questioned herself, accused herself over and over of not doing the right thing. She'd lain awake, trying to reach for an answer to the question her dad had just asked. But all she'd needed was for someone to voice it, because she found, then, that the answer was right there, on her lips, ready to be spoken.

'Because she's going to be a mother, and I wanted her to understand why she didn't have one,' she said.

Tom nodded, and Esme wondered what he was thinking, but didn't ask.

Bea had asked Esme to wake her if she slept for more than an hour, but Esme let her sleep on for two hours before going upstairs. She sat on the edge of her sister's bed, looked around her, tried to remember when this was Phoebe's room. She looked down at Bea, saw that she'd woken.

'Are you angry with me?' she asked, suddenly. 'With us? For keeping Phoebe from you for so many years?'

Bea sat up and rubbed her eyes. She placed a hand protectively on her stomach, and Esme tried to imagine the baby curled up inside. Earlier, Bea had leaned close and told her that it was roughly the size of a pea pod.

'I was a little, at first,' Bea said. 'I just wished you could have let me share in it. The good memories and the loss. But I think I understand it all better, now. It was too close, too painful.'

Esme nodded, smiled shakily. If she squinted her eyes, she could almost believe that the woman sitting opposite her was Phoebe, grown older and beautiful. But then there was no Bea. She couldn't have them both.

'Tell me more about the baby,' Esme said.

Bea lifted her shoulders and let them fall in a slow shrug.

'I can't wait,' she said. 'I feel so ready for her to come, now.'

'Her?' Esme asked.

'Oh, I don't know. Sometimes I say him, sometimes her.'

Esme smiled, wondering.

'It wasn't your fault, Esme,' Bea said, into the silence in the room.

Esme looked at her sister, her eyes filling. 'Thank you,' she said.

'You know, even though we never talked about her, Phoebe was everywhere in this house.'

'What do you mean?'

'The way Dad was always so careful with me, and the way you

looked at me sometimes, when you thought I wasn't looking. I know now that you were wondering who I would become, how I would resemble our lost sister. You see, half of the love you both had for me really belonged to someone else.'

Esme opened her mouth to protest, but found that she couldn't, in all honesty.

'It's no one's fault,' Bea said. 'The damage was already done, when I came.'

Esme nodded. She could see it, now. In keeping so quiet about Phoebe, they'd crowded the place with her. The air was thick with it. And all those years, Esme had been choking. No wonder Bea had left at eighteen and stayed away. Until now. Bea stretched and stood up and the two of them went downstairs, ready to move through the rest of the day, and Esme found herself repeating some of Bea's words inside her head.

It's no one's fault. She said them to herself all through Simon's visit, while she was watching him play charades with her dad and Bea, pleased at their easy laughter. She woke the next day with them in her head, and kept them in mind a couple of days later, when they dropped Bea at the train station and waved her off to London. She would hold them close, she decided, and bring them out when she needed them, and perhaps, one day, she'd be able to feel sure that they were true.

ACKNOWLEDGMENTS

This novel has been a long time in the making, and I will forever be thankful to my editor, Kate Evans, and publishing coordinator, Sam Brace, at Agora Books for loving it enough to give it life. Also for answering many emails, keeping me calm, and giving it its title.

In its first guise, the novel only made it to about 25,000 words, was called *As Yet Untitled*, and was the dissertation part of my MA in Creative Writing. Thanks to my tutor, Karen Stevens, for pointing out what was and wasn't working (the only part that has survived is the character of Esme). From my MA, I also owe thanks to David Swann, whose unparalleled enthusiasm has never left me, and fellow students Loree Westron and Meredith Andrew, brilliant writers and faithful readers.

Next up, it reached full novel length and was titled *A Sister-Shaped Gap*, and I owe a huge debt of gratitude to Ajda Vucicevic, who was my agent while I wrote it.

Throughout the writing and editing process, many friends have read the novel and told me what they thought. Jodie Matthews, Suze Wilding, Natalie Berry, Sarah Speakman, Gaby Robinson-Wright, Liz Jones, Paula Maxera, Pavan Bhullar, Jonna

Mather, Vanessa Barlow. Thank you. Thank you. Thank you. Every request helped me believe a little more that it might reach this stage.

In recent months, I've been so lucky to have Gillian McAllister as a mentor. Thank you for everything, Gillian.

Enormous thanks to writing friends, old and new, who've cheered me on and made me laugh. Rachael Smart, Rebecca Williams, Lia Louis, Christina McDonald. Thank you.

Finally, to my family for putting up with me and for believing. My in-laws, Sue and George Herbert, my parents, Sue and Phil Pearson, my sister, Rachel Timmins. My husband, Paul Herbert. My children, Joseph and Elodie. There are no words.

WANT TO HEAR MORE FROM LAURA PEARSON?

Sign up to Laura Pearson's Book Club to get:

1. An exclusive author Q&A with Laura and topics for your book group;
2. Details of Laura's publications as well as a sneak peak at her next book, and;
3. The opportunity to receive advance reader copies and win prizes

Interested? It takes less than a minute to join. You can get your Q&A and first newsletter by signing up at https://www.laurapearsonauthor.com/contactme/.

Connect with Agora Books
agorabooks.co

f facebook.com/AgoraBooksLDN

🐦 twitter.com/agorabooksldn

📷 instagram.com/agorabooksldn

Made in the USA
Middletown, DE
06 July 2018